MW00782278

the expert *of* subtle revisions

ALSO BY KIRSTEN MENGER-ANDERSON

Doctor Olaf van Schuler's Brain

the expert *of* subtle revisions

a novel

Kirsten Menger-Anderson

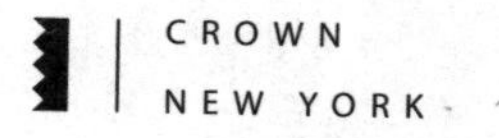
CROWN
NEW YORK

This is a work of fiction. All incidents and dialogue, and all characters with the exception of some well-known historical and public figures, are products of the author's imagination and are not to be construed as real. Where real-life historical figures and public figures appear, the situations, incidents, and dialogues concerning those persons are entirely fictional and are not intended to depict actual events or to change the entirely fictional nature of the work. In all other respects, any resemblance to persons living or dead is entirely coincidental.

CROWN
An imprint of the Crown Publishing Group
A division of Penguin Random House LLC
crownpublishing.com

Library of Congress Cataloging-in-Publication Data
Names: Menger-Anderson, Kirsten, author. Title: The expert of subtle revisions : a novel / Kirsten Menger-Anderson. Identifiers: LCCN 2024008013 | ISBN 9780593798300 (hardcover) | ISBN 9780593798324 (paperback) | ISBN 9780593798317 (ebook) Subjects: LCGFT: Novels.
Classification: LCC PS3613.E486 E97 2025 | DDC 813/.6—dc23/eng/20240223
LC record available at https://lccn.loc.gov/2024008013

Hardcover ISBN 978-0-593-79830-0
Ebook ISBN 978-0-593-79831-7

Editor: Amy Einhorn
Editorial assistant: Lori Kusatzky
Production editor: Natalie Blachere
Production manager: Philip Leung
Publicist: Bree Martinez
Marketer: Kimberly Lew

Manufactured in the United States of America

2 4 6 8 9 7 5 3 1

First Edition

For David Michael Thau

∞

To me, pure mathematics is one of the highest forms of art; it has a sublimity quite special to itself, and an immense dignity derived from the fact that its world is exempt from change and time. I am quite serious about this. The only difficulty is that none but mathematicians can enter this enchanted region, and they hardly ever have a sense of beauty. And mathematics is the only thing we know of that is capable of perfection; in thinking about it we become Gods.

—Bertrand Russell

I like crossing the imaginary boundaries people set up between different fields—it's very refreshing. There are lots of tools, and you don't know which one would work. It's about being optimistic and trying to connect things.

—Maryam Mirzakhani

the expert *of* subtle revisions

1

Hase

HALF MOON BAY, 2016

As far as official records go, I do not exist. There is no history of my life: no bank statements, no credit cards, no driver's license or passport. I have no birth certificate, no Social Security number, no pay stubs, no tax returns. No close friends, aside from Harriet, and Jake, who isn't particularly close. My only family is my dad, who isn't my biological father.

There is no adoption record, of course.

Call me Hase. Names are like lipstick or to-do lists. I have many. I choose one that suits my mood. For now, I choose Hase, because my father calls me that. I'm waiting for him, searching the horizon for his boat, the wind tangling my hair and clothes, the ocean lending me its odor. Here, I am Hase.

Elsewhere, I go by other appellations. The strangers who ask for my number or offer to buy me a drink call me Grace. The children I tutor call me Ms. H. On Wikipedia—I contribute as a hobby (anyone can, few do)—I go by TheRabbit, though I've used many handles there, most banned because I break the rules too frequently.

Untrustworthy, the editors call me.

For what it's worth, I don't trust them, either.

Today is my birthday. It's not the day I was born, but I always celebrate on June 11 because eleven is my favorite number and June has the longest days. Dates mean very little, my father taught me. You might as well choose a day you like.

And I did.

As a child, my father and I celebrated June 11 with Jell-O that I'd mold into shapes—a heart, a fish, a house—using pans we found in thrift stores. Each year, I picked a different shape and my father made up a story about how the next year would be informed by the Jell-O duck, or flower, or ghost.

I haven't eaten Jell-O since I moved to San Francisco, nor has my father told me a story, but as I wait for him at the dock, I think of the last time we celebrated. That story, for my nineteenth birthday, concerned a rectangle. At the time, I considered the rectangle dull if not disappointing after years of animals and hearts, but my father insisted it was a perfect form.

"A box will not look special if you don't open it."

When I pointed out that I couldn't open the Jell-O rectangle, he told me that humans are constrained by the limit of their imaginations.

In truth, I don't think I ever liked the taste of Jell-O; I'm simply fascinated by how the powder dissolves into water and how the water then becomes solid. The solid is neither rigid, like the mold, nor hard, like the table beneath it. However, these qualities did not prevent my father from telling the story of the Jell-O box, which served as a safe with no need for a lock, as no one thought to open it.

My father has never cared for the saying "hiding in plain sight," and the story of the Jell-O box is the story of why. The treasure inside the Jell-O box was not in plain sight. It was hidden by our failure to see beyond what we already know.

While my father told this final birthday story, I stared through the lemon-yellow Jell-O to the plate beneath. There was no way there was a treasure inside.

* * *

TODAY, THE OCEAN is playing like a wrestling child, bold but without malice. I hear both the gulls and the highway traffic. The water glows with the same muted light that illuminates the shops and parking lot.

Overhead, the skies are silent. I heard a helicopter hours ago, but I've not heard a return flight. The fog is thick, even now, just after noon. The boats stand out against the mist, shadowy but recognizable.

I watch them, though the view leaves me melancholy. There's a falseness to my life in San Francisco. I wander between living room and dining room, kitchen and bath, and feel uncomfortable in all of these spaces. I miss the smell of diesel and ocean.

I miss my father's boat.

I turn away from the pier and walk alongside the tourist-filled strip mall—seashells, seafood, books. The waiting has left my calves weary, my lower back and shoulders sore. I should have worn better shoes. I sit down on a bench that faces a bookstore and kick off my plastic sandals. I've worn down the soles unevenly. Perhaps I walk incorrectly. Maybe my posture's bad. I've spent too much time bent over my laptop.

A damp chill runs from the bench through my clothes. From here, I can't see the water, but I hear the waves. I used to think the ocean was speaking, that if I listened long enough, I'd understand its voice. The sea is telling us something, I explained, and my father agreed that the message, however unclear, must be very important. I sometimes think love is like this. We hear only the crash of its waves.

In the shop window is an advertisement for a weekly reading group and a display of books. I count seventy-four, only two by women. I count a second time to be sure. Then the salesperson emerges from the shop to ask if I need help. I know this question isn't concern but a warning: No loitering.

"No," I say. "I do not need help."

I recognize the salesperson, though I don't know his name. For the past few weeks, I've seen him when I meet my father. He's one of a dozen familiar strangers I will leave behind when my father decides to meet at another harbor. Before Half Moon Bay, we met in Sausalito; before that, San Francisco; and before that, Berkeley. Ever since Dr. Ord died, we've moved around. It's quieter, or easier, or safer, my father says, though I wonder if he's mourning the loss of his friend by fleeing the places where his memories include her. Dr. Ord was his best friend. The boat belongs—belonged—to her, actually.

The bookseller leaves, but I'm tired of sitting. I slip on my sandals and return to the pier and the spectrum of grays that join the sky and the ocean. Usually, when I meet my father, he arrives first. Usually, I don't wait for him. I'm concerned, but not worried. He's rarely late, though he's sometimes missed our meetings entirely: the harbor was closed and he couldn't sail out to meet me; he failed to account for the leap year and arrived a day early; he was consumed by work or correspondence and lost track of the time. When he arrives, he'll be happy to see I have a letter for him, tucked into my handbag. He won't notice that I dressed in a nice plaid shirt and the one pair of jeans I own that has no holes or stains. I know better than to wear torn clothes here. People judge me: I'm sloppy. I have no fashion sense. I'm stupid. Unrefined.

Online, I'm judged even more harshly, but I feel more comfortable there. I once explained this to Harriet, and she blamed my dad.

"You basically grew up alone in a cave," she said.

"That's not true," I said. "I grew up with you."

Though even with Harriet, I don't feel completely at ease—my breath is too loud or my stomach is grumbling. Something about me is always protesting.

But today is my birthday. I don't wish to dwell on such things. My dad will be happy to see me and thrilled to get his letter—a thick white envelope that, like the hundreds of others I've retrieved over the years, is addressed only to the P.O. box, with no return address.

I search the horizon once more. A foghorn sounds, then another. The wind whips my hair. Where is he?

* * *

THE DAY IS long and increasingly chilly. I hide from the wind behind the information kiosk and wrap my arms around my torso. The strip mall behind me is ugly, but I retreat there. The bench—my bench, as I think of it now—by the bookstore remains open.

It's my birthday. I should be with my father, hearing his dull accounts of tide tables, a breakthrough in the problem he's trying to solve, or why I should be more careful about whatever it is I last said to him. Over the years, he's become increasingly paranoid—about me, but also that someone might intercept his mail or that I'll misplace his letters. Paranoia is his peculiarity, but as he never bends to criticism, I've stopped mentioning it.

I once asked my father why he works so much. He blamed passion.

Most everything I ask he's answered—why we don't have paperwork (so we aren't imprisoned in anyone's database); why we don't get paperwork (so no one can steal our identity); why I can't do "normal" things (why strive to be ordinary?). I don't feel damned to the outskirts of society by these decisions. I am, in fact, freer than the people around me. My father himself taught me this, and that freedom has a price. Even when he hums, the tune is melancholy and always the same. The last time I saw him, ten days ago—when I met him empty-handed because the post office box, too, had been empty—he gave me a list of groceries, and not one was a luxury.

"You plan to stay here all night?" The bookseller is staring down at me. The shop has closed. Of the small strip of businesses, only the clam house remains open.

I try to smile but must fail because the bookseller looks unsettled. He strikes me as nervous, his crisp button-down shirt a false promise that life can be washed and ironed and worn like armor.

"I'm waiting for my dad," I say.

"Looks like he stood you up."

I finger my locket. The metal is even colder than my skin, but I play with it when I'm uncomfortable. Inside is my mother's picture, a photo of a portrait cut from a book. On the back of the page is a portion of a stranger's cheek.

Her portrait is done with a fine brush, the colors vivid and absurd—green for the lips, deep blue around the eyes—but is somehow more real than a photograph. I've spent hours tracing the brushstrokes. *She would have wanted you to learn math. She would have wanted you to learn German. She'd want you to be strong, and wise, and kind, just as she was.* My mother is a laundry list of wants, a fantasy composition of desire. If she truly wanted so much for me, she never would have left.

The woman in the portrait wants something unspoken, something I will never know. All I have of my mother is this necklace, and I wear it relentlessly, as if to prove to an indifferent world that she belongs here as much as I do.

"Do you need a ride somewhere?" the bookseller asks me.

"No," I say.

The sun will set in half an hour. Low tide arrives an hour or so after that. The next bus for San Francisco leaves before either. I'd stay if I could meet my father, but I don't see his boat on the horizon, and he doesn't sail at night.

My father wouldn't forget my birthday. And yet, he has. Did he fall and hit his head? Did he have a heart attack? I don't know what I'd do without him. He's the one person I trust completely.

I force the darkness from my thoughts. It's my father's paranoia, not mine.

When I return home, I will find him on the ham radio he and I keep tuned to the same frequency. He'll wish me happy birthday. He'll apologize and ask how I celebrated. We don't talk every night, but he's always there, like the city map I bought when I first moved to San Francisco and now pull out only when I'm lost.

"Maybe we can grab a drink?" the bookseller says.

He's looking at me kindly, and patiently, as if waiting for me to select the largest cookie from the offered tray. Maybe he really did want to help me when he asked earlier. If I didn't know he worked in the bookstore, I'd guess he was a teacher, or a tutor, like me. Like my dad.

I shake my head.

The last time I went out was weeks ago. I brought my laptop and bought a chocolate old-fashioned, which was all I could afford, and the man at the other end of the counter gave me a rolled joint. "For you," he said. "Because you're so goddamn beautiful."

The joint turned out to be oregano. I threw it into the ocean.

"I've got to run," I say to the bookseller, because I do. The bus is pulling up. If I don't sprint, it will leave without me.

* * *

THE WINDOW ABOVE the front door of my apartment building is patched with duct tape, and the lobby is dark. Half the lights have been burned out for months. The elevator's broken. On the wall beside the up button is a placard with the number for maintenance, but no one ever picks up. The last time I called, I didn't even get an answering machine.

Tonight the space is even more dismal than usual. Between now and when I left this morning, someone pried open the metal door securing the building's rectangular mail cubbies. The boxes hang open, their insides exposed. I feel vulnerable, though I rarely even check the mail because I never receive anything. Jake gets credit card offers and opportunities to renew magazines he doesn't subscribe to, but the box he and I share is empty. Still, most of the boxes are empty. The tenants are home, if not already asleep.

Only the security camera records me as I pass beneath it to the stairs: my plastic sandals, the cloth band that holds my hair away from my face, the red purse slung over my shoulder.

As soon as I get back to my room, I'll try my dad. I have just two more flights, then one, and then just a hallway.

* * *

THE APARTMENT JAKE and I share is the only one of the half dozen on the floor that doesn't have a welcome mat, yet there stands our door, open as an invitation. I'm thinking about this—how odd it is to see the door ajar at this hour, and how nice that I don't have to reach into my purse and rummage for my key—when Jake steps out. He's wearing jeans like mine, only a darker shade of blue and cinched by a belt that accentuates the ill fit at the waist, too big, even with his sweater tucked in. The sweater is beige, something my father might like, and wool. I'd thrown it into the washing machine sometime during the few awkward months we dated, and he pulled it from the basin mid-cycle, chastising me for being careless. From its neckline, half of a white button-down collar emerges, the other half lost beneath the weight of the knit. His hair is long and very fine, more blond than brown, and already receding. He's not yet wished me a happy birthday. Perhaps he's about to hand me a surprise gift.

"The police just left," he tells me. "Someone broke in and tore up pretty much everything."

"Everything," I repeat, taking in the news. "Did they—"

"They took the computers, all my papers."

My laptop is the only thing of value I own, and I can't afford to replace it. Jake's papers—the work he started with my dad and continues on his own—are basically garbage. Speaking of his hapless attempts to solve arcane math problems and my laptop in a single sentence, as if they are equal, is outright insulting.

I set down my purse. Nothing in the apartment is where it's supposed to be. The couch has been thrust into the center of the room, the cushions slashed, the coffee table upended. Scattered across the floor are books and shopping lists, plastic bags, a milk carton, disposable microwavable containers—the kitchen trash, emptied.

I have no idea what I'll do without my computer. I sit with it more hours than I do not, scrolling through the help-wanted gigs on Craigslist, editing Wikipedia articles or exercising my administrative privileges to delete pages that irritate me. But I'm thinking about my ham radio. If the thieves took that, I can't contact my dad. He could be calling me now, as I stand in the doorway. Happy birthday, he says. Happy birthday, my dearest Hase.

Happy birthday, into the silence.

2

Hase

SAN FRANCISCO, 2016

I've lived in Jake's apartment in San Francisco for three years, though I've known him much longer because my father used to tutor him. When my dad complained he wanted a P.O. box but couldn't bear the paperwork, Jake agreed to take care of the hassle. As a teenager, I came up from the boat to collect my father's letters, exchanging them for an envelope of cash to cover the box rental fee, and that's how Jake and I got acquainted.

I tell people I moved in with him because the wireless on the boat is spotty. The connectivity at the harbor is terrible, but I left because I had the opportunity. A room might not sound like much, but mine has a window, and Jake promised to help me move, and as soon as I closed the bedroom door, I stood alone in my own space.

He and I live together so well now because he doesn't actually know me. This is not because he doesn't like me—we dated for several months not long after I moved in. But even then, he was wrong about me. It was Jake who told me I wanted an intimate relationship, when the thought had not yet crossed my mind. Jake tells me I shortchanged myself because I did not, as he did, pursue my passion for mathematics. He tells me I am a perfect housemate because I'm a quiet person, very tidy, and never raise my voice. None of these are qualities that I would use to describe myself, and I've never had a passion for math.

Jake has ideas that he likes, and he ascribes them to me, and because he likes these ideas, he also likes me, even when the ideas are clearly not reality. If he were to look over my shoulder into conversations I have online, where I'm often chastised for screaming in all caps, he would see that much of my day is spent fighting, often quite fiercely, for something as seemingly insignificant as a single line of text.

What he also doesn't realize, as he's never asked, is that a line is not insignificant. If it's included, it becomes part of the story. If it's struck, it's forgotten. It's not, as Jake tells me, "a fact," and my editing is not "an addition to the sum of all knowledge." These are simply terms that he read about Wikipedia and now uses to describe what I do, just like he tells me, *oh, you were homeschooled*, or, *yeah, I know, you liked to travel*, whenever I try to describe my childhood.

But I don't mind that Jake doesn't understand me. If he did, he might not care for me, and our living arrangement might fall apart, and I'd rather that not happen.

* * *

Jake's clearly upset about the burglary, but I'm not in the mood to comfort him, or to explain that my father missed our meeting and I'm concerned, so I tell him I have to change my tampon. This way, he won't follow me into my bedroom, where I find my sheets and blanket stripped from the mattress and crumpled on the floor. My small library—the books my father calls seminal, all translated from the original German—lie on the floor beside the necklace Jake gave me before we broke up, which is pretty, though I'm fairly certain the gems are glass. My dresser drawers are open, my collection of T-shirts and jeans in disarray. The jackets and dress clothes I hang on wall hooks because the room has no closet lie on the floor, as does the one piece of art that usually adorns the wall across from my bed: the sheet music my father gave me on my fifth birthday. The frame is shattered—shards of glass everywhere—the paper carelessly torn from its backing, where the thieves found nothing because I've hidden nothing there. What did they imagine they'd find?

I remember how carefully my father handed the frame down to me from the boat the day I moved away.

"Do you have it?" he asked, though I was gripping it with both hands. The wind was strong and carried a chill, and the gulls flew low over the water, as they often do before a storm.

"I've got it," I assured him. I smelled the jam on his breath. His face was clean-shaven, the skin nicked and red in spots that marked unexpected waves. His lips turned neither up nor down, and yet he appeared to frown.

"You'll love San Francisco," he said. "I'm certain of it."

I knew he wasn't certain. He's not certain of anything. Proof isn't truth, he says of his own work, merely consistency. The world is inconsistent. One change upsets everything.

"Hase," he said. The sun was behind him, but he squinted, as if to better make out a faraway form. He handed me my suitcase. His hands are larger than mine, but veined and brown from sun. Whenever I look at his hands, I wonder how much longer he'll be able to live on the boat alone.

"I'll hang the picture in a safe place," I promised, though I have no such thing, only a room in the apartment I share with Jake. "Safe," I repeated, so softly I barely heard the word over the low, rhythmic thud of the ocean against the sides of the boat.

My apartment isn't safe. The thieves tore through everything, even the bedding. I imagine their hands on my sheets and shudder. My nightshirt catches the light where the glass shards collect on its fabric.

All they took is my laptop. I'm furious, but also grateful that the ham radio remains on my desk, the antenna attached. If the burglars had cast the cable out the window, I'd have to wait until morning light to set it right.

The radio was a gift from my father, the same make and model as the one on the boat. Neither he nor I are licensed operators, but we speak only to each other, and I doubt we'll ever get caught. We can't leave each other messages—my father doesn't have a landline, and he'd never be caught dead with a "tracking device," which is how he refers to cell phones—but we can always talk. When I first moved to San Francisco and still felt the rock of the ocean and the pull of the tides (the only time I've suffered seasickness was on land, when my body couldn't adjust to the stillness), he and I talked every night. Hearing his voice made me feel I hadn't moved so much as shifted, that I was driving in second gear, not first.

I pick up the handset and sit down at my desk.

"Dad? Dad, are you there? It's me, Hase."

I count to thirty in my head and repeat: "It's me, Dad. It's Hase."

It's nearly eleven, but my dad must be awake. He never goes to bed before midnight and often works all night. The closest I have to his passion is Wikipedia, but I write only because if I don't, my words will be left out; I'm motivated by exclusion, not love.

"I missed you today," I say into the radio. "Dad, are you okay? Is everything all right?"

"Everything's a mess," Jake says. He's standing in my doorway, but he steps into my room when I look up.

"I think we should get a smart doorbell," he says.

We have discussed smart doorbells before because Jake has no trouble with cameras that send video recordings to corporate servers, where the footage can then be turned over to the police or basically anyone.

"If they try to break in again, we'll have a record," Jake continues.

"No," I say. But he's standing and I'm sitting, my feet on the lip of my desk chair, my knees pulled to my chest. My voice is soft compared to his.

"This isn't about you. It's about safety," Jake says.

"It's not about safety. It's a doorbell that spies."

"It will protect us."

"A doorbell will not protect us."

"I'll pay for it."

Once, when Jake locked himself out of our apartment and couldn't reach me, he and I had a similar conversation. *You need a cell phone. Everyone has a cell phone*, as if a cell phone, like lungs or a heart, were required for survival. At the time, I thought there was nothing I wanted less. I was wrong. I can drop a cell phone into the toilet, but I can't conveniently lose a smart doorbell. If Jake insists on buying one, the Ding Dong–sized camera will record me even as I try to destroy it.

"No," I say.

"You can't say no, Hase. We're getting a smart doorbell."

I can say no, but I'm not in the mood to argue. I want Jake to go, but

I also don't want to be alone. My thoughts are scattered and unfinished. Even my memories—my father bent over me, pointing out the slack in the sail, the warmth of the sun the day we docked near the border of Mexico, the beige cabin walls—are fragmented.

"I'm very upset about this," Jake says, swinging one arm to encompass the disarray of my room and the living room behind him. "To be violated in this way."

My nod doesn't satisfy him.

"You just don't get it," he says. He said this to me when we broke up, too. And that I'm afraid of intimacy. I keep too much to myself. I won't let people in. I'm hurting myself by refusing to show emotion. Jake likes to tell me who I am and what goes on inside me.

"You just don't get it," he repeats, instead of saying good night.

He doesn't mention my birthday, nor does he close my bedroom door on his way out.

* * *

I TURN OFF the overhead light but not the radio, so I can listen for my father's voice. Outside, the city moves fitfully. A passing car. A swearing pedestrian, probably drunk. I lie on the bare mattress because I have no clean sheets. Above me, the darkness is cold.

I try to remember the last time I spoke to my father. Four days ago? Five? He told me about a neighboring boat and its resident who played the piccolo. *That flute is the thing of nightmares*, he said. He told me he'd see me today—yesterday, now that midnight's passed. I try to remember more but can't. When I try to fall asleep to the low hum of radio silence, I can't do that, either.

I trace the mattress seam with my finger, flick what feels like a sesame seed to the floor, try the radio again.

"Dad? Are you there?"

Each time I speak, my voice is strange—too loud or too tentative, like I'm a foreigner repeating an English lesson, hoping to say the words right.

"Dad?"

* * *

THE FIRST JUNE eleventh I remember is my fifth, when my father and I traveled to Dr. Ord's lake cabin to have a picnic and spend the night.

My memory, like most from that time, is a patchwork with missing squares: The shower was an opaque glass box. I was too short to hang my towel on the wall hook, so I pushed it as far from the water as I could, then carried it back to where my father waited outside on the grass. I worried the damp would stain my new dress. My father picked it out from the thrift store where he buys the sweaters he wears above ill-fitting trousers and the loafers he calls his leisure shoes.

Usually, I just wore Harriet's hand-me-downs. Harriet, Dr. Ord's daughter, is four years older than I, but we shared a nanny, and she's always been my best friend. She taught me how to roll socks into balls, how to weave ribbons through a barrette to make it more colorful, and how to stand in the first three positions of professional ballet. When I pulled on the new dress, I thought of how I'd show Harriet when we returned home and how she'd nod approvingly.

The dress was fashioned from a stiff red satin and trimmed with a row of beads. The previous owner must have applied these by hand, as the sewing thread was red on a dozen and a green-brown on the rest, and the knots on the underside were quite ugly. The collar was adorned with lace, also red, and the sleeves buttoned just above the elbow to form balloons above my shoulders. Around the waist was a red belt, decorated with beads larger than the ones along the hem but the same shade of red, their gloss so shiny I could see reflections. The garment fell umbrellalike over my calves, but pulled when I walked because the slip beneath the outermost layer was narrow.

Along with the dress, my father had supplied a pair of thick white stockings—"These will keep you warm," he'd assured me—that bunched beneath my knees, around my ankles, and under my crotch, as I hadn't pulled them up all the way.

The day was warm. I was uncomfortable but afraid to abandon the stockings, because my father chose them especially for me. He'd dressed up, too, in the jacket he usually wore to the university when he tutored.

He looked up from his journal and called out my name.

"Haaza," he said, the German pronunciation for the German word for *rabbit*. "Haaza," the way I say my name, too.

I must have appeared ridiculous in my new red dress and lumpy stockings, and I'd already muddied the feet as I hadn't worn shoes. My hair was wet from the shower. My father always combed it, so it was still tangled.

"Come," my father said, and I did.

That I was an obedient child might surprise those who meet me as an adult, particularly the men who repeatedly encounter me at the corner café and wonder why I don't arrive there the next day because they invited me. What they fail to understand is that I remain obedient, only to a different set of rules.

My father cupped my cheek in his hand and turned my face toward his own. I felt the stiff lace collar of the dress against my neck, and I imagined the cherry Jell-O rabbit we'd eat after our sandwiches.

"I wish your mother could be here," he said.

He gave me my birthday gift, and then admonished me to be careful as I ripped open the paper.

"It's glass," he said.

Inside was the framed sheet of music, the title penned at the top: *Himmelsauge*. Heaven's eye. I didn't go to school, but my father tutored me. Even then, I could read and write in both English and German.

My father ran a finger beneath each staff as he hummed. The melody struck me, even then, as sad, but also familiar, because he often sang it.

"We'll hang it in your bedroom," he said.

I nodded. Of course we'd hang this odd gift in my bedroom. It was mine.

The red dress was mine, too. After the picnic, when we returned to the cabin, I refused to take it off. The outfit was as ill-fitting as it was unsuited to the rustic living room, but this was also why I wanted it. I felt elegant and strange, encased in a protective bubble. I no longer stood on the floor. I floated above it. When I spun, the hem of my gown surged around me with the indifference of the birds who need only spread their wings to soar.

"Hase," my father said. The evening grew cool, then cold. He brought me my sweater from my overnight bag, but I refused to put it on. I didn't want to take off the red dress and I didn't want to cover it.

The night was still. Only my father saw me shivering. We listened to the news on the radio, and then to the ragtime music that floated across the lake to us.

I remember standing up and feeling at once exposed and powerful, the sweater I refused a distant past. I began to dance, though I have never taken lessons and knew only the three positions Harriet taught me. I was not graceful, nor was grace my intent. I simply raised my arms and spun.

Around me, I felt the skirt of the dress rise. I was dizzy, the drunk who got behind the wheel, the gambler who bet everything on red because I was wearing it. If my father tried to stop me, I didn't listen. I heard only the ragtime and the whip of fabric, and then the thud of my own body against the wood floor. A metal nail punctured my arm and tore the skin from elbow to wrist.

The sensation of pain drowned out all others.

Of the rest of the night, I recall only the hurt and the song, the syncopated accents and beats that didn't change when I fell.

Then my father was beside me and I was looking up at him from a strange bed. Not a hospital. People like us don't go to hospitals. My arm burned, but my father had bandaged it. He'd dressed me in pajamas and tucked me in under the covers. He was humming to me his hauntingly sad melody.

The cut healed, but the scar still runs jagged from my wrist to my elbow. Even long sleeves fail to cover it.

I never saw the red dress again.

* * *

At dawn, I'm still awake. I sweep the floor, smooth the crumpled sheet music, hang my jacket on the wall hook, count the cash I keep in the bedside table: $167.58. The burglars pulled the money from my drawer but didn't take it. I roll the loose change into paper tubes, which I'll bring to the bank the next time I pass by.

I empty my purse onto my mattress—nickels, quarters, dimes, an old pack of chewing gum, a few dozen bus tickets, two chewed pencils, the oval coin purse in which I carry a folded twenty-dollar bill, a broken pocketknife, the envelope for my father.

I've never opened my father's letters—I promised him I wouldn't—

but this envelope might contain a clue: the name of the place my father went, a student or colleague who might know his whereabouts.

I run my finger under the seal.

Inside the envelope are a half dozen pages, folded carelessly. There's no salutation at the top of the letter, nor—when I flip to the end—is it signed. I scan each page from start to end. Aside from a single note in the margin, the sheets contain only lines of math: wild integrals, curly brackets, unfamiliar symbols. I understand none of it, but I study the pages, hoping to find something anyway.

In the end, I feel as if the note in the margin is meant for me: "Is it hopeless?"

This is what my father waits for expectantly each month. This letter, or others like it, bring a glow to his face. This. And whoever wrote it didn't even bother to sign their name. I fold the pages and return them to the envelope.

It is not yet 8:00 a.m., but the telephone is ringing.

* * *

I NEVER ANSWER the telephone because the calls are almost never for me. The last time I picked up, well over a year ago, I spoke to Jake's sister, who's in prison for forging money orders. She called the apartment collect on her birthday and I accepted the charges, and Jake is still irritated about that.

Today, however, I think of my father. He doesn't use the telephone, and I'm not even certain he has my phone number, but the possibility that the call concerns him is enough to pull me from my room.

The living room smells of curry and the fried rice residue at the bottom of the strewn take-out containers. The phone rests on the floor instead of the side table. Jake is probably asleep, though usually at this hour he's making breakfast while I search the internet for work. Even when I have a job—or, more commonly, several of them—I have to line up the next opportunity: tutoring, assembling furniture, pet sitting, garden installation. Most gigs last less than a week.

I pick up the receiver. "Hello?" The number is local, but not one I recognize. The voice at the other end of the line is unfamiliar as well.

"Jake Laurier, please."

No one Jake knows would ask for him by his full name.

"Who's calling?" I ask.

"Forgive me for calling so early. It's rather urgent. It's about his former tutor, went by Herr Professor. We thought Mr. Laurier might know how to reach him."

"Is he okay? Did something happen?"

A pause. In the background I hear the beep of a microwave.

"He was supposed to pick up some papers, but he didn't arrive and I haven't been able to reach him by telephone."

My father doesn't use the telephone.

"I'm sorry," I say. "I didn't get your name."

"Peter Fury. Peter R. R. Fury. It's very unlike him to miss—he was quite anxious to meet with me. Are you Mrs. Laurier?"

"No," I say, though I realize I have diminished myself, or at least my right to be in this conversation. "I'm Jake's assistant," I say.

"The thing is, I'm about to leave for the summer and I really must get this work to him. Do you have his address?"

"I see," I say. I don't know Peter R. R. Fury, or how he got this phone number, but I know he's hiding something.

"Are you in San Francisco?" I say. "I can pick up the papers, and Mr. Laurier can pass them along."

"That would be wonderful," he says after a moment.

3

Hase

SAN FRANCISCO, 2016

I take the Muni to the Embarcadero and then the escalator up. When the steps reach the street, I jump, as if between dock and shore, exchanging the motion of water for the firmness of soil. *Are you Mrs. Laurier? I'm Jake's assistant.* I should have come up with a better response: I'm his sister, or mother, perhaps even his boss.

People pass me without acknowledgment. I'm not invisible, but unseen. Mostly, I scan the bay, searching for my father's boat. The air smells of kelp and bird shit.

At Broadway, I turn away from the water. At Grant Street, I turn again and press through the pedestrians. I count the sidewalk squares. The sky darkens. Once, a car passes so close I shudder, but then I turn into an alley and arrive at the address Peter R. R. Fury gave me: a building half as wide as it is tall, with metal bars across every window.

I push the front door, but it doesn't budge, so I press the buzzer and wait until the door opens to enter the lobby's musty opulence. The walls are covered with ornately framed portraits of bearded men, an old-fashioned display of refinement and wealth. I understand at once that I don't belong, though I'm reflected in the elevator's metal door, almost as if I, too, were a portrait: the ashy-brown hair my father cut until I was old enough to do it myself; the jacket I borrowed from Jake months ago and never returned—a pale green down, pockets full of crumpled receipts and a small stash of hard candies that I almost never eat but add to whenever possible. The bulk of the jacket makes my shoulders broader. Its hue lends my skin a sickly tone, and I look at once ill and incredibly strong.

A handwritten note tacked beside the elevator explains that it doesn't descend to the lower floor. To get to Peter R. R. Fury's office, I must exit the lobby and navigate a maze of halls that lead to a stairway. The stairs, covered in carpet worn through at the middle, are steep and lit with flickering sconces.

At the base of the stairs, I again must wait for a door to be opened, this time by a man who's both tall and heavy, too large to navigate the stairs with ease. His skin is damp from sweat or moisturizer, his hair is the uniform brown of do-it-yourself dye, and his clothes—a long-sleeve cotton shirt with loose-fitting pants—are mismatched shades of green.

"Dr. Peter Fury," he says, extending his hand. I shake it, but he doesn't wait for me to say my name before turning away.

I walk behind him to his office door, and he unlocks it with an anchor-shaped key and invites me inside.

A half dozen cushioned chairs are surrounded by bookshelves containing a mix of English and German texts, many on obscure topics such as *Movements and Habits of Climbing Plants* or *Of the Laws of Ecclesiastical Polity, Vol. 3*. The shelf against the far wall is dedicated to mathematics, with one full shelf devoted to Josef Zedlacher and his conjecture—the Zedlacher memoir, Zedlacher's few dozen published texts, a VHS cassette of the Zedlacher documentary, a DVD of the feature film, which was based on the documentary and released not long ago, four thick binders identified simply as PROOF, and even the Zedlacher comic book series.

The kindest critics refer to Zedlacher's work as fringe. Most call him downright insane. When he died in 1986, the newspapers referred to the Zedlacher Institute as "controversial" and "cultlike," Zedlacher's claim that we can travel forward and back through time—and already have—absurd.

I clearly remember the day I first learned about Zedlacher because Harriet was home from summer school and we were gathered in the yard that separated Dr. Ord's house from the guest cottage where my father and I lived then. We were barbecuing, but neither my father nor

Dr. Ord could get the coals to light. News of the Zedlacher Institute was all over the newspaper Dr. Ord was wadding up in yet another failed attempt to start the fire.

"Zedlacher can't even burn properly," she said.

My father snapped, "Don't speak of him."

My father is never sharp like that. Even when I spilled cocoa on a pile of handwritten work and ruined dozens of pages, he said only, "We can make another cup."

"You're right," Dr. Ord said. "But it boggles my mind that people believe it. That kid who died truly believed he was Haskell Gaul."

I knew better than to ask either my father or Dr. Ord what happened, but when I asked Harriet quietly and she didn't know, I took her back to my room, where we looked up the Zedlacher Institute on Wikipedia. I'd recently begun editing Wikipedia and loved to show off the site, as if it were my own personal web page, and so I insisted we go there, even though Harriet wanted to look at "a real website."

"See?" I said, pointing to the screen. "There's so much more here."

According to the Wikipedia page, translated from the German Wikipedia not long before, the Zedlacher Institute was founded by Josef Zedlacher in Vienna to "advance the science of time travel." The key "evidence" supporting his claim that we could travel through time was the work of a man named Haskell Gaul, who arrived in Vienna in 1933 from an unknown point in the future. Zedlacher claimed he witnessed a man "disappear in time" by winding a music box designed by Haskell Gaul and that he had searched for it ever since.

The Wikipedia page linked to Harry Houdini, who made an elephant disappear, and David Copperfield, who convinced his audience that he'd moved the Statue of Liberty, both added by an editor named FrogPrince, who also wrote: "People see what they are led to see. People believe what they wish to believe. I do not believe people can pop into the past as if it were a corner store. If anyone winds a box and disappears, it is illusion." This text had been removed and added to the page several times, and I deleted it once more, calling it "opinion."

The main purpose of the Zedlacher Institute was to identify the real Haskell Gaul so as to harness the power of time travel for "the good of mankind." This was why the institute held an annual conference, where devotees went to discuss "the great path forward." The Zedlacher Institute also ran contests, inviting the "world's best and brightest" to send in work pertaining to the Zedlacher Conjecture, the problem that would, when solved, allow the institute to complete its own music box regardless of whether Haskell Gaul was actually found.

The Wikipedia article had several sections dedicated to papers on related work, but I skipped over them, as I already knew time travel to be the philosopher's stone of modern crazy people. At the bottom of the page was a table containing the names of all the men who had at one point or another claimed to be Haskell Gaul. No one knew who the real Haskell Gaul was, but the table proved that an alarming number of young mathematicians wanted to be him: the man to solve the mystery of time travel. The most recent entry was the graduate student who was in the news that day because he'd died of sleep deprivation at the institute's conference. He'd claimed he was "in the mystical place where the spirit and physical worlds collide" and this was where "truth resides," and no one had intervened to save him.

My father found Harriet and me bent over the screen, still discussing the dead graduate student and whether any of Dr. Ord's current students were that crazy.

"What's this?" my father asked.

At first, I thought he was angry that Harriet and I were looking into the Zedlacher Institute, but I soon realized he was referring to Wikipedia itself. He'd never seen it.

He insisted I show him how to edit pages, and he was fascinated by the page histories, where he could see who added what to each article. And from that day forth, my father, who almost never used a computer and hated screens, became a huge fan of Wikipedia. I'd find him arguing in the math pages—he used my laptop to make contributions under my username, which is why people think I'm great at math—and I always knew when he was editing, because I could hear him muttering things like "Engelhardt is not a radical who incited violence. Who would say such a thing?"

Like me, he enjoyed the site because he could be invisible and visible, an outsider and a participant simultaneously, a contradiction realized. Over time, my father even made some online friends.

I'm remembering this when Dr. Fury hands me a manila envelope sealed with bright red wax.

"Thank you for coming on such short notice," he says.

He gives me his business card, a rectangle of cardboard with his name, phone number, and email address: fury@zedlacher.com.

"Please thank Mr. Laurier on my behalf," he says.

* * *

I STILL FEEL Dr. Fury's clammy handshake, even after I ascend the narrow stairs to the musty lobby and emerge into the foggy day. I can't imagine calling him, but I stick his card in my pocket beside the candies and turn toward Columbus Avenue. Normally, I'd stop at City Lights bookstore to browse for an hour or two, but nothing about the day is normal, and I just want to catch the bus.

I need to get home to try my father again. He'd never collaborate with anyone at the Zedlacher Institute, but he should know about the envelope and the odd meeting. I want to tell him about the apartment break-in. And most of all, I want to hear his voice and know he's okay.

"Hey," Jake says when I return. He must have popped home for lunch because he's dressed in one of the button-down shirts he wears only to the office. I suspect from his expression he's going to confront me about my jacket—his jacket, actually—how I stole it or ruined it because there's a small tear where the down shows near the cuff. Or maybe he'll tell me not to use his shampoo. I've repeatedly told him I never touch it, as it smells disgusting, but I do, in fact, use it because I'm usually too broke to buy my own.

"You're not going to believe this," he says.

While I was away, the police called to tell Jake that his P.O. box had been pried open. There's video footage of the post office—no shots of the vandal's face, but a clear view of the box.

"They assured me it was empty," Jake says. "There was nothing in it to begin with. Isn't that crazy, though? First the apartment, then this?"

"Yes," I say, but I can tell my response doesn't satisfy him because he's staring at me, waiting for more. "Just today?" I continue.

"You still owe me rent for the box, you know. Rent for the apartment, too."

"I know," I say. Jake pays for the P.O. box along with the utility bills and adds what I imagine is twice their total to the monthly apartment rent. I've confronted him about the amount, and he simply says I shouldn't take such long showers.

"I'm not in a position to cover it for you," he adds.

He is, though. He works as an actuary at an auto insurance company where he spends most weekends and his prospects for advancement are dim, but it doesn't matter because he doesn't want to advance.

I don't have the money. Nor do I have the energy to apologize and explain that I need more time.

"I've got to call my dad," I say, passing by Jake to go to my room.

* * *

I SET THE envelope on the desk where my laptop should sit and toss the jacket onto the unmade bed. The early afternoon light cuts across the room, dividing the desktop into bright and dark spaces. When I pick up the handset and try my father again, I, too, am divided by light.

"Dad? Dad? It's Hase."

I try again, then again. I've never spoken my name so often.

I once asked my father why he named me Hase, and he looked down at his hands. His forehead wrinkled the same way it had when he told me my biological father died before I was born.

"It's the name your mother gave you," he said at last.

A stranger named me, the woman concealed behind the metal face of my locket. I keep a stranger close to my heart. And yet, loving my mother, the idea of this woman defined in abstract and defiant color, is more real than the feelings I have for most people I meet in the flesh. She named me, and the name is mine. The name is whatever I'll make it.

Now, however, I feel useless.

If I had my laptop, I'd go online. Online, I don't forget my problems, but I can set them aside. I can sit in front of a keyboard convinced that I'm elsewhere. Online, I'm welcome until I'm not, usually because I've assumed an influential role—a forum moderator or administrator—and abused my power. My last Wikipedia bot inserted the words "History is not neutral" on several dozen pages before it was suspended, along with me.

Online, I can always return. I just have to create a new account.

Usually, when I'm feeling anxious, I edit Wikipedia or browse the deleted pages—drafts left too long untouched, content flagged as promotional or libelous, biographies deemed unworthy of note. I'm one of a handful of people who reads this shadow history. Most people don't even know it exists, but I'm a connoisseur of untold stories. There's a man whose biography has been deleted dozens of times. He claims he invented the blockchain, and sometimes he adds that he discovered DNA as well. I'm not sure if he believes these things, or if he's testing the limits of what he can get away with.

Over the years, I've deleted pages, too—sometimes because they are plagiarized; sometimes because they are duplicates; sometimes because they don't sit right with me. Twice, I deleted every page created by an editor who displeased me. Once, I was censured for this. Once, my deletions remained.

History can be this personal.

Most of my changes are subtle, however: details no one cares about, changes that draw no attention. I don't add lines; I shift language, the pattern of subjects and verbs, the verbs themselves:

killed to *murdered*
riot to *protest*
she was beaten to *he beat her*

Language, too, is never neutral.

* * *

I'M IN THE mood to change things, but the thieves have robbed me of the power. Instead, I twist the dials on the ham radio, past snippets of conversation and news to the frequency my father listened to when I lived on the boat, the space where the sailing community gathers to exchange tales of winds and weather.

Right now, they're talking about drugs.

"Coast guard is saying the boat was smuggling them."

"On the Farallons?"

"Smuggling eggs. That's why the whole crew jumped ship when the coast guard caught them."

"It's a real nice boat. Did you see the pic in the paper?"

My dad and I once anchored in a cove on the Farallons. He sailed out for the day so I could see the birds. A full day's sail because I enjoyed bird-watching. We couldn't go ashore—the wildlife was protected—so I sat on deck and observed the birds and the sea lions while my father worked on his proofs, and eventually the naturalist stationed on the island wandered down to glare at us.

My father wouldn't be out at the Farallons. The journey is crazy, even when two of us worked the boat. To go alone?

Still, I go to the living room to check the newspaper, which Jake receives every day, though he never reads it. Today's paper, one of four still rolled with a rubber band, lies on the counter beside a pile of junk mail and an assortment of kitchen items, retrieved from the floor where the burglars tossed them but not yet put away.

News of the abandoned boat made the front page. Beneath the headline "Ghost Ship" is a photo of my father's sailboat. The hull is storm-damaged, the finish uneven. The wooden mast, which Dr. Ord used to boast is stronger than hollow aluminum, looks like it might topple. I know this ship—the cramped cabin lined with plexiglass cupboards, the tiny stovetop that my father taught me to use, my narrow bunk.

Seeing my father's boat, I feel dizzy. The blood moves too fast inside me. My heart beats like a child's tantrum, furious and too loud. Everything—the newspaper spread on the kitchen counter, the voices still coming from my room, unclear and garbled by my distance from the radio, the creepy visit with Dr. Fury, the thefts—is terrible. I try to breathe slowly. Try again, then again. Tears blur my vision, but I force the panic deep inside me.

According to the paper, no bodies have washed onto shore and no corpses have been found floating. My father's ship simply appeared, fully provisioned but devoid of crew and captain. The coast guard saved the vessel from "certain destruction." A dockworker claimed that, as a child, he'd seen the same ship floating aimlessly through the coastal fog. He speculated that the vessel was hundreds of years old. Perhaps the ship was haunted. Perhaps a ghost steered it toward the rocks. Authorities were searching for the owner, for anyone with more information.

My father would hate this article, the public scrutiny and speculation. But then, his ship would never have drifted away had he been manning it. He is an expert captain.

My father cannot be dead. And yet, I hear his voice, the agreement I'd made without ever thinking I'd need to fulfill it: *In the event, Hase, you must get the book. Do you promise? Hase, you must. It is important.*

* * *

MY FATHER BRINGS up *the book* nearly every time I see him because he's adamant that I follow his instructions "in the event," as he calls it, the event being his death: I must go to Berkeley, because this is the place he has chosen, probably because it's close to the university and his one friend, Dr. Ord, now deceased, with whom we stayed years ago when my father first began speaking of the instructions. I must go to the library at the edge of town—a sleepy branch that's never crowded—and find *the book*. Over the years, *the book* is different (first it was *Everyday Reasoning* by Evelyn Barker, then *Volume II* of Kurt Gödel's collected works, and since then several others), but the gist of the plan is always the same, more like a treasure hunt than a final directive.

Now the instructions are all I have to act upon, the only way I can pull my father close. Retrieving *the book* is the one thing I can think to do, even though my father is not necessarily dead. I'll yell at him when he finally responds on the radio. Oh, how I'll yell.

As I walk out of the apartment, I can practically hear my own screams.

* * *

ON THE BART train, I imagine unbroken horizon and the gentle rocking of my father's boat. These are my canvas, the emptiness I return to again and again, the howl of the wind, the shadows of wings on water: cormorants, petrels, shearwaters. Birds were our only visitors. When I was fourteen, I cared for a bald-headed auklet chick. Two days I kept it before it died, and I placed the small corpse in a wooden box I used for pencils. I kept the box in my drawer with my underwear and toothbrush. One day, weeks later, I noticed it was gone. My father said he buried it, but I knew he could not do that in the ocean.

Buried in the ocean. I feel cold despite the warm press of bodies on the train. The news story makes no sense. The authorities suspect foul play, but my father keeps nothing of value on the boat. We own nothing worth stealing. Why would he go out to the Farallons without me? I am the one who passed the long hours watching birds. He's always been content with his mathematical work.

When the train arrives in downtown Berkeley, I step off, bleary-eyed, into the overly bright day. I've forgotten my wallet and have only my BART pass and a handful of change.

I sneak onto the local bus, overshoot the stop, walk several miles to the library, and find it closed.

The day is mocking me, and I damn the entire season.

* * *

THE LAST TIME I was in Berkeley was for Dr. Ord's memorial, and I walked, just as I am doing now, through campus thinking about how she died before my father and I could repay her many kindnesses: forgiving the rent for the cottage behind her house, paying our half of the nanny's salary, and, most of all, the welcome she extended.

From Dr. Ord, I learned about the mathematician Paul Erdõs—who moved from city to city, house to house, couch surfing, basically—because Dr. Ord fondly referred to my father as her Erdõs. She and my father often spoke late into the night about mathematics, while Harriet and I read or played Monopoly.

When Harriet went to college, I solemnly promised to write, and did, once a month, longhand accounts that filled several pages. I always imagined she read my letters in the same deliberate way I wrote them. It was Harriet who first learned that I tried to find my mother, even though my father told me she was no longer alive. I explained that I was unlike other girls because I wasn't interested in their conversations. I told her about the music I liked, how I preferred the piano—I'd started taking lessons—to the violin because the violin was whiny. I told her about the books I read, Johann Wolfgang von Goethe, Ingeborg

Bachmann, Helene von Druskowitz, most of which I discovered in my father's library. I told Harriet about discussions I had with my father on chance and truth and whether we understand time. In retrospect, my letters were tedious, and to this day, I'm not sure if she ever read them.

I haven't spoken to Harriet since her mother died, and she has never once visited me in San Francisco. Still, she is the closest person I have to a sister, and she lives just a few blocks from campus, in her mother's old house.

I want to talk to Harriet now, but when I try to sneak into the science building to use the pay phone, a middle-aged woman blocks the door with one arm and asks for my student ID. The security camera turns to me, or perhaps it has always been trained in my direction, a pinpoint of red light near its base alerting me to its purpose, recording. I consider the frayed hem of my shirt. I should have worn something nicer than jeans and my favorite blue shirt, so worn the color of my bra shows through. I don't have a backpack or a sweatshirt. I might as well be screaming, *Look at me, I'm trespassing.*

So I decide to drop by Harriet's house unannounced.

* * *

DR. ORD'S HOUSE, Harriet's house now, is practically on campus and yet protected from its bustle by a copse of near-ancient trees that Dr. Ord herself planted when she was a girl. As a child, when I expressed interest in one of the flowers, Dr. Ord insisted on giving me a tour: this one is a canyon live oak, the average canopy is over fifty feet; this one is a black walnut, the fruits are very important to Indigenous people; this one is a sycamore, its roots go deep.

The Ords' wooden porch is exactly as I remember it from my childhood. The swing no one is permitted to sit on hangs beside the cushionless deck furniture no one ever uses. All of Dr. Ord's potted plants are dead, probably because Harriet never thinks to water them. Plastered over the window of the bathroom (just to the right of the front door) is heavy cardboard. Harriet is developing film, or has been recently.

The last time I was inside the house, I stayed for two nights, because my father wanted to read through the mathematics archives down in UCLA, and I was too young to stay alone in our cottage. Dr. Ord gave me a potted rose to remind me of him while he was away, but the bloom fell off, and the mishap made his absence harder. I cried for much of the day. Everything in the Ord house was foreign and wrong—even the smells were of something else: lavender shampoo, coconut body cream, lemon soap.

Now I want nothing more than to sit on the Ords' worn sofa and stare at the collection of Japanese Noh masks that used to give me nightmares. I want to drink cocoa with hard mini marshmallows, curl my body into its fetal shape, and pass what I already know will be interminable hours between now and when the library opens again tomorrow.

"Hase," Harriet says, pushing open the door before I ring the bell. "Hase—my god, you look terrible. What are you doing here?"

4

Anton

VIENNA, 1933

I arrived in Vienna on the twenty-second of April, a Saturday that remains vivid for the stench of burnt wood and the eerie night-dark of smoke. I expected to meet my host at the station, but when I saw the smoldering rooftops and learned from the conductor that a factory fire had been burning for hours, I understood Professor Adler would not be waiting. He suffered from tuberculosis, a disease I knew well, as my father had died of it. Adler would not risk the smoke-filled air.

I had with me one small suitcase, having sent the rest of my belongings on ahead, and so I determined to walk, to let the city consume me. I left the station alone and walked without direction. I was not ready to present myself before my new landlady, Inge, who, I'd been forewarned, had a sharp tongue and a great interest in all matters related to the university, or to sit in the room Adler had mentioned was "dark" and "inhospitable." Housing was in short supply, and I was grateful to have found a place at all.

I'd not been to Vienna since I left for university, and though the war-weary streets had returned to life, the stone walls appeared uncertain, as if they might disappear if I turned my gaze away. I passed the imperial bank, which had collapsed when the markets plummeted, beside it a pile of stucco, detached and fallen from the facade like a final insult. Leaning against a wall beside the debris stood a man who'd lost one leg—in the Great War, he explained. "The years do nothing to heal such wounds."

Before I could respond, he turned his attention to a young woman carrying groceries—milk, butter, eggs—all of which I'd searched for futilely as a child during the war and which were now abundant. Behind her, the marquee announced a new production of *Hundert Tage*, which the liberal papers described as an artless homage to dictatorship, and the conservative press felt was an important work by Mussolini and Forzano. That the play was running here, in Red Vienna, heightened my fears that Austria's uneasy political tensions would devolve into civil war. Just last month, Chancellor Dollfuss had dissolved the nation's parliament, and though he maintained that the legislative body "eliminated itself," many felt, myself included, that he'd quietly staged a coup.

Only the coffeehouses remained unchanged, and I stopped in one, Café Josephinum, for a slice of Sacher torte. The university was in session and the tables surrounded by students, who looked up at me and, seeing a stranger, returned to their conversations. I sat, and the server brought me the *Völkischer Beobachter*, which I declined, as I'd already helped myself to a paper and had little interest in Nazi propaganda.

"You're with the university?" he asked.

"Yes." Even I could hear the pride in my voice. I knew from Adler that my application had been selected from among hundreds, and though I'd been engaged as an unpaid *Privatdozent*, I intended to prove myself worthy of promotion.

He studied me for a moment and then asked if he could sketch me. I had a balance to my features, and "balance was a thing of beauty."

The waiter himself was a striking young man, slight but imposing, if only because his eyes tore into me as he drew. His irises were a deep and imperfect blue, set off by dark brows. He'd first come to the university to study mathematics, he explained; one way or another, all philosophers wound up in coffeehouses. He set down his pencil and, glaring as if I'd offended him, selected a block of charcoal from the tin between us. With this unlikely tool, he sketched my likeness from eyebrow to chin. He then returned to the top of the page, where I saw my forehead emerge from the darkened background.

By this time, a small crowd of students had collected around us, and I learned my server's name, Josef Zedlacher, and his reputation, spoken in hushed and reverent voices. Rumor held that he'd once been fabulously wealthy but had lost his fortune and refused to speak of it. His drawings had been exhibited in the Secession's galleries beside Gustav Klimt and Helene Funke. He would certainly have become a world-renowned artist, but he'd decided instead to study mathematics and logic, which he called the only pure philosophy.

The boldest of the students gathered about us, a young woman in an absurdly beautiful gown, told me that Josef had talent in philosophy as well as art and was a "most promising" individual.

Josef, who'd continued to draw me throughout, only smiled, but I looked at him with new interest, as mathematics was my field as well.

At last Josef set down his charcoal and held up the portrait so I could view its entirety. He'd managed, with a single charcoal, to render both my eyes and the bags beneath them in such a way that I appeared more like a child than a man, my exhaustion no more than grubby finger marks left by careless hands. In the picture, I looked thoughtful, my head tilted slightly as I smiled, my gaze fixed on a point just behind Josef's shoulder, where the young woman in her shimmering gown had stood. She must be on her way to the opera or the concert hall, someplace where everyone would be dressed just as finely. Was she an actress? Her face was oddly familiar, but I couldn't place it.

Josef held out the sketch. "Would you like it?"

"Thank you." I reached to shake his free hand and, belatedly, introduced myself. "Anton Moritz. I'm the new lecturer of geometry."

"What a lovely portrait," the young woman said, placing a light hand on my shoulder. She stood close enough that I could feel her motion, the air enriched by her scent, spruce and pine. I was reminded of the Alps and of last winter's deadly avalanche.

My shoulder tensed.

Josef's gaze turned from me to the young woman, and he released the sketch into my possession as if I'd stolen from him the one thing he held most dear to his heart.

"Not as lovely as yours," he said to the woman.

She laughed, but I could see that he wanted her to say more, and that he was disappointed.

* * *

When I at last found my way to Inge's apartment building on Wiplingerstrasse, I took the second staircase at the second courtyard instead of the third and found myself in a warren of hallways that returned me to a stairway leading down. There I discovered a low passage, echoing with infants' cries and the slap of a rug beater. Addled, I knocked on the nearest door and waited for the resident—a woman, gaunt and gray—to answer.

She led me to yet another staircase and insisted I go up alone, as her back ached from needlework. From there, I found my way to Inge's apartment. The written directions Adler had sent me (and which Inge herself had typed, as she assisted the professor with such things from time to time) were moist with the sweat from my palms.

"I haven't cleaned the room yet," Inge informed me. She wore a pale blue dressing gown over bare skin, of which I saw a narrow stretch between the loosely knotted edges.

"I'm surprised you're here at all," she added. "I heard the train station closed after the fire. Up at the university they're saying the students started it."

I nodded. I'd heard about the demonstration at the café. The day's violence had been considerable, and several Jewish students had been badly beaten.

"Do the students parade every week?" I asked.

"They're always demonstrating." She looked me up and down, and I became aware of my crisp dress shirt, now stained beneath the arms with sweat. I'd not shaved since the day before, and I smelled of smoke and train grime. "You should be all right," she said approvingly. "But it's best to stay out of their way."

I took her to be forty, though she claimed to be a decade younger. Her skin was ruddy and lined deeply around her lips and eyes. Her hair, more gray than chestnut, was brushed into a gentle wave that reminded me of windblown bedsheets. As she showed me my room, she explained that she'd lost both parents as a child. She'd never married, but that didn't matter. Between the rent and the typing work she found through the university—lots of fancy thinkers without the faintest idea how to work a typing machine—she made ends meet.

Her apartment consisted of a kitchen, a living room, and my room, modest but appointed with built-in bookshelves and a writing desk. Inge slept on the quilt-covered couch in the living room beside a hanging cage where she kept a single yellow canary. The previous tenant had been a professor of biology, like my father, and left behind the complete works of Charles Darwin, each page X-ed and annotated with the word *drivel* or *monstrosity.* I thumbed through the volume, admiring his distaste, the strength of which I found amusing.

"You'll have to eat out," Inge continued. "Your first night in Vienna? You should be out."

She left me, I believed, to my own devices, but returned a moment later with a bottle of cognac and a single chipped glass.

"He left me that." She nodded toward the Darwin in my hands. "He took a position in America. That man! How I miss him. You know he used to sing to me?"

She began to sing, a song I took to be a lullaby and one I recognized from my childhood, though I couldn't recall who sang it to me. Afterward, she filled the glass with cognac and handed it to me before raising the bottle to her own lips.

I realized then that her robe had fallen open altogether and that I was staring at her breasts, each the size of a grapefruit and crowned with dark nipples that were, with unexpected modesty, gazing floorward.

I turned immediately to the Darwin, but I'm sure she saw I had no gratitude for the generosity of her bared flesh.

"My father was a biologist," I said, unable to raise my eyes from the pages.

I heard her pull her robe closed and worried I'd offended her.

"I bring the breakfast tray at seven," she said.

When she left, I replaced the book on the shelf and propped Josef's drawing against it. In this way, even I could look down upon myself, as a judge might a condemned man.

* * *

I DID NOT see Professor Adler until midway through the fall semester. His ill health and the smoky air (for he had, he explained, attempted to meet me at the station the day I arrived) necessitated a stay in the sanatorium, where the mountain air affected a cure or, as he put it to me that day, "I remain among the living."

We were both on campus, the sky an unbroken blue, much like it had been the day Adler and I first met in Berlin over a decade before. He was already a world-renowned scholar—a leading expert on knot theory—and an old man, though I'd learned in the intervening years that age is relative: he would always appear to me an old man, and I to him a young one, though at thirty-two I was already approaching middle age.

"You've settled in?" he asked, gazing at me through thick lenses.

I nodded.

"And Inge? She tells me she dotes on her tenants."

"Very much so."

He drew a handkerchief from his vest pocket, and though his cough manifested only as a silent motion in his chest, I could see that the fabric was speckled with blood. Adler had been my advisor. He first introduced me to Peano's axioms, Agnesi's *Analytical Institutions*, and Frege's *The Foundations of Arithmetic*. Had I not taken his course, I would have followed in my father's footsteps and gone into the natural sciences. To Adler, also, I owed my current position, as he'd put forward my name when he'd learned of my desire to return to Vienna and join its great university. I wanted to help him as well, but confronted by his ill health, I felt powerless.

"Professor," said a young woman. I hadn't noticed her approach, but when I looked up, I recognized her from the coffeehouse I'd visited my first day in the city. The curiosity in her gold-flecked eyes and the arched brows above them were unmistakable. She was again dressed as if going out for the evening. Her scarlet gown, trimmed in lace, was of a cut my grandmother might have worn, and yet—in a way that escaped me—it seemed unbecomingly modern. Around her neck, she wore a silver locket.

She fingered its chain and smiled. "I have the drafts of the new chapters."

"Ah, good," Adler said.

Noticing his handkerchief, she added, "Are you certain you're well enough to work?"

"Of course," he said. "Have you met Professor Moritz?"

When she turned to me, she appeared merely to be doing Adler a favor, though she did release her locket to take my hand.

"Sophia Popovic," she said.

"A pleasure to meet you," I said, deciding not to mention our previous brief encounter. "And you're studying mathematics?"

"I finished my doctorate last year." She stepped closer, and I smelled her perfume, more mossy than floral, a forest in the midst of Europe's most cosmopolitan city. Beneath one arm, she carried a thick ledger book, coffee stained but otherwise apparently new. A silver band snaked from her wrist to her elbow. I wondered if it might be a brace of sorts, though it appeared to have been wrought by an artisan, and her arm showed no sign of injury.

"Fräulein Popovic is working under Professor Engelhardt," Adler said, though he might as well have said Kant or Aristotle. Engelhardt was the reason philosophers came to Austria, while others, in China and Japan, studied German so that they might one day understand him. Even as a student in Berlin, I'd heard tell of Engelhardt's famed philosophical circle, the guests—from Albert Einstein to Eugenie Schwarzwald—the most innovative thinkers of our generation. Men vied for a seat around his table, but Engelhardt invited only a very few.

"He's taken me on as his assistant," Fräulein Popovic said. "The last one left for Paris."

"You're very fortunate to work with Engelhardt." I spoke as evenly as I could. I did not want to seem like a sycophant, or overly eager, though I wanted very badly to befriend the great man. I knew Professor Engelhardt mostly by reputation and considered him the greatest logician of our time. Twice, before coming to the university, I'd written to him, hoping he'd feel compelled to respond, though he was reputed never to reply to letters. He claimed to accept worthy contributions to his journal, but he didn't reply to submissions, and the issues he published consisted solely of his own work or that of his circle. I had every volume and had read most twice. Since arriving in

Vienna, I'd introduced myself to Engelhardt several times, and would likely do so again the next time our paths crossed, as he never seemed to remember me.

"He recommended *Principles of Topography* to me," Fräulein Popovic said. "It's not only fundamental to mathematics but all of physical science."

I blushed to learn that my work had come to Engelhardt's attention, and that Fräulein Popovic believed it had broader applications. Even Adler, my greatest advocate, insisted that my fascination for absurd—or what he dismissed as "fanciful"—spirals would doom me to professional obscurity.

Fräulein Popovic took Adler's arm.

"You should join us at Café Josephinum," she said to me. "The philosophers like to gather at Engelhardt's table."

Such was my surprise and excitement—an invitation to Engelhardt's circle was to me more exciting than the discovery of an entire continent—that I forgot my manners and the gratitude I should have expressed.

"I thought only Engelhardt extended invitations," I said.

"What an odd thing to say." Fräulein Popovic regarded me as if deciding whether to kill or nurture a young bird fallen from its nest. "The correct answer, of course, is yes."

And then she and Adler were walking away, and I was left alone to consider this unexpected good fortune.

* * *

On Wednesday night, I dressed in my good white shirt and permitted Inge to help me with my tie. I was very nervous but also thrilled to be joining Professor Engelhardt's circle. I hoped to speak of the work I was doing or to offhandedly note the successful approach I'd taken in my lectures, anything that might win his favor.

Inge, who often went out of her way to be helpful—offering jam in addition to butter at breakfast, or bringing a light supper, which she was not under contract to provide—was doing her best to bolster my confidence.

"You will look smart," she proclaimed, her fingers working the tie she'd placed around my neck. As she fastened it, she assured me the knot was the latest fashion in Paris and insisted it would "bring luck." She spoke of Professor Engelhardt's table as well. She herself had never been to a discussion or witnessed one in person, but she knew a tremendous amount about it.

"They say Engelhardt is the darling of the Jews," she said.

She pulled the knot too tight, and the cloth dug into the back of my neck.

"What do you mean?" I reached behind me to loosen the fabric, and she swatted my hand away. Engelhardt was a Protestant, though I—who'd long been familiar with his philosophy—often wondered if in his private life he believed in a God at all. What could not be verified was meaningless, and miracles and mediums were alike in his view. I did not know where his philosophy left his heart, but he was no more a Jew than the Catholics who claimed his ideas were blasphemous.

"Look what you've done!" Inge, displeased with her work, yanked the tie from my neck entirely. "I'll never finish if you don't stay still."

"I'm sorry." I bent so that she could again thread the tie around my collar.

"Do you know what they're discussing? You should always find out what they're discussing so you can prepare. Adler writes out his comments longhand. He has me type them.

"There," she said, pulling back. "That's better."

I would be late if I didn't hurry, so I thanked her and promised to report, as she asked, any gossip. Then, with Inge's knot around my neck—a monstrously large thing from the pull of it—I left the apartment and ran.

* * *

I ARRIVED AT Café Josephinum out of breath. I did not stop at the street corner to collect myself, nor did I take a moment to appraise my reflection in the window. My skin burned; my hair was tangled. My shirt had rumpled. Street damp muddied the cuffs of my trousers, and my socks, soaked as well, pressed the moisture against my skin. Only the knot Inge had tied remained in place, and I was surprisingly grateful for this small nicety.

The café itself was only half full, but I felt every eye upon me. I scanned the tables, recognizing no one, until I felt a hand on my shoulder and turned to find Josef, dressed as he'd been the last time I saw him, in his black waiter costume.

"Professor," he said. "Would you like coffee?"

I nodded.

When Josef returned, I learned that Engelhardt's table stood farthest from the window. The marble-topped disk could easily accommodate a dozen chairs, though only five were arranged in an arc on one side of it. Josef placed my coffee and water before the chair at the far end of this arc, and then pulled the chair out and away, so that it stood even farther apart from the others.

"Engelhardt is expecting you?" he asked.

My invitation had come from Fräulein Popovic, but I nodded.

"They went to the opera. Perhaps no one told you."

The last should have been a question, but Josef spoke as if it were fact.

"I'm sure no one will mind if you wait at the table." Josef smirked. He seemed to enjoy seeing me embarrassed, though mostly I was grateful for the opportunity to collect myself. I wished only that I'd had the presence of mind to bring a book, as I'd already read the newspaper. Still, I asked for the *Neue Freie Presse*, as I wished to appear occupied when my colleagues arrived.

After twenty minutes, Fräulein Popovic's voice pulled my attention from the newspaper to the door, where she stood between Engelhardt and Adler. I recognized Engelhardt at once, of course. He wore a gray jacket over a white collared shirt and vest. I'd heard he often wore gray because he was color-blind, and he wished to appear as he himself believed he appeared to the world. His hair, though confined by baldness to the sides of his head, was a youthful brown, despite his age, which I knew to be forty-seven. He carried a leather satchel that no doubt held his lecture notes. Rumor held that he slept with the satchel as well, now that his wife was in Paris with their epileptic son, and that he was happier for this companionship.

"Professor Moritz," Fräulein Popovic said. Her gown barely covered her knees and failed to conceal her clavicles, but I only noticed these shortcomings later. I stood to greet her and she took both my hands in her gloved ones. "We missed you at the performance."

Her concern at my absence seemed genuine, and I began to wonder if she'd invited me and I'd simply forgotten.

"I was very sorry to miss it," I said.

Engelhardt and Adler had made their way to the table by then, and Fräulein Popovic turned to introduce me. As I took Engelhardt's hand, I searched his face for signs that he recognized me but saw no indication that he did.

"I'm so pleased to be invited to your circle," I said.

In the silence that followed, I realized I'd misspoken, though I didn't understand how terribly until Engelhardt explained.

"We often come here after the opera. The circle gathers on Thursday nights, in the basement of the philosophy building."

"I see," I said. How impertinent I must have seemed! I hoped my dismay didn't show.

Engelhardt turned to Adler, whose conversation I'd interrupted. "I'm very sorry the administrator has been troubling you about this, too. Rest assured, I've nearly arrived at a decision. In fact, I promised to file the paperwork for Professor Huber's replacement tomorrow."

Josef appeared at that moment with four coffees, waters, and a slice of torte. He served the cake to Fräulein Popovic first, and then the coffees in the order in which we sat, with myself being the last recipient, though my previous cup was still full.

"Cream," he said, contriving to place the bowl in front of Fräulein Popovic, whose shoulder he brushed, either because he was looking at Engelhardt or because he desired the touch. In either event, he seemed nearly as distracted as I was, but by his own private thoughts.

Fräulein Popovic slid the cake before me, a wedge of dense pastry covered in chocolate sauce.

"You must try it," she said, and I was certain she felt pity for me.

I picked up the fork, broke the pastry's appealing surface, and raised the bite to my lips.

Before I could taste it, however, Josef's serving tray slipped from his hands, its impact against the floor as loud as a gunshot. His eyes, too, were fixed on the cake, and I felt I had somehow offended him by accepting it. I reached down to make amends by collecting the tray, but he knelt before my hand reached it.

"I'm afraid I can stay only an hour tonight," Engelhardt said, consulting his watch. "The séance begins at nine."

"The séance?" Fräulein Popovic seemed surprised.

"Maria Campioni's event. She claims to know the future and the past because she channels dead men's souls. It's possible, of course, that she can communicate with the dead. It's probable that her claims are trickery. I brought the camera to capture it."

Fräulein Popovic placed her hand on Engelhardt's forearm. "But Mother's expecting you. It's her birthday, remember?"

Engelhardt looked at her blankly. "I agreed to write about it for the paper."

Engelhardt's weekly column presented philosophy in straightforward language that excited even the trolley drivers, who debated each piece: Was it true, as Engelhardt wrote, that it's impossible to verify the German people's special relationship to the soil? And if so, does this make the claim meaningless? Is astrology science or nonsense? Is psychoanalysis? Thanks to Engelhardt, Ernst Mach was quoted in Vienna as frequently as Chancellor Dollfuss: "Where neither confirmation nor refutation is possible, science is not concerned." Of course the séance would appeal to Engelhardt, if only as a vehicle for promoting clear thinking.

"Send someone else." Fräulein Popovic waved away the commitment with a flick of her left hand. "You needn't be there yourself. Josef can go."

She indicated the waiter, who'd continued to linger beside our table, the recovered tray tucked beneath one arm.

"Do you know of Maria Campioni?" Engelhardt asked him.

Josef nodded.

"Do you believe she speaks to the dead?"

Josef nodded again. "I've seen her do it."

"I've seen a pencil bend when half submerged in water," Engelhardt said.

"You want the medium's photograph?" I asked, seeing an opportunity to redeem myself for my earlier mistake.

"There," Fräulein Popovic said. "Professor Moritz will do it."

"I can hardly send Professor Moritz to observe on my behalf."

"I'm perfectly capable of critical thought," Josef insisted. He was glaring at me, and I realized I'd offended him yet again. "There is nothing Professor Moritz will see that I will not."

"I would be happy to go," I said.

"Fräulein Popovic volunteered my name first," said Josef.

"Fine. You can go together." Engelhardt was clearly a diplomat, a man who could mend the gap between any two opinions, however jagged their edges. "Together, you'll study the famous Maria Campioni from both stage left and stage right."

I attempted to meet Josef's eyes to confirm the agreement, but he would not turn to me.

"There," Fräulein Popovic said again. *There*, as if she were pointing to the door and sending us on our way, an offhanded order that—over the course of a single evening—would forever darken my life. "It is decided."

5

Josef

OPATIJA, 1914

In June, the year Josef turns twelve, he takes the Southern Railway from Vienna to Pivka, and then on to Matulji, where he catches the tram to Opatija. Every summer his family makes this journey, only this summer his twin brothers arrive and everything changes. Their screams make Josef want to jump out of the tram, even though he knows that waiting for him at the hotel is a box of chocolates, each wrapped in Dalmatian lace and decorated with candied flowers.

When he steps off the stuffy train and into the warm summer night, his mother tells him, "You are a young man," and he knows that with this designation comes responsibility. He must ask nothing of his mother, and if he finds her in bed in the middle of the day, he must sternly speak the words his father orders: *Come, come, darling. Your behavior is unbecoming.*

The summer promises long evenings on the veranda and days spent on the beach or in the famous baths. Kaiser Franz Joseph himself spent months beside the turquoise waters of the Adriatic Sea. All the best families, among which Josef counts his own, holiday along this Riviera of Austria-Hungary.

That he first encounters Sophia Popovic in Opatija that summer is less surprising than the fact that he has not over the previous twelve. She is just his age, but wears her hair up in a way Josef has seen only at formal events, dark locks framing her face and bedecked with yellow flowers. She carries a book, which rests in her lap, and though the bench is stone, designed to provide an exquisite view of the Adriatic waters, he prefers to gaze at her. She is dressed all in black despite the season, and he wonders if she is in mourning.

Contemplating her sorrow, he feels a deep sadness himself.

"What's wrong?" she asks. "Why are you crying?"

Only then does Josef understand that his face is moist with tears.

"Have you been here long?" he asks.

She shakes her head. "I don't care for the seaside."

"But the coast is beautiful."

"The people are dull."

"I'm not."

"No?" Sophia turns her gaze to him, and she must recognize that he speaks the truth because she adds, "If only I met you earlier. We leave today."

Her father is conducting for the Vienna Court Opera, she explains. Kaiser Franz Joseph will be in attendance.

Josef's father works for Kaiser Franz Joseph, too, as his personal physician. Josef's voice is full of pride when he tells her.

"And your mother?" Sophia asks.

His mother is most likely in bed. "She is a doting wife and mother," he says.

"My mother's a pianist. She plays six hours a day."

"And still has time for—"

"For me?" Sophia laughs. "Of course."

Josef wonders what Sophia does with her mother—board games? Bridge? Whist? Needlework?—but only common people ask for what is not freely given. His father taught him manners. Curiosity should not be indulged, though Josef's questions grow inside him like an untended garden. Why does Sophia not have a chaperone? How long has she been sitting alone? Does she play piano, or does piano bore her?

Would she like to stroll with him?

"Have you ever been in love?" Sophia asks him.

The question is flummoxing. Either Josef admits he has not, in which case he will appear ignorant to matters of the heart, or he declares that he has, in which case Sophia will call upon him to provide details. She leans closer. A lock of her hair brushes his shoulder.

"I love my country," Josef says, blushing.

"That's very noble."

She stands, pressing her book against her chest.

"I should go," she says. "Perhaps I'll see you here next summer."

She leans forward and kisses him goodbye, a light brush of her lips on his cheek. Hours later, he still feels it.

But he does not see her the following summer. The hotel where his family stays becomes a makeshift hospital, and no one goes on holiday due to the war.

* * *

WHEN JOSEF'S FATHER leaves for the front a year later, he tells Josef that he's now the head of the house and must discipline his young brothers. This Josef does, as his father taught, with an open hand to the rump.

In school, Josef packages cigarettes and chocolate to be sent to the soldiers. In physics, he learns to predict the trajectory of a cannon shot. Over time, Sophia becomes less present in his thoughts and more like the portraits he draws, something he has to construct. By the time he finishes grade school, the war has ended, and though Josef boasts he's been awarded a medal for transporting munitions through the Dolomites, that accolade belongs to his father, who lost an arm in the fight. Soon Josef will start university, where he will study math and logic despite his talent for art, and Sophia no longer figures into his thoughts.

Josef, like his father before him, applies to a fraternity. The other young men—there are eleven at his interview, most older and returned from the front—are unimpressed.

"You look like a Jew," they say.

Josef is slight, not much taller than he was at twelve, but he draws his shoulders back to make himself seem larger. His father lost one arm in the war, he tells them. He would not marry a Jew.

The fraternity grants his application, but Josef remains an outsider. When the men gather, Josef sees himself through their eyes: *You look like a Jew*.

And so, when his peers don their hats and ribbons and parade through campus, Josef is the first to shove the Jewish students from the walkways. When the students call for the "undesirable" faculty to leave the university, his voice is among the loudest. He collects names for the yellow list of tendentious professors, the ones who are poisoning youth with their thoughts.

In this way, he makes himself welcome.

* * *

ON WEEKENDS, JOSEF sits in the dining room of his parents' flat. The portrait of his grandmother—his father's mother—hangs beside the window. His mother will remove it as soon as her husband is sent to the sanatorium. The room smells of herring and the pine that Josef's father has taken to whittling despite the loss of his arm.

The man who taught Josef that he must dress smartly now wears his dressing gown at the dining table. He has not repaired the water damage beneath the front window. The broken cabinet door hangs open just behind him. He no longer disciplines with blows, nor does he lead the evening prayer. Josef has tried to assume such duties, but he feels foolish performing small tasks in the shadow of the one he can never complete: to regain the family's position in an empire that no longer exists.

Josef is the only son remaining. His brothers have died of the Spanish flu, and Josef feels this tragedy acutely. Why should he survive? What will he do to deserve it?

The pieces of wood his father whittles become soldiers, each deformed—heads chopped flat, thighs concave, limbs lost entirely beneath his father's shaky single hand.

* * *

JOSEF FINISHES HIS degree and then his doctorate. His family moves to a smaller apartment in a less prestigious part of town. Their savings were lost in the war, and now that his father is ill, they have no income. At night, in addition to his studies, Josef works as a bookkeeper, first for a shopkeeper, whose front window is broken twice in the six months Josef works in the shop, and later for Café Josephinum, where he will become the night manager. Work is hard to come by. He would teach if he had the opportunity, but the one job offer he receives requires that in addition to mathematics he teach singing and handicrafts, an insult to his intellect, and so he turns it down.

Between his studies and the bookkeeping, he has little time for politics. He rarely has time for more than a few hours of sleep. He is not out protesting the day the one-eyed man and his young nephew are killed at a left-wing demonstration, though he reads that the court agrees the young patriots who fired into the demonstration are not guilty of murder. It was, as Josef sees it as well, self-defense.

He would think nothing more of the matter, except the socialists—hearing the verdict—storm both the university and the Palace of Justice. The police fire into the crowds, killing eighty-nine people and injuring hundreds more. Josef will call it a socialist revolt and the socialists will name it a massacre. The workers themselves express their dismay with a general strike, which is why the trolleys stop running and the telephone service ceases. But Josef remembers July 15, 1927, for another reason.

On the Ringstrasse, as he makes his way to campus, the press of the protest slows him. He worries he will not be permitted to pass, that he'll never make it to the safety of the lecture halls.

The crowd's energy frightens him. He feels the heat of the day and of the bodies beside him: a bearded man with a placard that he thrusts above his head; a pair of children in tattered pants; a woman in a wide gray dress who hands him a leaflet. On the front is a drawing of the dead child.

"This was not self-defense!" she insists.

Josef crumples the flyer, tosses it behind him. He does not share her contempt for the court's decision. Already, he sees that this demonstration promises violence.

He would return home, or at least take a side street, but he can return no more easily than he arrived through the throng of students and the men dressed in the uniform of the Republikanischer Schutzbund, the workers' army.

Josef presses his fingers to his temples, turns away as the man beside him raises his placard and calls out, "Justice for the workers!"

Then the man's gone, pulled into the crowd of bloodthirsty Bolshevists. Josef tries to walk faster. The streets are littered with flyers and broken glass. From ahead, he hears that the windows of the philosophy building have been broken. From his right, he hears the half hour chime. Will he ever get through?

From his left comes a woman's voice.

"Justice for the innocent!"

She is standing above the crowd, as if onstage or beneath a spotlight. Josef sees the firmness of her chin and cheekbones, the shades of gold and brown that fight to dominate her eyes, her hair as wild as the violence in the city streets.

He recognizes her at once.

* * *

JOSEF PRESSES THROUGH the protestors toward Sophia and reaches her only because she is not moving herself. She stands on a concrete bench, not unlike the one where he first met her more than a decade earlier. Her shoes are bright red and buckled twice, once across the instep of her foot and a second time around the ankle. He has never seen shoes like them before and suspects by their perfect fit that they were made for her. The color matches her gown. Its satin catches the light.

She should not be out in this crowd—he can still hear gunshots—and he is about to grasp her leg, and so catch her attention, when he realizes she's not alone. Standing on the other side of the bench, his face blocked by the skirt of her dress, is a man who must have urged her to leave, as she steps down from her perch.

Josef finds himself unexpectedly staring into her face, his tongue immobilized by the recollection of their brief meeting that long-ago summer, or by his change in circumstance. He remembers her voice—*Have you ever been in love?*—and the kiss that felt like a whisper. What is she doing here? What does her smile mean?

"Are you hurt?" she says. "Can I help you?"

"Op-Opatija," he stammers, a place that no longer belongs to him, or even to his country. "We met in Opatija."

She takes his hand between both of hers.

"Of course," she says, her eyes resting just beyond his shoulder, as if she were trying to discern his past. "Of course I remember you."

"You shouldn't be here," Josef says.

"I should be at the library," she agrees. "But we got caught up in the—"

"It was you who decided to jump up on the bench," her companion says, and Josef turns to him.

"Professor Engelhardt," Sophia says, half an introduction. She waits for Josef to announce his own name.

Josef does not. Engelhardt should know him. The famed professor read Josef's thesis just last year, pronouncing it "sufficient," the lowest passing mark. Engelhardt's radical views warp his understanding of the world as well as his appreciation for Josef's work.

"Are you headed to campus?" Josef asks Sophia. "I was on my way—"

"The campus is closed," Engelhardt says. "Lectures canceled. It's best you go home."

"Are you studying at the university?" Sophia asks.

Josef has finished his doctorate, but before he can teach at the university, he must earn the right to do so, a privilege that will require at least four more years of study—for Josef, likely longer. The process is designed for men with means, and Josef only manages because in addition to his studies, he keeps books at the café. If Sophia were to ask him again about love, he'd say he has no time for it, and yet, seeing her, time becomes irrelevant.

"Mathematics and logic," he says.

"How funny," Sophia says. "I work with Dr. Engelhardt."

Josef must have misheard. A logician of Engelhardt's status would not mentor a woman. And yet, there the professor stands, one hand on Sophia's shoulder, gently guiding her toward the campus, and against his own advice.

"Our paths will no doubt cross again," Sophia says.

"Yes," Josef says, but he knows she cannot hear him.

He can scarcely hear his own voice.

* * *

At home, Sophia still dancing in his thoughts, Josef learns that his father—electrified by the city violence—descended from the family's flat for the first time in weeks to participate more fully. Although he was not himself hit, the sound of the gunshots distressed him. Believing himself wounded, he waved his one intact arm and insisted he was bleeding. Then he insulted the men who calmed him in so ugly a fashion that Josef blushes when the incident is described to him.

Josef would have taken his father to the sanatorium that evening, but the trains are not running due to the general strike, and he worries that the air will again be broken by gunfire. Instead, he spends the night beside his father's bed, nodding while his father blames the violence on the Jews and communists, who have taken everything. But not from him. They have not stolen his fortune, because he is wise and buried it, where it will remain safe until the unrest is over.

"Where?" Josef asks. He is both surprised and angry. How could his father have buried the fortune and left him to work tables? To struggle each day to earn rent? Did he realize his decision imprisoned his own family in a squalid flat, far from the city center? "Where did you bury it?"

"They will never find it," his father says. "They will never take it from us."

This victory brings a tortured smile to his father's face, and though Josef asks again where the fortune is buried, his father looks back at him blankly.

A stay at the psychiatric hospital will permit the old man to regain his wits, Josef decides. He takes his father the next day. Soon after, he receives notice that his father has escaped the sanatorium. His corpse is found in the Danube.

Josef learns this horrifying news while at the university, and not only does he feel guilt—he was the one who took his father to the hospital—but he is confronted by the sympathy of the students who are present when the news is relayed. Josef does not wish to share his grief with these near strangers. Nor does he wish to return home, where he must share the news with his mother, but this is what he does, the loaf of bread she asked him to pick up sitting between them unsliced. He will throw the loaf away the next day, but his father's death will continue to haunt him. The last words his father spoke to him—*They will never find it. They will never take it from us*—keep Josef awake at night.

He tells no one of his efforts to discover the buried fortune, other than Sophia, whom he contrives to see often: at the library, on campus, or sometimes at the café where he keeps the books. He despises the work, and yet he agrees to more hours when he becomes the night manager. He makes little more than he did before, and he must now serve the frivolous fools who quote Karl Kraus, but he chooses to be on the floor because Sophia spends her evenings there. He's not in a position to take a seat at her table, but he can listen to her conversation. At times, he is so excited, he forgets his waiter's costume and all that his family has lost.

On campus, she sits in the front row of all Engelhardt's lectures, and Josef sits behind her, near the back of the room, where he can study her without being watched. Some days, Josef hears nothing, so intent is he on the curve of her shoulder. Whenever he passes her office—a small room off Engelhardt's larger one—he stops to eavesdrop. Her laugh is multifaceted. Josef imagines sapphire, blue and sparkling. She articulates each word as if it were a rock she's polished. If he could, he'd collect them in a box so no one else could have one.

Sometimes he follows her. If she is alone, he offers his company. He prefers not to share her attention, nor does he like to discuss philosophy, as her views—on religion or a unified science—do not sit well with him. One day Sophia will realize her arguments are undermined by the weakness of her sex. Until then, he tolerates them. He will do anything for her, and he has told her this.

"You are a good friend," she says.

She is a good friend to him as well. When Professor Huber dies suddenly in the fall of 1933, his position is not advertised, but Sophia tells Josef that Engelhardt will fill it quietly. There are no academic opportunities in Vienna, yet someone must teach the dead man's classes, and the man appointed will likely remain on.

"I will write to Engelhardt on your behalf," she tells him.

With her recommendation, the job will no doubt be his.

* * *

WHEN PROFESSOR ENGELHARDT agrees to send Josef and Moritz to the séance to observe Maria Campioni, Josef begins to close the café at once. Engelhardt's words swirl in his head: *I promised to file the paperwork for Professor Huber's replacement tomorrow.*

He turns away a respectable customer and angers a dozen more by removing plates and cups from tabletops he will not wipe down that night. He cannot wait while men linger over conversation. He cannot refill glasses or ask if anyone wishes for more. The séance begins at nine, and he will be there. Moritz will not snatch away Sophia's favor. Let the customers be angry! Josef will not work at the café much longer.

He does not look up from his labor, though he knows Sophia taunts him with her naked calves crossed demurely beneath the marble top of Engelhardt's table at the far end of the room. Her gown, a silk charmeuse with a yoke of lace and a flounce of netting that covers but does not conceal her skin, cost more than he earns in six months, but he is not angered by her wealth. The dress is absurd in the coffeehouse. This is no doubt why she wears it. Had she instead gone to Hotel Sacher, where the patrons dine in *chambres séparées*, she would have donned a maid's costume, or carried a paper bouquet of red carnations.

She dresses so only to titillate him, he thinks, as the mop moves beneath his force until even the stains his colleagues deem unyielding succumb to his will. His colleagues. The term is as perverse as Sophia's gown. None of his coffeehouse colleagues attend university, and none dream of being more than what they are, paid servers, glad for the work and the meal they take home at the end of the day. If they aspire at all, it is to his position, night manager, for which one must know numbers well enough to close out the register.

Josef pours the filthy mop water into the street, locks the side door, hangs the mop from the wall hook limned by mildew. He's already counted the monies, bundled the cash, placed it in the lockbox beside the pistol the owner keeps in case of brawls. Ever since the war, the streets have been violent—good, honest men fighting the socialists, who blither endlessly about public housing but instead build their army. They say the Schutzbund exists to protect party parades, but Josef knows better. An army is a tool of power, and the Reds are intent on revolution. They will destroy what his family built: Austria for Austrians.

For the first time since he began closing, Josef raises his eyes to

Sophia. She sits beside Moritz, and though Josef is certain she feels his gaze, she does not turn from her conversation. Her lips are pursed in concentration. Her eyes are closed. What was it she said about darkness? Not that it exists only relative to light, but that it belongs to the world.

He wants to leave with Sophia, to walk her home, to make a joke so that the night might sparkle with her laughter, but instead he gets Moritz, whose necktie is arranged in a ridiculous bow that makes his head appear to float on an ocean of fabric. Has no one the courage to tell him that he looks foolish?

Even Josef, in his waiter's costume, looks more presentable. He may reek of coffee, but his trousers are not covered in mud. His hair is neat—he carries a comb in his breast pocket to ensure this is so. Last night, his mother agreed to trim his hair, and though his neck feels tender and exposed, he knows that he looks better for the close cut. He might not be tall, but he carries himself well. Women delight in him. Moritz, though only a year older than Josef, already has a stoop to his shoulders.

* * *

AT LAST, THE café empties, and Josef takes the key ring from the wall hook. Moritz and Sophia alone remain seated. Josef hears her speak Wittgenstein's name.

Wittgenstein. Why should one man be so revered?

He feels the weight of the key ring in his pocket. On the nights he closes, he takes the keys with him; once Engelhardt offers the new position, he will never have to do so again. One day, his wardrobe will be tailored in London. He will hire a barber to attend to his morning shave, own homes in Vienna and Paris, an estate in the countryside. When his family is as wealthy as the Wittgensteins, he, too, will be well known and respected.

When she stands, Sophia's heels click against the tiled floor. Over her silk gown she has wrapped a stole. Secured by nothing but the shape of her shoulders, the garment is meant to be removed. He considers telling her how he would like to pull it off to reveal her perfect skin but decides not to. Even if he whispers, Moritz stands close enough to hear him. He knows better than to speak intimately to a woman at the wrong time. Josef has always known what to say to women.

"Thank you for going to the séance on such short notice," Sophia says, addressing both Josef and Moritz.

Josef nods but feels slighted.

* * *

AT THE DOOR of Maria Campioni's apartment, a silver-haired woman hands Josef branches of dried sage. Moritz is here on Engelhardt's behalf, Josef explains, and the woman charges neither for the evening. Josef would not have paid for himself, regardless. In exchange for handing out the medium's cards at the café, Maria Campioni grants him free entrance. In truth, it is through Josef that the medium first came to Engelhardt's attention, though Engelhardt does not remember this.

Ever since his father died, Josef has attended Maria Campioni's séances. For years, as he's sat in this room waiting for his father's spirit and been discouraged by the silence, he's clung to the belief that his father will speak, that Josef need only reach out to him more intently, that Maria Campioni will at last bring them together and he can ask the question that only his father can answer: Where did you hide the money?

His father must have buried the money in the woods, or secured it beneath a stone beside the Danube, or entrusted it to someone who now withholds it, when Josef needs it most. Had his father simply sewn the money into the lining of his coat or quilt, Josef would have found it. He's searched the obvious places again and again, tearing fabric until his mother, eyes wide with fear, throws him out of their rented rooms. No matter. Soon, he and his mother will move to better quarters. The university might not pay enough for him to resume his childhood lifestyle, but the salary will sustain him while he waits for his father to speak. And he will command respect, which is also a currency.

Josef leads Moritz down the hallway decorated with photographs of Maria Campioni, a plain woman with unruly eyebrows and thin brown hair. In each photograph, she stares into the camera, her lips arranged in a playful smile, as if she is unaware of her plainness. Though she appears alone, the plaque beneath each image bears two names, hers and one belonging to a dead man. She does not summon women, Josef tells Moritz. Women despise her. They are jealous creatures, even in death.

"I see no one else in these photographs," Moritz says. He has stood for some moments before *Frau Campioni and Herr Buchleitner*, in which the medium stands before a lake, a scarf wound around her head like a turban.

"You don't see the dead in photographs," Josef says.

"I see," Moritz says, raising one hand to Engelhardt's camera, as if he might photograph the photograph, but he does not.

* * *

THE SITTING ROOM is empty of furniture aside from a wooden chair where Maria Campioni sits. Its legs are of uneven thickness, appearing to have come from different makers. Aside from the walls, painted to look like red silk, the room is without pretense, the lamps mismatched, the rug woven from scraps of cloth and bare in places, the floor gouged with wear. The lower third of the walls is covered in mirrors that make the space seem larger.

When Josef sits beside Moritz, the circle around the medium is comprised of eleven guests: six men and five women.

"You doubt me," the medium says, fixing her eyes on Moritz.

"I have only come to observe and take photographs," he says. "It is, to me, quite remarkable."

"He will ruin it for us all," says a woman who's dressed, much like the medium herself, in loose black fabric that falls around her in such a way that Josef cannot tell if she is thin or fat. Her companion, another woman, young enough to be her daughter, begins to cry.

Maria Campioni shoos away the objection. "His doubts silence neither the living nor the dead. They see all, the past, the present, the future."

The future, yes. Josef imagines Sophia. She will have fresh peaches in winter, a castle in the south of France, a metal cage of butterflies that will flap their perfect wings. He sees his corner office at the university, tastes the venison served on a marble table covered with a fine white table linen. He will hold Sophia in his arms and press her face to his chest, and she will be content.

From down the hall comes the sound of a violin, and Josef knows the medium's assistant has placed the recording on the gramophone. He's heard this song at every séance. He knows the melody well enough to hum along but does not.

"Tonight we will speak to our loved ones on the other side." The medium closes her eyes. "I will bring them to you, if they are willing to come."

Josef feels this last remark is directed at him, though it is not his fault that his father has not arrived here.

He hears the snap of the camera and knows Moritz has taken a photograph.

If the night follows the pattern of the previous ones, the medium will soon be possessed by a spirit and rise from her seat. She will sway where she stands in the center of the room, her arms extended to either side as if she might take flight. Her features will shift, her nose becoming smaller or upturned, her lips growing full or narrowing, her irises deepening to black or paling to a hazy blue. She will appear to be the dead person who is commanding her voice, though only the person to whom the spirit speaks will see the likeness. Only the person who receives the spirit's message will be transported by the contact. The camera in Moritz's hands will capture nothing.

Tonight, the medium remains seated for nearly an hour, the eleven guests shifting their legs beneath them to ensure the flow of blood. Josef feels their impatience. He wonders at the silence and fears Moritz has inflicted it upon them. Perhaps the dead hide from those who dismiss them lightly.

The music has ceased. Josef cannot remember when it stopped, or if this silence is also usual. From previous séances, he remembers only the medium's voice, low and monotone when she is possessed by a spirit.

The minutes pass. From the far side of the room comes a dull ring, not unlike the sound Josef's knuckles make against his metal wait tray.

The medium rises, her eyes now open, though her arms do not spread wide and she does not sway as she should. Her hands are fisted; her face appears pained. When she falls to the floor, her thin hair spreads across the carpet.

Moritz's camera clicks, and Josef feels angry. How can the lecturer think of photographs?

The medium begins to writhe. From her mouth comes foam, a gray-green ectoplasm. Across the room, a woman prays that the Lord will deliver them.

Could it be? Could his father have come at last? Will he tell Josef the location of the fortune? Will Josef even have a chance to boast of his promotion?

"Father," Josef says aloud, though he does not see his father, only the medium. He has not yet heard his father's voice.

The camera clicks again, and then the lights go out.

6

Hase

BERKELEY, 2016

Harriet has cut her hair short since I last saw her, at Dr. Ord's memorial. The style makes her seem older and very serious. She wears a green headband that suits her henna-red hair, and a cropped sweatshirt and jeans that end at midcalf. Beneath these, and despite the late afternoon heat, she wears black stockings patterned with pink and green flowers. Her fashion sense, at least, has not changed. Nor has the house. Harriet left her mother's old art—the masks, which I notice at once, as well as the framed etchings of Ernst Mach and Olga Hahn-Neurath, whom both Dr. Ord and my father admired.

I sit down on the couch, a bastion of cushions upholstered in an orange and gold paisley fabric that probably influenced Harriet's taste in clothing. Stacked on the coffee table are dozens of manila folders, each bulging with papers, and several mathematics journals.

"Do you want coffee?" Harriet is already headed toward the kitchen. "Excuse the mess—I'm working on a book. I started it with my mother, but now it's just me, so it'll never be finished."

I pick up a folder, flip open to a ledger sheet with my father's handwriting, his arrows and brackets, the flourish of the elongated S-shaped integral sign. My father's papers are like a religion to him, a meditation, a touchstone. On the boat, he keeps his correspondence in a box beneath his bed, as if he fears being apart from his work even for a moment.

I ignore the urge to slip the ledger sheet into my pocket.

"I was thinking about you just the other day," Harriet says, returning with two coffees, though it's closer to dinner than to lunchtime. The wall clock reads 4:42, but Harriet may not have changed it for daylight savings. She sits beside me, and her mother's gray-blue irises meet mine. Harriet's eyes are not yet padded with bags, but I can see a hint of them, almost as if her mother's face is behind the skin, trying to push through. I straighten my shoulders reflexively.

"There was this odd librarian who came by," Harriet says. "From the Zedlacher Institute. He told me he's documenting the Engelhardt circle, and he—"

I startle. Not only had the Zedlacher Institute contacted me, but the book my father asked me to retrieve "in the event" is Walfried Engelhardt's *A Treatise on Logic and the Foundations of Mathematics*.

"—he was hoping to interview my mother, the Engelhardt circle was one of her interests, but—"

"I came out here to get the Engelhardt book," I say. "My father—"

"I have a copy upstairs," Harriet says. "The guy was really odd," she continues, her voice like the ocean, soothing, constant. The ocean never cares if I respond, and Harriet doesn't leave me time to, anyway. My knee touches hers, and still, I feel far away. I hear her voice, but we might as well be on the telephone. "Even if he weren't from the Zedlacher Institute, I wouldn't trust him. He kept going on and on about Haskell Gaul's Wikipedia page. So, of course, I thought of you. Are you still wasting your time on that site?"

"No," I say. Harriet has never cared for Wikipedia, and has actively disliked it ever since some bonehead deleted her mother's biography. "I'm changing history."

"Right, well. He shoved Haskell Gaul's Wikipedia page under my nose and asked me to identify—"

"No one can identify Haskell Gaul."

"Not Haskell Gaul," Harriet says. "The math on the page. He wanted to know if I recognized it."

Harriet, like her mother, has a PhD in mathematics, only Dr. Ord specialized in string theory, while Harriet, who is also a Dr. Ord, though I never think of her as this, is more interested in probability and statistics.

"Did you recognize it?" I ask.

"It was garbage. The reason the page contained an image of the formulas and not normal lines of text is that the symbols don't exist. It wasn't even math. But the guy insisted it was extremely important that I identify the author. He claimed it had to do with time travel and the conjecture and the fundamental nature of *all of reality*. Do you remember the mathematics conference the Zedlacher Institute had, when that graduate student died of sleep deprivation?"

"I do," I say.

I realize I'm moving too much, crossing and uncrossing my legs, leaning back in the cushions, then forward. I can't find a comfortable position. I want to tell Harriet that my father's missing, that he might be dead, but if I do, she'll tell me to go to the police, and I can't do that, so I stare at her necklace, a locket like mine, only engraved with her initials.

"Can you show me the Wikipedia page?" I ask.

She extracts her laptop from beneath the piled folders, an old machine, slowed by the number of open files, but I keep these observations to myself. She navigates to the web page and then turns the screen so I can better see it.

The Haskell Gaul page is long, because it contains a section with photographs of all the men who claim to be Haskell Gaul beneath the known details of the man himself: that he arrived in Vienna in 1933 and that Josef Zedlacher conducted a thorough investigation several years later and found no trace of a Haskell Gaul before then. There are notes about Gaul's time in Vienna and a brief paragraph on his death in 1934.

"Here," Harriet says, pointing to the image containing the strange math. "It's attributed to Anton Moritz, but apparently, it's not published anywhere, and the notation is nothing Moritz would have used in his time. I mean, no one used notation like that in the thirties, or in any time, for that matter."

"I've seen it," I say, because I have.

"Where?" Harriet asks.

"In a letter," I say. "I have it back home. I was going to give it to—" I stop, because I don't want to talk about my father. I don't want Harriet to ask how he is. I don't want to answer, and I don't want to lie.

"You can see who added the image," I say instead, bending across her to click the page history tab and reveal a long list of edits—a large number of them reverted, content added and then deleted, due to a passionate argument over whether the Haskell Gaul page should be categorized as "fictional character" or "biography," and whether the Zedlacher book can be used as a reliable source.

"Who is it?" Harriet asks.

"Oh, wow," I say. "It's Manifold."

Manifold, like TheRabbit, is an online name used only on Wikipedia. I've come across Manifold so often I've searched other forums for his handle, without luck, to see what more I could learn about him. In truth, I don't even know that Manifold is a man, but as everyone on Wikipedia refers to Manifold as a "he," I do, too. He edits mostly math pages and is widely considered a genius. Manifold himself achieved notoriety a few years ago because he recategorized all the computer science pages as "mathematics," and the FBI had to be alerted when he began receiving death threats. I've never interacted with him, but I often come across his edits. His editor biography says only: "Don't contact me."

"Oh, well," Harriet says, snapping closed the screen. She turns to me, and I feel her eyes dart from my unbrushed hair to my lips, which are pressed and must betray my distress, because she frowns. "You still haven't told me what brought you out here."

"The Engelhardt book," I say.

"Right. Let me grab that—"

"I have to get the library copy. It's out at the north branch."

"The branch library has that?"

"No one ever checks it out," I say.

"Do you need a ride out there?"

"It doesn't open until tomorrow. Can I stay here tonight?"

A part of me wants to ask if it would be okay to sleep in Harriet's bed with her, just like we did when we were kids.

Harriet is staring at my hands, the dirty fingernails, the chipped burgundy polish.

"Okay," she says. "I don't mean to press, but if you want to talk about anything, I'm here. Okay?"

"Okay?" she repeats.

I nod.

When she hands me a blanket, her fingers brush mine, the contact so brief that I feel my memory of it is unreliable. I could not have felt warmth in so quick a touch, but I did—I do.

* * *

I WAKE TO the murky light of early dawn. The blanket and pillow Harriet gave me have fallen to the floor, as has the magazine I asked for and didn't read, though holding *The Atlantic* and turning a page every now and then at least gave me the appearance of being engaged.

Harriet is already awake and sits at her computer. She's wearing a black T-shirt with the word *Average* printed across the front, as well as pink shorts that nearly reach her knees and pink-framed reading glasses. From the beeps and explosions emerging from her laptop, I can tell she's playing a video game.

"Hungry?" she asks. "I have yogurt if you like. I picked out some fresh clothes for you, too."

I turn down the yogurt but accept the outfit: a close-fitting yellow spaghetti-strap top and a lavender skirt that is simply a tube of cloth I can pull up or down to expose a customizable expanse of bare skin. I suggest a T-shirt, like hers, but Harriet insists I look amazing.

"I'm right," she says. "I'm always right."

The hours between waking and the library opening feel like days, but at last I slip into the passenger seat of Harriet's car and pull the seat belt across my shoulder. The armrest is cold, but I clutch it when the car lurches forward, then back, and we pull away from the curb.

Harriet's car is a mess. The dark gray seats don't conceal the numerous stains; the fabric roof liner is torn, even shredded in places, as if someone has tried to claw their way out. I tap my fingers against the armrest but don't realize I'm doing this until Harriet tells me she can't drive with the "incessant racket."

She has the radio tuned to a pop station, and I ask if we can turn it off.

"I like tinny, happy pop," she says, but she turns it off.

As she drives, she natters: *he's speeding, she's speeding, that truck's going 128*. She calculates the speed in her head based on various observations that she sometimes shares as well: *I timed him from the bridge*, or *he covered fifty meters in twenty seconds.* Harriet does everything using the metric system, and I find this annoying, though for no good reason.

When we arrive, the library is just opening and the parking lot is empty. Still, Harriet insists on pulling in and out of her spot until she feels the car is "centered."

"The university library is a lot closer," she says.

"The university library doesn't have what I need."

"Thanks for going out of your way," I add.

* * *

THE LIBRARY HASN'T changed much in the decade since I was last here. The roof still looks like it's about to cave in; the grounds remain unplanted. I don't remember the picnic tables, but they look old and worn and were probably here then as well.

Inside, the books displayed in the featured case are new, but otherwise, the place is as it was when my father led me to the mathematics section, where the books he added were sure to be safe. He'd gone through the entire collection himself, and none of the books had been checked out in decades.

As I run my finger over the spines, I wonder how long the overhead light has been out. The books are so old, my father should have worried the library would throw them away, though I also know such a fear would never cross his mind. Throwing away Euclid's *Elements* would be like burning a Bible or tearing a treasure map to shreds. No one would even think of it.

In the event, Hase, you must get the book. Not that he's dead. I don't know that. Life is like innocence: assumed, unless proven otherwise.

"Not a bad collection for such a small library," Harriet says. "They have my mom's book," she notes approvingly.

I scan the spines for Engelhardt's *A Treatise on Logic and the Foundations of Mathematics*, a surprisingly slim volume that looks more battered than studied.

I flip open the book to the page my father specified, seventy-one. The math itself might as well be written in kanji for all I understand of the symbols, but I recognize my father's handwriting at the top, a neat line of numerals:

26573

I expected to find something useful: a map with an X; a set of instructions I can follow, continue to follow; a cassette tape I can listen to again and again, whenever I need to hear my father's calm voice.

The cryptic line of numbers cannot be what my father meant.

I turn to the next page. It's empty, a chapter break, but even before I'm confronted with its blankness, I know seventy-two isn't right. The page my father meant is the previous one. Seventy-one, a permutable prime and my father's favorite number.

Harriet reaches over my shoulder to replace the spiral-bound calculus text she grabbed while I was looking at the Engelhardt volume. I shut it, and a business card falls out: Dr. Monica Ord, Professor of Mathematics. On the back, again in pencil, are the words "office hours, 2–3 Monday."

Was I supposed to ask Dr. Ord what the numbers mean? Dr. Ord can't help from beyond the grave. Dr. Ord can't laugh and say, "Oh, how like your father," and then explain, as she'd done for the trees surrounding her house, what the numbers actually are.

I feel the urge to tear the cover off the Engelhardt book, scatter its guts across the library floor, kick the shelf, watch the volumes fall into a tumbled mess—though, of course, I'll do none of these things. As long as everything's neat, no one will know my quiet is just a facade.

"Are you going to tell me what this is about?" Harriet's voice comes as if from far away.

I'm trapped between the library shelves. I hadn't planned on telling Harriet about my father's disappearance, but I am not prepared for the dizzying possibility that *the book* will lead me nowhere.

"My dad's missing," I admit. "The coast guard found his boat—"

"Oh, god," Harriet says.

I accept her embrace, feel the rubbery texture of the *Average* logo on her shirt against my arm.

"You should have told me," she says.

Her brows, which she always darkens and shapes with a color that doesn't quite match her skin tone, press down. I expect she'll say more, but she's waiting for me.

"He's missing," I repeat. And then, because Harriet's concern is plain on her face, I explain, "I only came here because he asked me to. He was supposed to leave instructions."

I hold out Dr. Ord's card as if it's evidence.

And then the whole story emerges from my lips, how my father had not come for my birthday, how I saw his boat in the paper, how I know Dr. Ord would have been able to help, but she is gone, too.

Gone, I say, not *dead*. I can't bring myself to speak the word *dead*. All my father left me is a number, a code without a key, instructions I can't follow.

"Maybe I can help?" Harriet offers. "I mean, my mother and I worked together pretty closely."

She takes the Engelhardt book from me, and I tell her to open to page seventy-one and wait as she reads the lines, considers, and then, with one hand, directs my gaze to each spot on the page as she speaks.

"This symbol means strict implication. And this"—she points to the second line on the page—"represents the set of all real numbers."

"It's the numbers at the top of the page," I say.

"Right. It's hard to say what any of it has to do with the numbers on top. Maybe they're a code of some sort."

"Great," I say, too agitated to discuss the conclusion I'd already come to. "Thanks."

I slip the Engelhardt book beneath the fitted yellow shirt I borrowed from Harriet, and then fold my arms across my chest to hide the lines that show. I've never had a library card, but the book does not belong to the library. This book, like my father—and me—has no proper identification.

7

Anton

VIENNA, 1933

I arrived at the séance confident that I would debunk the charade, if not with Engelhardt's camera, then by my own observations. I could see contradictions in forty-page derivations. The corporeal world—filled with bodies and matter obeying physical laws—was, in comparison, relatively simple to verify. Whatever happened in Maria Campioni's sitting room would obey the forces of the living world, however the medium conspired to make events appear otherwise.

I was only surprised that Josef believed the woman possessed abilities beyond base trickery, for he was a student of mathematics, as well as a pupil of Engelhardt's. How earnest he'd been when he told me the dead do not appear in photographs! Of course the dead would not appear in photographs. What Engelhardt hoped to capture with the camera was not the dead but the medium's hand attempting to deceive us. When I presented my evidence against the woman, Josef would have to reconsider his position. No logical person could believe in spiritualism when, by one's own senses, one could clearly see it was a hoax.

All this I thought as I entered her sitting room, which was empty of the drapes and the bulky furniture I expected. The walls were bare aside from a low row of mirrors that were no doubt intended to confuse us. The starkness surprised me, as a framed picture could conveniently conceal a hole between one room and another.

I sat down in the circle and, like the others, turned to the medium. I thought of all conjurers as fabric-draped crones, but Maria Campioni was about my age and looked much like the portraits of Kaiser Franz Joseph. I wondered if her mother or grandmother had been a maid at the palace. I wondered if she had a family herself.

As the minutes became an hour, the hardness of the floor entered my muscles. The odor of smoke and cooking fat grew stronger. I shifted my weight. The medium herself never moved. Did she fear me? My collared shirt and jacket, and the tie—knotted in the fashion of the academics in Paris—betrayed me as a wise and observant man. She would do nothing that might compromise her deceptions.

Had I not felt obliged to sit until the end, I would have left. However, I could not in good faith report my observations to Engelhardt if I failed to endure the séance in its entirety, and so I remained.

My thoughts began to wander.

Before me was a blue-green lake that I visited long ago on a class outing. On the shore stood a group of boys, my old schoolmates. The day was bright and would burn us all before dusk, but we paid no heed. Who would be first to cross the lake? We bet against one another. We dove into the water. I don't remember who won, but I know I did not, because I remained behind Heinrich, who was older than the other boys, and strong. I hadn't thought of him as strong until I saw him in the water and became transfixed by his thighs, how he spread them wide and then drew them together, shooting forward, away from me.

I wanted to touch him.

I was horrified by this desire but felt it all the same. Heinrich was my classmate. We sat two rows apart.

I remember how he kissed my forehead and pulled my body—still moist from the lake—close to his own.

"We can be free here," he said.

"What do you mean?" I asked, and he laughed. He placed his lips against my chest, and I held my breath, as if I were underwater, unable to breathe.

If only we'd been invisible, far beneath the surface of the water.

But we were not invisible, for this is how I appeared, Heinrich's body above mine, when our instructor returned to tell us it was time to go.

"Anton, is it you?"

I startled to hear Heinrich's voice now, in Maria Campioni's sitting room. I hadn't seen him since that day at the lake. He'd gone from the outing to the headmaster's office, and after that, his desk remained empty. The schoolmaster relayed the news of his death a few months later and then asked us to turn our algebra books to page forty-seven. I did not. My eyes remained on Heinrich's desk; beside it, a window no one was permitted to open.

"Anton? I've never ceased thinking of you."

A chill ran through me—fear or sorrow, a blend of both. I wanted to flee the séance, but instead I pulled my gaze from the floor.

Heinrich stood before me. His blond hair appeared gray in the low light, and his features, though still perfectly balanced and finely drawn, wore an expression I didn't recall. This Heinrich was terrifying in his intensity, the dark hold of his regard enough to make me tremble. I wanted to rise, to run, but could not. Nor could I move my lips. I had fallen into a trancelike state, a nightmare, a hell. I could not turn away from Heinrich. I could not respond. Had I been drugged? Hypnotized?

I heard the click of Engelhardt's camera. The click, again. From far away, I heard a woman's voice. My head became light, my fingers numb.

When I woke, the circle of guests had broken apart. The camera sat beside me on the rug. The medium had risen, and the lights were on. A man asked for the time, another for directions to the train station.

Across from me, the wall mirror reflected my countenance: face pale as the moons of my fingernails, my lips without color, my eyes open but unfocused. I felt the chill of Heinrich's breath. Where he'd stood, the mirror reflected nothing, though Josef was in the glass, still beside me.

Legs weak, I stood.

"Did you know that Maria Campioni once summoned Colonel Redl?" Josef asked me.

Of all the dead men in Austria, why mention Redl? When the colonel placed a gun to his head and fired, all of Vienna knew the reason. Even before the papers reported that he'd traded Austria's secrets to the Russians, everyone knew he'd been blackmailed. His brief affair with an Italian soldier had already doomed him.

"No," I said, though my expression must have betrayed my disquiet, because Josef smirked.

"I look forward to your report," he said. "I'm sure Engelhardt will find it interesting."

* * *

I LET MYSELF out of Maria Campioni's apartment and was surprised to find the streets lit with early dawn light. I wanted to divorce myself from the séance and its torments, but the door did not lock behind me, nor did it close completely, and the murmur of voices followed me. I shivered. Did the other guests see the dead man with me? Were Heinrich's words spoken aloud? Or was his voice simply part of my nightmare, an expression of the fear I always carried, that even if I refused to act on my desires, I could not hide them, either.

I was shaken and exhausted, my thinking no longer clear.

The street itself was empty, but I heard chanting in the distance, the sound of breaking glass. Another rumble, more disquiet, a further terrible extension of the night. I longed for a jacket or scarf to wrap around my body. My arm trembled when I raised it to check my watch, which I could not read in the dimness. I walked until I needed to rest, and then sat down in the street like a madman. I felt the curious stares of passersby, but no one paused to ask if I needed a doctor.

I stopped four times on the journey that had required half an hour the night before, but I reached the campus before the morning's first session began.

The grounds, perfectly manicured when I'd left, were now littered with torn books and papers. The door to the philosophy building had been pried open and was covered in flyers, hammered with nails into the wood. Inside, the halls were marred with hateful slogans. The administrator insisted the university's extraterritorial immunity was fundamental to intellectual freedom, but the campus now proved so hospitable to rioters that it failed to serve all other purposes. The academic year was not even halfway through, and we'd called the painters twice already.

I didn't know if I'd find Engelhardt in his office, but I headed straight there, planning to leave the camera on his desk regardless. A student from my Thursday lecture greeted me, and I had the presence of mind to answer his question, which concerned topography. I would speak more about it in class, I said. He looked at me oddly—classes had been canceled for the week, he informed me—and then made mention of my tie, so I explained it was the current fashion in Paris.

I made my way to Engelhardt's office, ignoring the press of confusion. Word of the campus closure was just getting out. Engelhardt's door was closed, but I knew by the line of light that peeked out from beneath it that he was in. As I neared, I heard the sound of conversation as well. I had no wish to interrupt or to leave the camera in the hallway, where it could easily be trampled or stolen, and so I waited for a minute or an hour, I don't know.

At last, the door to Engelhardt's office opened, and Josef strode out in an expensive suit that was far too large for him. He'd managed, despite my early arrival, to preempt my visit. He did not meet my gaze, and I took this as a sign that he'd betrayed me in some way. He seemed, in general, uncomfortable, though he'd dressed up, no doubt hoping to impress the chair of philosophy. His face was clean-shaven, his hair neat. I, by comparison, appeared a mess, my clothes the same today as last night.

"I see you made it through the rubble," Engelhardt said, extending his hand in greeting. "Josef was just telling me about the séance."

Josef's expression revealed nothing about the conversation, not even his usual smirk. He did not wish me a good morning, nor did he acknowledge that we'd spent the evening together.

Engelhardt waved me into his office, and I passed between the two men as they exchanged goodbyes. Then Engelhardt followed me and closed the door. I suspected Josef would eavesdrop, but this fear was dwarfed by the illogical fear that he'd been privy to my nightmare.

If my secret were revealed, I feared that not even Adler, who still called me his most promising student, would vouch for me.

I set the camera on Engelhardt's desk.

"Did you get many photographs?" he asked.

"Some." I thought of Josef in the hallway, listening. "What did Josef report?"

Engelhardt smiled the half smile we all knew, because he smiled just so when he thought us idiotic. "Ectoplasm, but he had none to show me."

He patted the camera, and I continued to search his face for signs that his understanding of me had changed. I read a dozen dark meanings into the gaze he fixed on me, not unkindly but critically all the same. At last his eyes fell to my rumpled shirt.

"When I was a younger man, I worked all night, too," he said. "There's nothing more satisfying than throwing oneself against a problem like that."

"Yes," I said.

"You seem like a man with ambition."

I couldn't tell from his tone if Engelhardt thought ambition good or evil, but I lowered my eyes in what I thought was modesty. "I hope always to arrive at the truth."

Engelhardt smiled his half smile.

"Please," he said. "Join us tonight in the basement of the philosophy building. The university is closed, but we are still meeting. Adler will be sharing his thoughts on Esperanto."

"On Esperanto," I repeated, the weight of Engelhardt's words not yet fully striking me.

He'd invited me to his circle—not a condemnation, but an honor—yet all I could think about was Josef, outside in the hallway, listening.

* * *

ENGELHARDT INVITED ME to his circle as if on a whim, but he rarely invited newcomers, and I labored over my remarks for the rest of the day. With classes canceled, I had time to practice my points before Inge, who assured me I was "a smart one." However, I knew from experience how conclusions that seemed well substantiated when I sat alone at my desk could be questioned or thrown down like playing cards. Around Engelhardt's table sat men with the sharpest minds in Vienna, and as much as I admired my colleagues, the very intellect I revered could easily pierce my arguments and leave me bloody. To further upset me, on my way to the philosophy building, I twice crossed paths with the old woman I recognized from the night before as Maria Campioni's assistant. Each time I noticed her, I found her eyes boring into me, and I felt extremely unsettled.

When I arrived at the basement meeting room, Adler clearly picked up on my anxiety, as he looked up from his thermos of chicken soup and regaled me with stories about his most incompetent students. One had proved, through a series of assertions, that a number divided by itself was undefined. Another had decided that addition was devil's work and fled the department to become a poet.

I did my best to smile, but my thoughts remained blackened and etched with the lines of the old woman's face: her narrow cheeks and deep-set eyes, the dry lips that hung apart as if she had just spoken a dark omen or condemnation. By then, the circle members, whom I knew by reputation, had gathered at the table: two physicists, a half dozen members of the philosophy department, an architect, Adler, and Fräulein Popovic, who arrived with a stack of papers and sat down beside the empty seat at the center of the table. Her black dress struck me as something one might wear to the theater. Framed by the chalkboard behind her, however, it resembled a clear surface, possibility.

"Ah, Professor Moritz," she said. "I have the séance photographs."

I hadn't expected to see the images so soon, nor did I wish to look at them, but Fräulein Popovic rotated the photographs so that they appeared to me in their proper orientation, and I bent forward to better see.

The image on top of the stack was of Maria Campioni. She sat on her stark wooden chair, her eyes closed. Behind her, I could make out the faces of the guests across the circle from me, and even the reflected face of myself, though I remembered that the light had been low and wondered how the camera caught such detail.

"This is the first from the night," Fräulein Popovic said. She set it aside, revealing a second image of Maria Campioni. The medium appeared as she did before. Again, the image was startlingly clear. The only evidence that the first and second photo differed was in the background: a head turned toward or away from the medium, a hand resting on a knee or against the floor.

Again and again Fräulein Popovic removed the top image from the stack. Each time, I caught my breath, afraid anew.

"Really, quite remarkable," she said. "She never moves."

She uncovered the last of the images, and my eye was drawn to where I was reflected in the mirror glass. I sat on the floor with the camera to my chest, only I was not looking at the medium. If anything, I appeared to be looking at my own reflection, my face pale.

Then Fräulein Popovic covered the image with the rest of the photographs and slid the pile in front of the empty chair.

I wanted the meeting to start so that I might forget the haunting photographs of that wretched night, but the meeting could not begin until Engelhardt arrived and called the discussion to order.

* * *

AT LAST, THE door to the basement opened, and Engelhardt entered along with the administrator, whom I recognized from the portrait he'd commissioned of himself and hung in the library. He carried a portfolio case that no doubt contained the memoranda with which he regaled us. I received at least one a day, each demanding that I adhere to some new policy or another: we must include more Catholic philosophers in our syllabuses; at dusk, the windows must be fastened shut to discourage unlawful entry; we must fill out yet another form declaring our allegiance to the Fatherland Front, the single political party that Chancellor Dollfuss had established, with himself as head.

I worried that the administrator had come to force us to leave the closed campus, but he stopped in the doorway, and I realized that he was on his way elsewhere and only pausing to finish his conversation.

"You will take immediate action?" he said to Engelhardt.

Engelhardt smiled his half smile and said, "Thank you for bringing this matter to my attention."

With that, the administrator bid Engelhardt farewell, and the door closed behind him.

"The man is an idiot," Engelhardt said, sitting down beside Fräulein Popovic, who covered his hand with hers. She'd painted her nails a bright red, but I only noticed when their hands were joined.

Engelhardt then explained that the administrator had arrived that afternoon with a list of "tendentious professors" who were causing "unrest" among the student body. The students themselves had put together this list in the interest of protecting their own well-being, and the administrator explained that he was simply acting on their behalf, appealing to the faculty to amend their behavior. Today, Professor Engelhardt was distressed to discover his own name upon this list, along with the usual "undesirables," which we all understood to mean the communists and Jews, whose names had been circulating under the banner of various slanders well before I arrived at the university.

"Such madness," Engelhardt said. "I hold the chair!" He looked down, and I thought he was simply collecting his thoughts and would offer his reflections. Instead, he said, "Professor Moritz, are you ready to present?"

I was not ready to present. My understanding was that Adler would be sharing his thoughts on Esperanto. This was clearly Adler's understanding as well, and I was deciding how best to respond when I heard the tinny song of a music box. Then the door opened.

A strange man stood in the doorway. He appeared priestlike, in a dark jacket draped over his shoulders and an odd cap festooned with red roses. His hair was long, with ringlets that reminded me of Archimedean spirals, of which I've always been quite fond. His eyes—a moiré of blue, greens, and gray—were trained on me, and I was at once unsettled and drawn by his gaze. His lashes were startling even from where I sat across the room, each long enough to half wrap around my forefinger.

Did I know him? He was looking at me as if he expected an embrace, or perhaps I merely wished to pull him close, to confirm the existence of this stranger, who seemed more specter than man. I could not tear my eyes away from him.

He unfastened his coat and tossed it onto the table, revealing a pinstriped jacket and trousers that fit him so closely I could imagine the muscles beneath. He alone was standing, but with a confidence that implied those seated were mistaken.

"I am Haskell Gaul," he announced. He spoke loudly, as if to the room, but his gaze remained fixed on me, or, rather, through me, piercing my jacket and the shirt beneath to my flesh, of which I was suddenly conscious.

"And why are you here?" Engelhardt asked.

"I have come tonight just as I did before." He turned his gaze from me, and I felt at once relieved and emptied, invisible outside the line of his sight. "In the past, or in the future."

I could see that the words intrigued Engelhardt in the same way the séance did. "You've been here before?" he asked.

"Indeed," Gaul said. His accent was heavy and unplaceable. His clothing, too, was foreign: the flowing jacket, the oddly cut trousers. Even the fabric of his shirt, a white cloth that reflected the light in such a way that it sometimes appeared blue, was exotic.

Gaul considered the low ceiling and water-stained walls, and only then did I notice that the baseboards were blackened with mold. Only as he surveyed the room did I realize that the windowless walls blocked the night.

He pushed his hair back from his forehead, placed one hand against his own torso, where, were I holding him, I would rest my palm as well.

"This place is a hole," he said.

I thought the observation rude, but Engelhardt seemed oddly delighted.

"It is," he said. "Was it a hole in the past or future, the last time you were here?"

"Most likely." Gaul turned his gaze back to me, and I nodded stupidly, as if I had an opinion on this absurd claim. He frowned, consulted his watch. Perhaps he was in a hurry, though he made no move to leave.

"Shall we go elsewhere?" he said at last.

"Did we before?" Engelhardt asked.

"Yes," Gaul said. "We went to Café Josephinum."

"Very well, then," Engelhardt said. "Let's go to Café Josephinum."

* * *

WALKING TO THE café from the university, I was more moth than man, flitting behind Haskell Gaul so as not to miss his words. His German was heavily accented and he sometimes used the wrong tense, and though no one corrected him, he grew tired of the mistakes and switched to English.

I paid no attention to Engelhardt's responses, so intent was I on Gaul himself: how he leaned forward when he awaited a reply, interjecting when he found a statement lacking. He spoke as if hurried, though his gait in no way corroborated this.

The moon lit the night with an eerie glow. The streets were slick with light. I was anxious to get inside and command a good seat at the table; still, I held the door for my colleagues and, from the doorway, watched Haskell Gaul walk into the café as if he'd never entered it at all. He didn't stop to remove his coat or brush the dust from his trousers. He didn't raise his gaze from the floor or turn to ensure that the rest of us had followed. He didn't slow or speed his pace, and I imagined him walking just so till he hit his head against the far wall of the building. When he at last stopped, a dozen paces into the room, he said only, "Ah, so this is Café Josephinum."

The café had changed since I'd been there just the night before. The left front window was boarded up, and the room was noticeably darker for want of streetlight. The tables had been rearranged to provide access to the much-reduced view; even Gaul, the thinnest of us, could not navigate between them without inconveniencing others by asking them to move. The guests themselves seemed different as well, bundled in layers of dismal browns and grays, as I was myself.

"A socialist threw a brick through the window," Josef explained when he brought the coffee. He walked more slowly than usual. The weight of the tray seemed to pain him. "Late last night."

"But you were at the séance," Engelhardt said.

"Yes." Josef turned his gaze to me, and I felt his contempt.

"How do you know a socialist threw the brick?" Engelhardt asked, leaning forward. I thought he might begin lecturing on observational evidence, but Josef set down the last of the coffees and spoke first.

"Only a socialist would do such a thing," he said. "This is why we keep a gun in the safe."

When he turned back to the kitchen, Engelhardt shook his head. "There's something not right about that man."

"Josef was the one I wrote to you about for Professor Huber's position," Fräulein Popovic said.

Engelhardt laughed. "Even if he were suitable, he hasn't completed his habilitation."

Before she could argue, he leaned closer to her and lowered his voice.

I suspected he was speaking about Josef, or the position, or both, but I sat too far away to hear what he said. Our party was arranged in such a way that I, though last to reach the table and the farthest from Engelhardt, sat beside Haskell Gaul, who did not notice or chose to ignore the empty seat reserved for him between Engelhardt and Adler. My heart soared at this good fortune.

"Anton Moritz," I said, as I'd not yet had an opportunity to introduce myself.

"It's wonderful to finally see you. After all these years," he said.

I did not recall the name Haskell Gaul, but I said nothing so as not to embarrass him. He rested his palm on my thigh, and I felt the hair on my forearms rise.

"You found me, and now I've found you," he said.

He pressed his hand against my leg once more, and I shifted my weight, readjusting my position, close, but not too close, a natural distance, though I could not recall what natural was. My heart raced. I hoped no one saw my blush.

Gaul himself seemed untroubled by my distress.

"I found you?" I said.

His answer made no sense, though perhaps I misheard because of his accent: I'd written to him many times. We were close collaborators. "The way your mind works—it's astonishing."

I like to think that I said thank you, or better still, that I was honored that he remembered my work, or even that he'd taken the time to read my letters. I like to think that I had the wherewithal to propose that we discuss my ideas further, perhaps at another time, just the two of us. But my head had begun to throb; my words, when they tumbled from my lips, were like those of an awkward child.

"But I've never met you."

"No," he said. "You always refused to meet in person. Every time I asked—no, no, no.

"I understood, of course," he added. "But there was nothing I wanted more, Anton."

He spoke to me as if we were close, choosing the familiar "you" instead of the formal one, and now speaking my first name. No one in Vienna called me Anton. Herr Professor, Herr Professor Moritz, but never Anton.

His knee touched mine. I felt the warmth of his shoulder against me, and then, like a sudden chill, the curiosity of the others gathered around the table.

8

Josef

VIENNA, 1933

Josef has always had an interest in secrets, transgressions he discovers—overheard in the café or late at night when he walks home: Professor Leitner is having an affair with a student, Professor Fuchs has fallen in love with a prostitute, a Jewish student has lied about his last name. Most are shared in hushed voices, but Josef arranges his body so that he can hear, leaning over a table to wipe a second time or preemptively sweeping up crumbs of pastry. Secrets are valuable. He dutifully reports each to the administrator, and the administrator returns this favor with a small sum that Josef discreetly pockets.

The most recent payment, which Josef received after reporting that Professor Ladstätter once again assigned Arthur Schnitzler's pornographic play, now permits Josef to sit alone at a table at Restaurant Lichtenegger. He has not eaten here since he was a child and he and his twin brothers sat facing the window. Now he sits where his father once did, observing the bar and its assortment of brandies and bitters.

His glass has been empty for nearly ten minutes, and yet the waiter idles behind the counter as if the passing seconds are simply sheep he must count before he drifts to sleep entirely. This restaurant was once known for its service. When his father brought the family every Thursday night, and sometimes on Saturdays for lunch as well, he didn't even have to look up. Now the table linen is coarse, the cloth napkin folded carelessly. The woman at the table to Josef's left is speaking too loudly.

She wears her wealth ostentatiously, thick gold chains around both wrists and gems on every finger. Who does she think she'll impress? The waiter? He's attended to her needs—bringing coffee, refilling her water glass—twice since Josef arrived, and this irritates him.

Josef, too, is dressed finely. The fabric of his jacket is gray with a subtle sheen of silver. It dangles on his shoulders (altering the jacket would insult his father's memory, his mother insists), but its enamel buttons, each bearing the double-headed eagle of the Habsburgs, speak of prestige and confidence. His hair is brushed; the bare patch just above his right ear, where he pulls when he feels anxious, is covered. He looks respectable. Only he knows that in the satchel at his feet is his waiter's costume, which he carries, even though he intends to give notice tonight.

Today's lunch was meant to be a celebration. He reserved the table this morning, planning to invite Sophia to join him once the news became official: that he would fill Professor Huber's vacant *Dozent* position.

He's expected Engelhardt to offer the position ever since Sophia told him about the vacancy. He knows she wrote to Engelhardt on his behalf, because he's read the letter himself, alone in her office, where the envelope is filed with the rest of Engelhardt's correspondence.

Josef deserves this position. He is a Renaissance man, master of both art and logic, the most brilliant of Vienna's most exceptional students. The university will do well to count him among its salaried employees.

And yet, this morning, when Josef visited Engelhardt's office to present his report from the séance, the chair of philosophy did not extend the offer. Why does he make Josef wait? Had Moritz not arrived while they were talking, would he have done so? That must be it. And yet, Josef feels uneasy. He would cancel this celebration, except denying himself this fine meal is an admission of failure, and he has not failed. He did not invite Sophia to join him, but he still dines in anticipation of the good news that will surely arrive this afternoon.

"Trout with tarragon," the waiter says, depositing the plate before Josef as if it were a pair of torn gloves.

Josef spreads his napkin across his lap, lifts his fork. He is hungry, but the fish is nearly raw. It does not give way beneath his fork.

Josef calls the waiter back.

"It's underdone," he says.

The waiter smirks. "Would you prefer it burnt?"

In his pocket, Josef has more than twice the sum required for this meal. This waiter won't insult him.

"May I speak to the manager?" he says.

The waiter retrieves the plate, and Josef ignores the sympathetic glance the man receives from the woman at the next table. Her opinion means nothing to Josef. He spends far too much time impressing fools already. That Engelhardt should hold the chair! How can the university be blind to the man's shortcomings—the tedious pauses where he gropes for words (and is applauded for deep thought!), the lectures insulting God (while students nod approvingly!), the many times he's neglected to implement the administrator's policies (for the good of Austria!). Engelhardt's best years are behind him. No amount of work can compensate for the absence of original ideas, or the presence of questionable ones: *Religion, like spiritualism, is not a science; what cannot be verified is meaningless.* On several occasions, Josef has reported to the administrator that many feel Engelhardt is godless and too radical. He should not hold a position of power. Were their positions reversed, Josef would release Engelhardt from his service immediately. Instead, he must flatter the man, awaiting his favor.

The trout, when the manager returns with the plate, tastes like rubber. Josef must use a knife to cut it. The bell peppers, sliced thin and arranged like reaching fingers, are cold. But as the manager has served it, Josef pretends to relish the dish.

The bowl of liver dumpling soup arrives just as he finishes, the smell of the broth overpowering the lingering scent of fish. This soup was his childhood favorite, but now its scent reminds him of all he's lost: his status, his childhood home, his twin brothers, his father.

The memory of last night's séance turns in his thoughts. His father had been in the room, he's certain of it. He felt the presence as one might a blow to the chest or a bad case of indigestion. His father had come to him, to bless him before his promotion with the location of the buried fortune. Josef should have heard his voice, but another spirit forced him from the room.

To be so close and then denied! The night was wasted, and yet, it was not. The spirit was not the one Josef desired, but it was not entirely useless. Moritz had spoken very little, but he had called out a man's name. His voice was soft, but strong enough to capture Josef's attention, and he'd said enough—Josef leaning closer to listen—to betray his secret.

Such a secret is valuable indeed.

The third course arrives, and Josef's soup is untouched. The woman at the next table has departed. The restaurant is closing, the waiter says. They must prepare for the dinner guests.

Had the waiter thought to come earlier, Josef would have told him to take the bowl away. He does not say this, however, because his job is not to instruct the incompetent.

Before him, the pheasant, shriveled, skin blackened with char, sits beside mashed potatoes flecked with bits of red-brown skin. The English beans are withered.

"And bread?" Josef asks. The smell of the flesh, oily and rich, makes his stomach snarl.

"You would like to order bread?"

"I would like bread. And wine," he says, as his glass is still empty.

The waiter brings neither. Josef pays for the meal and leaves.

A wealthy man does not argue for discounts.

* * *

THE LATE AFTERNOON is chilly, but the shop-lined streets still bustle. The street musicians with their accordions force Josef to step out of his way, and he glares at the man who extends his cap as if expecting payment for this disservice.

The tram is too full to ride comfortably, and so Josef walks through the throng of hats and overcoats, past the tobacco shop and the bakery. He wants to get back to the university. Very likely Engelhardt is looking for Josef now. Josef should be there. He readjusts the strap of his satchel, concerned that a wrinkle has formed in the jacket beneath.

He turns toward the Ringstrasse, but two teenage boys block his way. Their hair is cropped short in the current fashion, and the shorter of the two clears his throat. His jacket is wool and expensive, not nearly as fine as Josef's, but fitted. His trousers are perfectly tailored to stop just short of his polished shoes.

"Are you with the university?" he asks.

Josef nods. He is headed to the university now, though he does not say this.

The taller of the two wraps his arm around Josef's neck and pulls him close. "All the Jews in Vienna are at the university. Are you a Jew?"

Josef shakes his head. His father fought for Austria. When he drowned, years later, his corpse went to the dissecting room, where the students of anatomy extracted a bullet from the muscle of his thigh. His mother received the metal wrapped in butcher paper, as if it were a gift.

"Of course he would deny it," the short boy says.

"I'm not a Jew," Josef says, his heart beating rapidly. In his pocket is the remainder of the sum the administrator gave him for his services, but he knows better than to hold this out as proof. Josef is nothing if not Aryan. He detests the socialists and the Jewish communist Marx, and yet these boys see nothing but Josef's dark hair. They are younger than he is but strong. They will leave him bruised and bloodied should the conversation turn to blows.

"I work for Café Josephinum," he says. He does not wish, in this context, to draw attention to the university. That the institution itself is seen as corrupt is testament to how far the radical elements have distorted its principles.

Once he has power and a permanent position, he will see that respectability is restored.

The tall boy releases his hold, and the shorter jabs his elbow into Josef's stomach.

"I'm tired of dealing with filth," the boy says.

Josef feels the pain like hunger, pulsing and intense.

He is fortunate that they walk away.

* * *

INJUSTICE PAINS JOSEF more than the blow. Likely his skin is already discolored, but he does not stop by the lavatory to confirm the bruise. He must hurry—Engelhardt may have left the offer letter at the department office. He is probably wondering why Josef has not yet accepted.

"Is there a letter for me?" he asks the department secretary.

The department office, with doors on four walls that permit visitors to enter from all directions, unnerves him. The counter is too high, the light gloomy. Beneath his feet, the parquet flooring is splintered and discolored with age.

"Your name?"

The secretary should know this, but Josef conceals his irritation. "Josef Zedlacher."

The secretary shakes his head.

"I was expecting a letter. Will you please look again?" Josef says.

The secretary thumbs through a stack of envelopes.

"Nothing," he says. "Is there something more I can do for you?"

"No." Josef feels like screaming, but he thanks the secretary—he knows to express gratitude to those who serve him competently—and leaves by the closest of the room's four doors.

He expects to find Engelhardt in his office, as it is open, but he is not there. Josef steps inside anyway. His abdomen remains tender from the blow, and he feels off-balance and out of sorts. He will wait where he can sit comfortably. Engelhardt may have left Josef's offer letter on his desk, though Josef searches through the papers and fails to find it. He paces the office, consults his watch. Engelhardt could not have left already, though as the minutes pass, Josef begins to suspect that he has. He must not have finished the paperwork, or he left it at home by mistake and has returned to collect it. What else could explain the silence?

Josef, too, should leave, but instead, he steps into Sophia's annex.

He has joked with her that her office is no bigger than a closet. He himself does not have an office, but he's noted that his bedroom is no larger than a closet, either. Sophia has never been to his apartment, but she knows the size of the room where he sleeps, and this thrills him. Perhaps she imagines him, as he does her, in bed, the blankets sliding off her torso. In his vision, she wears her hair down, and he brushes this wilderness away from her face to behold her ear and cheekbone. In sleep, she is innocent, her breath matching his, as if she and he were one body, as if nothing had changed for either of them since the day they first met.

He breathes deeply, hoping to find her in the office air, the scent of moss and fern, storm-rich and alive, but all he smells is chalk.

On the wall is a miniature he painted of her. She does not know how many likenesses he composed before finding one he felt adequate, and even this picture, over which he labored, insults her beauty. He captured the shape of her eyes, but not their intensity; the thickness of her hair, but not its urgent desire to spring from its styling. The angle of her head is thoughtful but removed. She watches the world as if amused by it. He traces the line of her cheek. The color is wrong. The paint is too thick. He wants to scrape the tinctures away and reveal the original lines. The truth is somewhere between these two curves, the visible and the obscured, the present and the past.

This portrait angers him. He would destroy it, but he has no better one, and he quiets the urge to drive his finger through the small canvas.

"Perhaps the next one," he says. "Perhaps she will sit one more time."

He knows Sophia stands to gain nothing from posing for him. Dozens of artists have painted her, some on commission, others, like Josef, of their own accord. She has told him that in her mother's home, there is a room filled with family portraits.

Sophia sits for him because she admires his talent. She must. "Josef is a gentle soul," she wrote Engelhardt. "Given an opportunity, he will go far . . ."

He will go far. Josef slides open the bottom drawer of her desk, where she files Engelhardt's correspondence, his fingers searching for the envelope he knows by feel, her stationery. He has read much of the other correspondence as well: old letters from Ladd-Franklin and Wittgenstein, which he secretly copies; memoranda from the university; scented envelopes from Engelhardt's wife, who has taken their only son to Paris to undergo X-ray therapy for epilepsy. The boy is wracked by the disease. No one expects him to return. Most prevalent among the letters are petitions that point to rampant unemployment and the need to limit the number of Jews and foreign students. Engelhardt has never once responded, and each time Josef meets with the administrator, he reports this troubling silence.

At last, Josef finds Sophia's letter and reads it again. He has not copied it, as the words are most beautiful in her hand. Nor has he stolen the letter so that he might more easily read it. If he took it, Sophia might notice its absence. She, too, might wish to reread it, and she must not find it missing. He is careful to replace her letter among the other candidate recommendations—all of which he's reviewed and none of whom are worthy—before closing the drawer.

It's then that a note in Engelhardt's hand catches his eye. Sophia has not yet filed this correspondence, a single sheet of notepaper fastened to a stack of paperwork with a metal clip and partially obscured by a draft of Adler's latest manuscript.

Josef sets aside the manuscript—the book is no doubt as dull as the old man himself—his excitement growing as he recognizes that the papers are for the *Dozent* position, his position, Professor Huber's replacement, though already Josef can see there's been a mistake.

Please pass this irksome paperwork along—I cannot bear to speak to the administrator again. And inform Professor Moritz once processed.—E

Josef reads Engelhardt's note again. Anton Moritz? When was this decided? And how? He turns the note over. It bears no date. The position should be Josef's, would be Josef's if a decent man had the power to decide. How dare Engelhardt choose Moritz over him! Moritz does not deserve to lecture at the university, not to mention hold a salaried position.

Josef envisions Moritz, wrinkled and wild-eyed, as he'd been that morning. Clearly, the man had not slept after the séance. Had he any sense, he would never have come to campus, but there he sat with Engelhardt's camera, hoping—despite his ghastly appearance—to earn Engelhardt's favor. Clearly, he had.

Josef tastes bile, risen from his injured gut. He is by far the better thinker. And yet, even if he were to inform Engelhardt that Moritz is unsuitable, he suspects the chair of philosophy will not listen. Engelhardt is poisoning the university. More and more, the faculty resembles Engelhardt's philosophical circle, a haven for Jews and other degenerates.

But it is not too late. Josef tears the note in half, then the paperwork. He will see to it that all is made right.

9

Hase

BERKELEY, 2016

Outside, the day is hot and the library parking lot nearly full. I half expect the librarian to call me back, even though Harriet and I passed through the theft detection system, the Engelhardt book pressed against my stomach, without disturbance.

I can tell Harriet's not happy that I took the book without checking it out first, but I don't want to talk about it. I don't want to think about the book at all, but when I bend to sit down in the passenger seat, it digs into my gut.

"Where to?" Harriet asks.

We can't sit in the parking lot all day, but I don't know what to tell her. I don't want to go back to Harriet's place, and I don't want to return to my apartment. I don't want to talk to Jake, and I don't want him to accuse me of withdrawing into silence. I came to Berkeley with a single goal, and now that I've collected the book and discovered nothing useful in it, I have no thoughts other than disappointment.

She turns on the motor, then the radio, and replaces her reading glasses with shades.

"You should eat something," she says.

My stomach feels hard, like a muscle worked to the point of exhaustion. I'm not hungry. There's no food that will comfort me, no taste I desire.

I shake my head.

"When did you last eat?" she asks.

The last meal I remember is the birthday dinner I was supposed to share with my father. We would have eaten together on the boat: clam chowder, because it was my birthday and I got to choose. Clam chowder, because each bowl comes with a plastic bag of hard, salty crackers like the ones my father used to carry in his jacket pocket for me. Sometimes they were so broken by the time I ate them that they resembled bits of broken eggshell, and I'd place each fragment on my tongue as if it were whole. I'd make a single bag last an eternity.

I fold my hands into each other to hide their trembling. Across the parking lot, a mother and her young daughter walk along the curb as if it were a balance beam. The girl doesn't fall, but her foot slips often. When they reach the path leading to the library, the girl turns and retraces her steps. I can't decide if she and her mother are waiting to be picked up, or if they simply don't care if they go inside. Or maybe the child will not go inside until she can walk the whole curb without falling off.

Maybe she's like me.

Harriet's phone rings, and she picks up, though I can tell by her expression that she doesn't recognize the caller. I watch the child on the curb and try not to listen to her conversation.

There must be more to the Engelhardt book, something my father wanted me to understand, some place he wanted me to go, something he wanted me to do. Are the numbers a combination? And if so, to what lock? Are they a code? A message?

I pull the book from beneath my shirt. Blue and green lines decorate the cover, Engelhardt's name and the name of his translator in a small font below them. My father insisted I find this volume. Had he ever considered the possibility that I'd never understand why?

"Yes," Harriet says, but not to me. "Yes, that's right. Okay. Thank you."

She hangs up and sets the phone back in the open storage compartment between our seats.

"That was the coast guard," she says. "They towed in your dad's boat."

"What?" I say. "They called you?"

"Well, technically, it's my boat," she says. "But it's still registered to my mom, so it took them a bit to find me. They said they're still searching the area for—"

"Where is it?" I picture the sailboat as it was in the newspaper, floating empty, sails loose and silent. It was lost, just like my father. I never imagined I'd see it again.

"San Francisco, the Marina Yacht Harbor. They asked me to come in and fill out some paperwork."

"When?"

"I don't have class until tonight, and it's just a lecture I've given before, so I could go today. What do you think?"

"You don't need my permission."

"I mean, would you like to go with me? It could be upsetting—and I can take care of it by myself, so it's just if you—"

"Yes," I say. "I want to go with you. Can we go now?"

"No," she says. "First we're stopping for lunch."

* * *

MY DAD'S SAILBOAT is tied to the end of the pier, but I can't board it. Harriet has to fill out paperwork first. She's the one who speaks to the harbormaster and who waits patiently in the office while he makes a few calls. I'm too anxious to join her, so I wander away from the waterfront joggers and toward the waves that press the boats against the dock and then suck them away again. The air smells of waffle cones and fried garlic—carnival food—though the only source is a single food truck that looks like it made a wrong turn and got stuck at the edge of the parking lot.

I'm still carrying the Engelhardt book. I can't leave it in the car because I might not return to it, or the car might be stolen, or I might need the book while I'm on the boat. My father insisted I get this volume, and I refuse to leave it carelessly in the front seat, or even the trunk, which Harriet offers.

My father's boat is tied lengthwise beside the community corkboard, which is covered with advertisements for hull cleaning services, boat shares, and "magical" journeys to Baja. Its hull is storm-damaged, its finish uneven, but it looks no worse than the last time I saw it. The sailboat has always been a collage of imperfections, repaired and concealed beneath paint that's faded to an assortment of mismatched colors. The teak door protecting the cabin has blackened; the railings have splintered. Lettered across the back, the boat's name—*The Paradox*—is so pale it could easily be mistaken for shadow.

The boat is the last place I saw my father. I know he's not on board now, and yet I still feel he's sitting there waiting. He would hate being here now. He'd hate the paperwork. He'd hate to see the boat in the newspaper and know that strangers have gone through his things. He'd hate that he has no say in these matters because the sailboat was never actually his. It was never ours, despite the many years we spent on it.

We were always guests.

I think back to my last visit with my father, how he reminded me, again, about the Engelhardt book. What had I said just before he broached it? I'd done most of the talking—but then I always did most of the talking: I'd made stale bread into bread pudding; I'd gotten into a fight on Wikipedia, and though I was right (the source the other editor cited was Nazi propaganda), I was overruled; I was reading the *Ultimate Guide to Wiring*, because it seemed from the help-wanted gigs on Craigslist that installing light fixtures and fixing broken dimmer switches might be a simple way to make more money.

Somewhere, in the context of my near monologue, my father mentioned *the book*. Something I said reminded him of it, but what? I can think of nothing unusual between when we met and when we said goodbye and he promised to see me again for my birthday. We parted just as we always did, me on the docks, him on the boat, turning to wave as he pulled away, his cap pulled down to cover his ears, though the wind was low and the afternoon, though cool, didn't warrant it.

"Hase," Harriet says, joining me on the dock. "You ready?"

She studies my face, decides I'm ready, and waits for me to step onto the boat before following.

"They told me the cabin was locked when they found it," she says. "They had to cut the padlock to make sure no one was—no one was inside."

"Huh," I say, but I am thinking about the rowboat, which isn't fastened to the side of the boat. Nor is it tied to the back. For the first time since I heard the sailboat was discovered floating, I feel hope. Had my dad rowed away? He would not have locked the cabin if he were on board. He only locks the cabin when he leaves, and even then, only if he travels to visit the library or to meet a student. Had he simply gone up the dock to use the bathroom, he wouldn't have bothered.

On deck, I see my father's absence everywhere: the seat cushions that remain in the hold, the socks that aren't hanging over the rails, the empty cubby where he rests his coffee cup so it doesn't topple over, the silent radio. The sails are down but uncovered. The lines tangle in a pile beside the motor.

I feel like I'm trespassing. I shouldn't be here, either. I'm overly aware that I'm wearing Harriet's clothes. The skirt she lent me is short; the tank top clings to my torso. I don't wear clothing like this. I feel distant from myself. Nothing about the moment is right.

The broken padlock lies beside the closed cabin door, and I pick it up and enter the combo, 628, the first three digits of the mathematical constant tau. Seeing the numbers, I can almost hear my father's voice. *Tau is far superior to pi. Why use pi with a factor of two when tau alone is far more elegant?*

The lock clicks, but it's already cut open. I have no need to enter the combination other than confirming that it remains unchanged.

I remove the wooden slats that enclose the cabin, feel the swell of the ocean. Harriet groans.

"How did you live here?" she asks.

I shrug. The boat was perfect for me and my father. I liked that it was never still, because, as my father taught me, the earth is always moving, and any feeling of stillness is wishful thinking. I preferred my narrow bunk to my old bed in the garden cottage, and loved that I could wake up in the dark cabin and emerge into the brightness of the day, sunlight amplified by the water. I never had to watch the other children leave their homes for school, or the adults, dressed in suits, head for the office, or the automobiles pull out of driveways and speed off to far-flung destinations.

At the Ord house, I was always aware that we didn't live the way most people did. We didn't invite people over. We didn't have a telephone. We didn't even have a television. We didn't belong to a church or a sports club. We never flew on planes. I didn't have a regular doctor or dentist, and I was homeschooled by my father, who liked to be called Herr Professor. When people pressed him for his name, he simply made something up: George Fredericks, or Greg Martin, or Martin Cummings, and then refused to respond to it. I was Hase, just Hase, but I made up last names when required, which was almost never, because no one cared or asked.

I rarely longed for a different life: to go to Harriet's school with the mean kids, the multiple-choice tests, the adults who assigned the busywork she complained about. I didn't care for sports. I was never jealous of Harriet's large house—or her new clothes, which I knew I would one day inherit. I loved my father and he loved me, and we carved out what he explained was a simpler life. Not all those around us valued simplicity, he said, but their disapproval was a form of ignorance, and we must not judge them harshly.

"I still miss the boat," I say. "If the wireless wasn't so awful, I never would have moved away."

Below deck, the linoleum covers the floor like a miscut carpet, not quite large enough to touch the sides of the boat. I know the light switch is just to the right of the door and that it doesn't work. I know the netted pockets filled with odds and ends—flashlights, headlamps, maps—and the drawer where my father stores the compass, flare, and extra batteries. The cabin is well lit by daylight, but I flick on the switch at the base of the lamp out of habit.

The air smells musky, sour, but the space looks eerily normal, as if my father has just stepped away. I see no signs of a struggle, nothing missing.

I check the cabinets, the familiar plastic glasses and plates, a pot for tea, sponges, soap. The binoculars hang in a holster just above the drying towels. I notice nothing out of place in the closet, just the sweaters hanging beside undershirts, the pants folded on top of the bin of socks and underwear. My father's bed is made. The radio is off but tuned to our frequency. Beneath the counter, where we've always stored groceries, are what remain of the supplies I last purchased for him: cans of beans and chili, dried fruit and nuts, pasta, cereal, powdered milk. In the trash, an empty tin of tuna.

Fastened to the countertop is the shopping list, the things I would have purchased for my father had we met.

I run my fingers over his handwriting:

3 cans soup (tomato)
1 bag dried apricots
6 cans green beans
1 bag lentils

Groceries for one. I feel tears forming.

"I think I better lie down," Harriet says. "I feel every bit of that chicken salad—"

She's holding on to the cabinet and looks like she might pass out.

"Down here's the worst place to be," I tell her. "Go up. Find a point on the horizon."

"I don't want to leave you alone in here," she says.

"I'm fine," I say, though I'm not, and I can see she knows this. "There's no reason for you to get seasick. I'll meet you on the dock."

"I won't be long," I add, and she nods, reluctant but agreeing.

As I watch her ascend the steps to the deck, I realize she'll probably sell the boat. This may be the last time I'm on board, and I will take as long as I need despite what I just promised.

Beside my father's bed, the wall calendar taped to the cabinet is illustrated with a black-and-white photograph of Yosemite. Only two dates are marked, the first and the eleventh, the days he was supposed to meet me. My eyes linger on the ring around June 11.

I unfasten the cabinet where he stores books in watertight bins. One of the few times my father raised his voice at me was after I left a volume out in the cabin, where it might become damp. His library—these few dozen titles, most in German—is one of his two most prized possessions. The other is the box of letters beneath his bed. These are in English, a few from me, but mostly from students, and mostly just math,

Jake's "progress reports" among them. My father showed me Jake's letters before I moved into his apartment because I *should know what sort of mathematician he is*.

I reach beneath the bed for the box of letters and find it where my father keeps it. The box has a combination lock built into the side, and I type in the key: 235711. My father showed me this combination only once, long ago, but I never forgot it because he also showed me how to pull the number apart. *See*, he said, running his finger beneath the six digits, *the first five prime numbers: two, three, five, seven, eleven*. This is how my father sees numbers, the patterns inside, the way one relates to the next.

I look at a string of digits and see nothing.

How could my father expect me to understand the meaning of the number written in the Engelhardt book?

I open the book again to page seventy-one, this time so I can look for primes: 26573. Two, five, seven, three. I break them out: 26 5 7 3, but I see no pattern, no progression, no meaning.

I toss the opened book onto the bed and flip up the lid of the box of letters. Usually, the birthday card I made just after I learned to write sits on top of the correspondence. Today, it doesn't.

The box is empty. All the letters are missing. Gone.

My father loves those letters. He would never leave them out where moisture might destroy them.

Were they stolen? I think back to my ransacked apartment, my swiped computer, the sheet music torn out of the frame, the furniture upended, the belongings strewn across the floor. Here, nothing is out of place. No one forced open the box. Whoever took the letters knew the combination—which leaves just me or my father.

I look down again at page seventy-one, run my finger beneath the digits: 26573. All I see is how they might mean something else: a phone number, a street address. But even if the numbers were something that common, they're not the right length.

26573

Five digits, no comma. There's only one thing I think of when I see a number written in a style that's easier for a computer to read:

Wikipedia, where each page has a unique ID. A numerical Wikipedia page ID has none of the elegance of my father's thoughts, none of his mathematical imagination.

And yet, my father spent hours editing Wikipedia.

Perhaps, he, too, would have thought of that.

10

Anton

VIENNA, 1933

The night I met Haskell Gaul, he remained in my thoughts until morning, when I woke with excitement because I had an appointment with him. He'd asked to talk about my work, and I'd agreed to meet him in the department library. The campus was closed, and the reading room would be empty, and I had no classes to pull me away.

I had several hours before the appointed time, but my thoughts were consumed by anticipation and I was unable to focus. Inge found me pacing the room and proclaimed that I looked like a madman.

My room by then had become cagelike, and I had no appetite. I left the breakfast tray on my bedside table and fled the apartment.

The campus was quiet when I arrived, and I felt very much alone as I pushed open my office door. On my desk were two missives from the administrator, one regarding additional paperwork and another relating to the campus closure. Both memos bore yesterday's date, so the plain white envelope beneath them must have arrived yesterday as well.

I thought at first that the note was from Haskell Gaul, or rather, I feared he could no longer make our appointment and had left an apology. This conclusion made little sense, as the envelope was beneath the flyers and had obviously arrived before the meeting with Gaul was even arranged. My thoughts were distorted by expectation, though what I expected—other than seeing Gaul—was unclear to me.

Reading the letter, I knew at once that it was not Gaul's work. The writing was jagged and uneven, each line rising and falling in diagonals of ink that pooled in places and failed to complete a stroke in others. And yet, the writing did not seem hasty. Even before I began to read, I understood that the author deliberated before setting down each word.

> *Anton Moritz:*
> *I trust you understand both my meaning and my generosity when I say that I will do nothing that might compromise your vulgar secret should you agree to my demands. I have the ear of men of great influence—*

I could bring myself to read no further. The séance had afforded Josef a view of my private life, a long-ago trespass. I was powerless in the face of this accusation because it was true, yet the sum he requested was more than most men earned in a lifetime. Even his stated generosity was absurd.

However, I soon calmed down and saw the note for what it was—a farce. How could Josef have the ear of men with great influence? And what evidence could he hold against me? The words of a medium? A photograph that revealed nothing?

I tore the letter to shreds and then, reassured but still unsettled, decided to go to the library, where I hoped to find peace before meeting Gaul.

* * *

THE DEPARTMENT LIBRARY, like the rest of the university, was locked. However, as faculty, I carried a key and could come and go as I wished so long as I had strength enough to push open the door, designed by its weight alone to keep lesser men out. The wood was a sort found nowhere else in the building, a gift from a Spanish monastery, though I could think of no reason why Spanish monks would send a door to Vienna, or why the university would feel compelled to hang it. Some years before, Adler caught his left hand between the door and the frame and his fingers remained deformed—the price he paid for knowledge, he joked. I often thought of him when I passed over the threshold.

Set into the door were metal ornaments: spheres, cones, cubes, and a single solid torus. Pressing the torus released it, and though small enough to fit into the palm of my hand, it alone could prop open the door—not from its outer edge, but the inner one.

In anticipation of Gaul's arrival, I hung the torus over the door hinge before entering the library. Josef's letter still darkened my thoughts. Even if he had no case against me, I could be destroyed by rumor. Whispered gossip required no validation.

The law could be unforgiving, but men even more so.

In the dimness, the lines of the chairs and carrels merged. I made my way past the unattended reference desk and a cart piled with journals and into the reading room. The air, illuminated by daylight, was a veil of dust, though bright enough that I immediately made out the form of Haskell Gaul, seated at the farthest table. He could not be sitting there, not without a key, and yet, I recognized him. Again, he'd cloaked himself in his capelike jacket, but I knew him by his curls. I felt suddenly shy.

Gaul did not notice my approach, and I stood behind him for some moments while he sat transfixed by the figures on the page before him. I did not wish to disturb him, but curiosity compelled me to peek at his work. I leaned forward, and he slammed closed his ledger book.

He looked up, frustration on his face—whatever he'd been working on was not a simple problem—before he recognized me and smiled with such warmth that I felt he'd embraced me.

"I'm sorry," I said. "I didn't mean to startle you."

"I lost track of the time," he said. "Time, time, time. Would you believe me if I told you I traveled back through time to see you?"

"No," I said. Was he joking? Did he expect a smart retort? I would have asked what he was working on to change the subject, but we were interrupted by the arrival of Fräulein Popovic, who emerged from the stacks with a pile of well-worn books. She must have let Gaul inside, and they must have spoken, as she extended a book to him.

"The book I mentioned," she said.

Turning to include me, she added, "A few of us from the university are going out to the countryside. Campus is closed, classes canceled. You have no reason not to join us."

I began to make an excuse. I may have said something like "well" or "unfortunately," but Gaul surprised me by agreeing for both of us.

"Of course we'll come," he said. He took my arm, and I felt the thrill of him. "We do go," he assured me. "It does happen."

His command of German was not very good, but perhaps he was right, and time away was what I needed most. If nothing else, Josef would see my response to his demands when he came to my empty office.

I laughed, and Fräulein Popovic looked at me oddly.

Gaul looked at me as well, waiting for the yes I'd not yet spoken.

* * *

FOR NEARLY FOUR hours on the drive to the Popovic country estate, Gaul and I sat in the back seat of Fräulein Popovic's automobile, and I marveled at how easily he and I spoke and how much I enjoyed his presence. We discussed Gödel's incompleteness theorems, Kovalevskaya's studies of elliptic integrals, Noether's work in topology, Zermelo and Fraenkel's contributions to set theory. I agreed with Gaul's analysis of Cartwright's latest paper. I admitted that I hadn't noticed the contradiction on page 216 of Adler's latest work. I assured myself that our conversation was no more than professional interest, but I also knew this was untrue.

Gaul was studying me with a generosity that thrilled me. Even when I misspoke, he leaned forward, as if my bumbling were terribly interesting. He admired my work, he said. He'd read every one of my papers and would love my thoughts on one troubling aspect of a baffling problem. Never once did his attention stray from me. At times, I was so distracted by his gaze, I could not recall which words I'd uttered and which were still forming inside me. I feared I'd revealed my private thoughts, that he knew I was thinking about his shoulder or his thigh or his knee, and how it had touched mine. I blushed and could do nothing. I was trapped beside him.

When we arrived at the estate, however, I immediately missed the intimacy of his attention. That he now gazed at the red and white flag flying from the turrets of the castlelike residence made me oddly melancholy.

The Popovics' estate, Corydalis, named after the flowers that grew wild around Vienna and had been Gustav Popovic's favorite, was constructed with a burnt-orange stone from Africa, Fräulein Popovic explained as she led us to the doorway. Between the drive and the entryway, we passed six storks, three rhesus monkeys, and a single peacock that glared at us as if we intended to steal its dessert. The menagerie belonged to Fräulein Popovic's mother, the famed pianist, who, in addition, kept four large snake terrariums, a pair of squirrels, and a darkened room that housed three species of bat.

Around us, the grounds were planted with spirals of flowering plants that permitted enthusiasts to wander into the depths of each garden by following the ever-smaller circle of its path. Fräulein Popovic's father had overseen their construction, but they were only completed—if a garden could ever be said to be complete—after he died, leaving Vienna without its foremost conductor and composer.

* * *

KATARINA POPOVIC GREETED us at the door with the confidence and poise I recognized in her daughter. Had Fräulein Popovic not addressed her as "Mother," I would have taken the two to be sisters. Only when she smiled and the lines around her eyes deepened did Katarina Popovic's age show. At those moments, including the one in which I first kissed her extended hand, a pianist's hand, remarkably strong, I found her even more beautiful than her daughter.

"The others are in the sitting room," she said.

We followed her through a grand hall, where she and Gaul exchanged a few quiet words about composition.

In the sitting room, Engelhardt and Adler rose to greet us. They appeared delighted to see us, and particularly happy to see Gaul, who, they said, had impressed them tremendously at the circle's meeting.

Fräulein Popovic guided me to a sofa. Had she not, I might have remained standing, so awed was I by the room itself. The light fell in through several stories of windows. The walls were papered but scarcely visible beneath a cacophony of portraits and landscapes, each framed and hung within a palm's width of the next. Instead of cut flowers, live ferns decorated each corner. The rug, again a spiral, was woven with scarlet and silver.

Just then, I heard footsteps, and Katarina Popovic exclaimed, "Ah, good, we're all here."

I looked up and was startled to find Josef, dressed in a starched shirt and collar. By his expression, his surprise upon meeting me was as great as mine. For an instant, before his gaze became cold, I felt that he, too, was afraid, but he managed to contain his emotion and nod curtly.

"Such a pleasure," he said to no one, and sat down on a wooden piano bench, the room's most uncomfortable seat.

My muscles tensed and I stilled the impulse to excuse myself. I had every right to be here, I reminded myself. I was a guest of this house.

I felt Gaul's curious look but did not turn to him.

"You're just in time," Adler said. "Engelhardt was about to baffle us."

"Is this the puzzle, then?" Fräulein Popovic indicated a large paper upon which Engelhardt had written:

send
more
———
money

"It is," he said. "Replace the letters with numbers so that the words become a proper sum."

I stared at the puzzle as if considering it, though my thoughts were muddied. In Vienna, I'd dismissed Josef's demands, but I could not so easily ignore the man himself. Guilt was a curious companion, clouding my thoughts with the fear that I'd be destroyed and that I deserved to be.

"A proper sum?" Gaul asked, no doubt believing the trick to lie somewhere in the rhetoric. His eyes sought mine, though he did not seem to desire my approval, just my attention. If a man is speaking, one should heed his words, I assured myself, and yet, I also knew that my regard was not merely out of politeness, and that my face, however hard

I tried to still my expression, might reveal my thoughts. I knew better than to allow my gaze to linger on Gaul with Josef's critical stare upon me, but I couldn't help but glance at him.

"A plus b equals c," Engelhardt said. "Where a equals 'send,' b equals 'more' . . ."

"M equals one, of course," Fräulein Popovic interjected.

"Ah, yes. The trick to the puzzle lies exactly in that observation," Gaul said.

The light lent his curls a silver cast, and he showed no sign of dismay for having solved the puzzle only after our host.

"It's no fun when you always answer first," Adler said.

"She hasn't answered," Josef said. "Not until she provides the full solution."

"The rest is simple." Adler waved away the complaint.

I was consumed by the awkwardness of my situation and could make no sense of the puzzle at all. To be together with Josef was both absurd and uncomfortable. However, the longer we sat together in this room, the more clearly I saw that while we were with the others, neither he nor I could discuss the situation he'd imposed. Beneath this restraint, I had the upper hand. I was a lecturer; he had not yet completed his habilitation. I was an invited guest, and he, I soon learned, had been at Café Josephinum when Fräulein Popovic invited Adler, and had been invited but also asked to help with the old man's luggage. Most in his position, anxious to impress their professors, would speak too much, but Josef lingered as he did when he worked at the café, as if grudgingly waiting to serve us. He moved only when Fräulein Popovic rose to retrieve more cream from the tray, and he insisted he do it himself.

Engelhardt then began to speak of our administrator, who'd demanded we invite Professor Bretz next year instead of Professor Aschheim, whom the administrator referred to only as "the Jew."

"Aschheim is one of the finest physicists in Europe," Engelhardt said. "Bretz? His work is imitation."

"If you defy the administrator, he will retaliate," Adler said.

"But Aschheim's work is far superior."

"Enough of this talk," Katarina Popovic interjected. "I'll speak with the rector when we get back. He won't risk losing my patronage."

The house phone rang then and Katarina Popovic stood to answer it. I could tell by her side of the conversation that the cook was conferring with her about dinner and that we would be having fish, though I could not imagine eating. Adler shared a joke with Engelhardt, who laughed politely, though I remember the lines were not at all funny.

When Katarina Popovic excused herself, we all understood that our time in the sitting room had come to a close.

"Come," Fräulein Popovic said, taking Engelhardt's shoulder. Her dress sparkled beneath the early evening light. "Let me show you the lake before dinner."

"I would like to see the lake, too," Josef said from the hard bench across the room. He sounded pathetic, almost desperate.

"I need your help with the luggage," Adler said. "The books—"

"Can't they wait?" Josef snapped, but he must have realized he'd been impolite, because his tone was softer when he continued. "Of course. Of course I'll help."

Josef followed Adler from the room, his body tense and expectant, as if he were waiting to be called to return. Through the light fabric of his shirt, I could see the line of his spine.

He spun around then, though it was not me his gaze sought, but Fräulein Popovic. His eyes traced her form, and then rested on the arm she'd offered Engelhardt.

I, too, noted how his arm entwined with hers, but my thoughts were dismayed by my own situation.

"Come now," Fräulein Popovic said brightly. "We have a whole weekend ahead!"

* * *

I ROSE THE next day before dawn broke. Between Josef and Gaul, both of whom now resided in my thoughts, I had not slept. I craved the thrill of the car ride with Gaul, but knew Josef would be watching and I must do nothing to confirm his suspicions. That I considered knocking on Gaul's door was a symptom of my distress. I did not even know what I wished to tell him. No good could come of it, which is how I felt about this entire weekend.

I went downstairs, hoping my footfalls wouldn't wake the others.

The darkness imparted the sitting room I alone occupied with a feeling of immense space. I walked to the window, thinking I might watch the sunrise and that it might bring a sense of peace. Peace, I was thinking when the piano notes sounded, muted by their journey from the far wing of the house but still very beautiful.

I followed the notes through a hallway narrowed by statues of famous men—Mach, Boltzmann, Mahler, Rilke—until I arrived at a closed door. The door, too, seemed narrow, but this was an illusion imparted by the width of its frame.

The door was unlocked, and I opened it, revealing a second stretch of hallway, also narrowed by statues of men—Doppler, Haydn, Schubert, Bruckner. The music still sounded far away, and I wondered if I'd set off in the wrong direction. However, I kept walking and at last stood before the door I sought. Because it was open halfway, I could peer inside, where I saw Katarina Popovic in silhouette as she sat at the keyboard playing. Before her was a single sheet of paper, which she never turned, and only then did I realize that I was listening to the same few bars of music again and again.

With this realization, I could listen even more intently, and I noticed that each time she repeated the melody, she changed it, not dramatically, but enough that I'd been fooled into thinking the piece much longer. I would have listened for hours, only Katarina Popovic turned, and though she could not see me, she was aware of my presence.

"Sophia?" she said, mistaking me for her daughter.

I felt sheepish pushing open the door to reveal myself, but I knew better than to give in to my first impulse and run.

"The music is exquisite," I said.

"It's all wrong," she said.

"Wrong?" I was confused by her assessment and surprised when she took the sheet of music from its stand and crumpled it. The floor was littered with similarly crumpled papers, but the room was otherwise—aside from the piano and bench and a tall vase of roses that sat beside her—empty. A single window faced the surrounding forest, still indistinct in the early morning light. The windowpane retained a ghostlike imprint of fingers.

"I'll have to start again," she said.

"But it's perfect."

"No," she said. "It's not right."

"I didn't know you composed."

"I used to compose with my husband," she said. "I stopped when he died. But this came to me as a symphony."

"It's marvelous."

"Here," she said, tossing me the crumpled paper. "You can have it, then."

Even the wadded paper was exquisite, soft and warm to my touch. I smoothed the sheet, pressed it flat between my hands. How could she throw it away?

"The only way to fix it is to begin again," she said. "I'll never see the melody if I keep looking at the errors."

"Do you always begin anew?" I asked.

"I keep the title."

I read aloud the single word at the top of the sheet: *Himmelsauge*.

"Yes," she said. "Do you know the flower?"

I shook my head, and she pointed to the roses beside her, three tall stems arranged with ribbon and a handful of cut glass that colored the bottom of the vase a deep red. "I keep them beside me for inspiration. These are among the last we'll get this year."

The blossoms were full, each nearly as wide as my palm, with a carmen red at the center that faded to pale lavender at the edges.

"Such a beautiful color," I said.

"They are beautiful, and the only rose I could grow this time of year, because it resists the frost. It was bred to resist frost. Some say that's unnatural."

"A rose is not unnatural," I said.

"No?" She seemed surprised by my answer, and I wondered if I'd offended her.

"Well, then," she said. "Breakfast should be ready. Let's join the others."

* * *

AT BREAKFAST, SEMMEL and kipfel, fresh baked and served buffet style, I took only *Milchkaffee*. I brought my cup to the library and sipped as I watched Adler, who was already at work. Perched on the back of his chair was one of Katarina Popovic's rhesus monkeys. I'd encountered this animal several times already that morning, and my shoes still smelled of its feces.

Adler did not look up, nor did he acknowledge Gaul, who arrived just after I did, his long black coat billowing around him like rising smoke. He wore dark glasses like the ones I often saw in advertisements. Where his eyes should be behind the lenses, I saw nothing aside from my own reflection, which unnerved me. He stopped near the grandfather clock by the far wall, and only then did I become aware of its ticks. Each second sounded inside me like a drum.

"Katarina Popovic tells me the flowers in her garden are arranged to open at all hours," Gaul said, removing his glasses. "Would you like to have a look?"

He addressed the room, but I could now see that his gaze was on me.

I should have said I had work to finish, a paper to complete or a lecture to prepare for when campus reopened. And yet, like the men who drink until they can no longer control their muscles, I was imprisoned by poor judgment. Perhaps—and for a moment I thought of Engelhardt with his hand on Fräulein Popovic's—married men experience such imprudence when tempted by a beautiful young woman.

"I would," I said.

* * *

OUTSIDE, GAUL LED. He knew a surprising amount about every plant, information he shared enthusiastically before urging us to move on to the next bed—lavender, herbs, roses, palms.

"The true beauty of a garden," he explained as we walked, "is how the idea is rendered in physical space. You need a very deep knowledge of plants, and also of how to arrange them. At the center of this spiral, for example, is a flower that opens exactly at noon."

He must have felt my gaze, because he looked up at me and smiled.

"Nothing opens at exactly noon," I said. "I think it's safe to say—"

"How do you know what's safe to say?"

I laughed. "Nature doesn't adhere to a clock."

"No?"

Gaul was particularly captivating when he disagreed with me, as he disputed with his entire body. He shook his head no and sliced the air with both hands, as if to decapitate the very words that displeased him. Only then did I notice how graceful his fingers were.

He placed one hand on each of my shoulders and pulled me close.

"These are the moments that make life worthwhile," he said. "Don't you think?"

I felt his breath on my cheek. His lips brushed my skin. Had I not pushed him away, they would have engulfed mine entirely.

"What are you doing?" I said.

"Don't throw this away," he said.

I took a step back. What if Josef saw us? Gaul must not be seen with his arms around me, though already I found myself longing for the embrace I'd aborted.

"Anyone might look out and see us," I said.

"What does it matter? You must feel this. I can't be the only one."

"Are you mad? We could—"

"Anton, I don't care."

"I do," I said. "You—we—must not do this."

"Is that really what you want?" he asked.

When I nodded, he looked as if he'd been emptied, a bottle of the finest wine woefully spilled across the soil.

I'm not sure how long we stood together in silence before Gaul removed his watch and dangled it with its face toward me. "Ten minutes till noon," he said. "Let's see what opens."

I watched the second hand make a complete circle.

"When I was a child, I constructed a sundial," Gaul said. "I spent hours deciding on the best location, calculating the angle of the face, painting the hour markers and gnomon. It was only accurate in the summer months, but I checked it every day. Somewhere, I still have the ledger book with the readings. Line after line after line."

Movement caught my eye, and I looked past Gaul to the lawn abutting the wing where we slept. There, Josef stood in the same starched shirt he'd worn the day before, gazing up at the windows. His back was to us. Had he seen us? I didn't want to return to the house, nor did I wish to stay here. The view was beautiful, but I stood at the edge of a cliff, or perhaps I was already falling.

Gaul knelt beside the flower bed.

"There, nothing," I said, reading the time on his watch. "Noon has come and gone."

"You weren't looking," Gaul countered. He pointed to a pale yellow flower, though he couldn't have seen it open, either. He'd been looking at me.

"It's wormwood." He wiped the dirt from the knee of his pants and stood. "They say it's the flower of regret."

He looked at me, perhaps waiting for my response, but I had none for him.

"Come," he said. "We should get back."

* * *

WE WERE LATE and walked quickly despite my reluctance. I didn't want to climb the steps to the elegant stone patio where Josef stood waiting.

I hoped vainly he would realize how late he was and go inside, but his gaze remained on me as I approached. When Gaul and I reached the base of the stairs, he stepped closer.

"You will agree to my terms?" he called down to me.

My heart raced. Josef had trapped me between his body and Gaul's. I could not step back, nor could I step up without confronting this tormentor.

"You have no reason—" I began.

"Reason?" Josef interrupted. "You think you're better than me, with your evidence and reason. You think I'm foolish to believe in spirits, but men are ruled by the heart. Do you think I don't know yours?"

"What's this?" Gaul asked.

Just then, the door burst open and Engelhardt's voice ripped through our conversation. "I've been charged with collecting all stragglers."

The interruption startled me, but Josef even more so, as he was standing with his back to the door. He had turned toward the voice and lost his footing. The words struck him like a blow.

He toppled, one foot caught under the other, his head striking the lip of the stone step with an alarming crunch. Then his body hit the ground, blood already pooling near his brow.

11

Josef

VIENNA, 1934

When the driver pulls up in front of the Popovic house, Josef does not get out, though the car has, as he requested, stopped in front of the estate, the measure of the Popovics' wealth and his ambition. One day, he will own just such a great house. One day, he will gaze upon the world from his own third-floor window. The war and its aftermath have taken his father, disease his twin brothers, but Josef remains. He will restore the family's glory, ensure that the Zedlacher name is revered.

In his breast pocket, like an identification card he must show should the police stop him, is a note from his doctor proclaiming him cured, though he feels no different from the way he did months ago, just after the accident, when Katarina Popovic brought him to Purkersdorf. Either he remains ill, or he was cured long ago and the months of convalescence were a false imprisonment, his symptoms—his obsession with work, his refusal to engage in insipid conversation—misconstrued as "psychopathic tendencies." Society forgives its geniuses far greater eccentricities. Why did no one recognize his intelligence? His drive?

That he must thank Katarina Popovic for paying for his doctors irritates him, which is why he did not call ahead, though he realizes now that he should have. The Popovic house is magnificent but silent. The shutters, even the ones in the piano room that always remain open so Katarina Popovic can play by natural light, are fastened shut. The carpet at the top of the stairway has been removed, leaving a rectangle of pale white stone. The fountains between the street and the front facade are off.

"The Popovic house," the driver says. "Vienna's finest pianist. Have you heard her play?"

Josef shakes his head. He does not care to impress the driver with tales of the Popovics' summer estate. He will not admit that Vienna's greatest pianist paid for his care the past few months. "It is a small amount," she'd written. He kept her letter for weeks, because it smelled of Sophia. When he was well enough to realize that the paper reeked of mold, it had been eaten by beetles. Beetles were everywhere in Purkersdorf. At night, he felt them crawling under his nightshirt. During the day, they scurried in the shadows.

"It's a shame the maestro died so young," Josef says. "He was a most remarkable talent."

"Are you getting out?" the driver asks.

"The house is shut."

"Yes," the driver says. "She's been unwell."

"Sophia?"

"Katarina Popovic. Are you a friend of the family?" The driver has the long thin hands of a pianist, but his posture is poor. Perhaps his sight as well, because his eyes narrow.

"I know Sophia Popovic," Josef says. "We were at university together."

"Then you were with me as well," the driver says. "I studied physics—"

"Have you seen her?"

"She's in America."

"America!" Josef feels this news with his entire body.

"I plan to go there as well—there are no jobs in Vienna. Half the academics are driving taxis, the other half are unemployed. Professor Engelhardt's at Harvard. Fräulein Popovic, as his assistant—"

As his assistant. Josef still hears the sound of her laughter. When he closes his eyes, he sees her as he did from the grounds of her summer estate, where he found her in Engelhardt's bedroom. Through the window, her dress appears more gray than green. The silk moves with her body, the lines of her thighs and shoulders. Engelhardt places his hand on her.

How dare he take her to America! She belongs to Vienna. It's she who pumps life through the streets. Without her, the city is cold.

But then, so is Engelhardt.

On his darkest days at the sanatorium, Josef wrote to the chair of philosophy. Engelhardt might think he is above the law, that he can bed whomever he wishes and promote whichever foul thinker he fancies most. But Josef is watching.

He signed each letter "A patriot."

"Please take me to my apartment," Josef says. "I have no time for idle chatter."

* * *

RETURNING TO HIS life after the months of forced recuperation is like crawling into bed just as the day begins and everyone else already sits before breakfast. Josef is too late. He's missed the date of what was to be his final exam—the day he would have at last earned the right to lecture at the university. He's failed to collect the money from Moritz, or to prevent the man's promotion from going forward, though for this, Josef blames Engelhardt. Engelhardt gave Josef's position to another man, Engelhardt stole Sophia, and Josef could do nothing. He's not even certain that Engelhardt received the letters he sent from the sanatorium.

Josef considers pressing Moritz for the debt still owed, but power and appearance are tightly woven. Should Josef, in his worn clothing, attempt to make demands, he will gain neither respect nor acquiescence. Besides, Moritz is evidence of Engelhardt's poor judgment, which Josef will bring to the administrator's attention.

"I am an old friend," he insists when he visits the administrator's office. He considers pushing past the front desk and demanding an audience, but he knows this is impossible. The administrator, now an advisor to Chancellor Dollfuss, refuses to see him.

He returns to work at Café Josephinum. His muscles remember: wipe the tables, grind the coffee, clear the dishes. He rinses each cup, sets it back on the shelf. He is no longer night manager. The owner has allowed that hiring Josef back at all is a kindness.

While he washes the cups, he thinks of Engelhardt's hand on Sophia, and of the Engelhardt circle, and how he was never invited. Josef should be in America with Sophia.

He sets one wiped cup beside another. He will wash dishes until he is dismissed, and then he will walk to the tram, which will carry him to his family's apartment at the edge of the city. His body bends with the sag of the mattress. His muscles ache from the stairs he climbs each day. The months of convalescence have aged him. His hair, though remaining true to its brown color, has become brittle. Beside his eyes and lips, blue-green veins show. His forehead wrinkles; his lips turn down. Even at rest, he appears to frown. He feels like an old man. His thirty-second birthday is in two weeks, but all he anticipates is the February chill.

"Josef!" The night manager is irritated. A customer waits.

Josef scans the tables, sees the new party near the back of the café, a single man in a deep gray overcoat. What remains of his hair is cropped short, but otherwise he looks as Josef remembers—Professor Engelhardt, pulled fully formed from Josef's thoughts.

Has he returned from America? Has Sophia?

"He's been sitting there ten minutes," the manager says.

Josef sets down his towel, then takes it up again so he can fold it. Once, twice. Dissatisfied, he shakes out the cloth and starts again. The manager will not bully him. Josef will not serve Engelhardt on the manager's request. Yet, Josef wants to see the chair of philosophy. He wants to look Engelhardt in the eye and say, what? Even before Engelhardt stole Sophia, Josef despised this godless, arrogant man, his endless lectures and the adoring students who accepted his blasphemies as if they were truth. How could Sophia have chosen such a man over him? Was it the chair he holds? His influence? His power?

The café lights are on, the daylight fading. From the corner of one eye, Josef sees a woman hail him, but he pretends not to notice. The floor is filthy. The night manager does not clean it properly. The air is stale. The night manager does not know to open the doors early to freshen it. Josef folds the towel a third time and then sets it aside and walks toward Engelhardt's table.

Engelhardt bends over a book. He must have come straight from the station, as he still has his travel case. The fabric of Josef's uniform brushes the professor's dark gray overcoat.

"Coffee," Engelhardt says, looking up. Behind the lenses of his reading glasses, his eyes are hazel.

Josef nods but does not leave the table.

Engelhardt closes his book, Tolstoy. He is only at the beginning, the first or second chapter.

"I thought you were in America," Josef says.

Engelhardt studies Josef's face, no sign of recognition in his expression.

"We came for the conference."

"We?" Josef asks. "Sophia, too?"

Engelhardt shakes his head. "Myself and a few students. Things have been so uncertain politically, we weren't sure we could come. But it's the very first conference on logic and the exact sciences. I'm speaking tomorrow. I couldn't miss it."

In the pocket of his waiter's costume, Josef has his doctor's note asserting that he is well. He, too, should be at the conference. He, too, should be presenting work.

"One coffee," Josef says.

In the kitchen, he pours grounds into the cup. Perhaps Engelhardt will choke on them. Perhaps they will clog his throat.

* * *

THE NEXT DAY, the first day of the conference on logic and the exact sciences, Josef stands at the window of the fabric shop, where he has fingered a roll of silk brocade cloth for what feels like hours. The gold thread forms a pattern of birds, but he has not looked closely enough to know this.

"Are you sure I can't help you?" the shopkeeper asks. He is young, but the cut of his jacket is outdated. Josef is the store's sole customer, and he feels the shopkeeper's desperation.

"I will ask for help when I need it." Josef still wears his waiter's costume. He has not been home since Engelhardt did not deign to recognize him. Josef could not bring himself to wipe the man's table, or to wash the cup that had touched the man's lips, or to take the money he left for the bill. Never again will he serve him. Never again will Engelhardt make him feel small.

"We have other silks," the shopkeeper says. "My father just received a shipment from—"

"I do not care for silks."

"But this one here, that you're looking at, is silk. Look. See how it shimmers? You could hang it on the walls."

Across the street and behind a cobblestoned square, the conference hall stands like a palace. The steps leading to the entrance are stone, the doors framed with columns. A wide balcony casts its shadow over the front doors. Josef has seen dozens of men emerge from the building, none of them Engelhardt.

"I also have some fine muslin," the shopkeeper says. "People don't think of muslin as fine, but this cloth will convince you. This muslin is divine. I have it in back—"

"Bring it to me." Josef has no interest in the fabric, but he wants the shopkeeper to leave. Doesn't he realize Josef wants to buy nothing?

With each of the shopkeeper's steps away, Josef feels lighter. He runs his fingers across the top seam of his trouser pocket, feels the weight of the gun, which he stole from the café safe.

Engelhardt must be inside the conference hall, unless there's another door at the back? Josef should find a better vantage point, but the shopkeeper has returned, his arms bending beneath the weight of the spooled cloth, already frayed at the edge. Josef could easily pull the weave apart, thread by thread.

"Touch this. See?" the shopkeeper says. "Fine muslin."

"Set it there," Josef says. "Beside the silk."

"Yesterday, I had a customer buy three spools, this size. It won't last. Not at my prices."

"Has the conference broken for midday?"

"Hmm?"

"The conference. Across the street."

"There is a conference?"

"Of course there is a conference. Do you know nothing?"

"I know fabric. Look." The shopkeeper rubs the silk between his fingers. "See how it holds its form?"

Josef, unable to suffer the clerk a moment longer, turns to the door.

"You will be back?" the shopkeeper calls. "You heard what I said. This won't be here long."

12

Hase

SAN FRANCISCO, 2016

My father and I often passed hours in silence, and yet, I find nothing calming about the silence on the boat today. I can't fade into my old routine, my father with his notebooks and pencils, consumed by work but gazing up at me periodically, as if to make sure I've not disappeared. Alone on the boat, I'm aware of each of my footsteps, and the solitude thunders.

This visit to the boat might be my last, but I'm not tempted to take my remaining belongings: collected shells and sea glass; the bowl I painted from a kit my father gave me; the field guides to ocean birds.

These things belong to the past.

When I turn off the light and close the cabin, the boat belongs to the past as well: the ghost ship I read about in the paper.

"Do you want me to take you back to your place?" Harriet asks.

I slide into the front seat of her mother's old car, and though Harriet assures me she has not been seasick, I smell vomit. My clothes are moist from the ocean, but not wet enough to leave a mark on the seat. Still, I am careful to set the Engelhardt book on the dash, where I will not dampen it.

"I can drop you off on my way back to campus," Harriet continues.

"Can you drop me at the library?" I ask.

The main branch is open until eight, and if I'm lucky, one of the computers will be available. I prefer not to use a public terminal, but the thieves have left me little choice.

"If you need me, I can cancel—"

"I'm okay," I say, though I'm not. I still feel both the rock of the boat and the emptiness of its cabin, though mostly, as I sit beside Harriet, I think about what's missing: my father's letters, but also his laptop—and the rowboat.

Was he onshore when the wind pulled the sailboat out to sea? Did he abandon the boat in the ocean?

"It will be okay," Harriet says.

The light pressure of her hand on my shoulder slows my thoughts, which are nonsensical: the nature video Harriet and I laughed about years ago because the host acted out what to do if one encounters a bear. Remain still. Wave your arms. If the bear attacks, drop to the ground and make yourself as small as possible. *It will be okay.* The first time Dr. Ord recovered from cancer, Harriet poured champagne and spoke the same words while I sat across from her thinking that in a week, or a month, or a year, the cancer would come back. It did.

I stare blankly at the clock on Harriet's dashboard. I've missed not one but two tutoring sessions and will have to call both families to apologize. That I must apologize in addition to everything else seems grossly unfair, but my work is like that.

I want to walk into my room, close the door, ignore Jake if he calls out after me, and find my dad on the radio.

"Hase," he'd say, as if he were sitting next to me. We'd share a frequency, a moment in time if not space. We'd be together, my father and I. No one can tell me otherwise.

"Hase?" Harriet asks.

She has pulled up beside the library, but I'm still thinking about my father as if he were present, as if I'd met him just now in Harriet's automobile.

"I'll come by tomorrow," Harriet says. "Okay? And call anytime before then. Okay? Hase?"

I've already opened the car door. Blown trash carpets the gutter. The traffic screams. Only an hour remains before the library closes. I feel the urgency like hunger.

"Do you have a bag?" I ask, suddenly worried the library will take away the Engelhardt book if I bring it inside uncovered. "I need a bag."

Of course Harriet has a bag. Folded inside are the clothes I wore yesterday, which is good, because my keys are still in my jeans pockets. I slip the Engelhardt book inside and say goodbye.

"Don't forget this," Harriet says, handing me Jake's jacket. "It's colder here than Berkeley."

Only after she pulls away do I realize that I did not thank her.

* * *

TONIGHT, THE LIBRARY isn't crowded. The open seating area on the ground floor is empty aside from a bearded man I recognize from previous trips here. He's probably crazy, but he manages to look as if he's just come from a rough day on the job, his expression a mix of exhaustion and triumph. Before him on the table are three paper coffee cups, all empty, and a pile of rocks.

Summer break has left the usually crowded workstations empty, and I sit for a moment to copy the digits from the Engelhardt book onto a slip of paper: 26573. I check and double-check the digits, running my finger beneath each as I write—2 6 5 7 3. I don't trust my memory.

The slip of paper, unlike the book, is inconspicuous, though no one glances up when I make my way to the computer nook. I can use the machine of my choice, and still, I feel I've chosen the wrong one.

The screen brightens, casts a cool light over my hands.

Technically, I need a library card to use the computers, but I don't have one and this has never stopped me. A card might be the most straightforward way to access the system, but there are always other techniques. Occasionally, a librarian will demand I make a reservation, but I've developed ways to deal with librarians, too.

I pull up an internet browser, more concerned about the slow connection speed than the system expelling me. As I type the digits into my page request, I worry someone behind me will see. I'm just a woman at a library computer, and yet, I can't see myself with a stranger's indifference because I'm so anxious my hands shake.

That the number from the Engelhardt book is a Wikipedia page ID is a long shot, but certainly possible. My father would have known—after all the years he contributed to the site—how to access a page by its ID number.

It isn't difficult, just not common.

Normal people don't browse by page ID, but I'm not normal, nor is my father, who contributed to my impressive body of work—over 350,000 edits—because he never bothered to create his own account.

I've been banned or suspended dozens of times under as many different names on Wikipedia, but TheRabbit is the one name I'm careful with, not just because my father uses it, or because it's the English version of my name, Hase, but because it has the largest edit count, and with that comes power.

I look over my shoulder one more time, and then the page pops up.

* * *

AT THE TOP right side of the Wikipedia page, where my eye lands first, is a photograph of a brown and white rabbit, its ears turned toward the camera as if it is listening to the shutter click. Its feet, one white, the other brown, are firmly planted on the soil, and yet the creature looks as if it's about to spring.

Rabbit.

The English Wikipedia has over five million pages. That the numbers my father jotted down brought me to the page for Rabbit is not a coincidence. My father left the number of this page knowing only I would see that it is meant for me.

I scroll through the text—habitat and range, biology, eating habits, folklore and mythology: "pregnancy tests were based on the idea that a rabbit would die if injected with a pregnant woman's urine . . ."

The words stick inside me like a bone in my throat. *The idea that a rabbit would die*. The idea. Ideas require thought. Not all are equal, but some don't even warrant the word.

I change:

idea to *misconception*

And though some might argue that this is a minor edit, I disagree.

Alongside the text are more images: an illustration from a nineteenth-century book depicting two rabbits with two snakes, several obese rabbits described as "a nuisance," a photo of a baby rabbit, another of a rabbit leaping through grass. At the bottom of the page are the usual references and a link to the "Rabbits and hares portal." Nothing unusual. Nothing that reminds me of my father, except for the page itself.

Rabbit. I run my fingers over my locket. I normally keep it hidden beneath my shirt, but the cut of Harriet's tank top is too low. I find the groove between the halves of the lid, but I don't open it. I know what's inside: on one half, the painted image of my mother, on the other—where once there'd been a photo of me—nothing. I threw the picture away when the paper curled and pulled away from the metal. The blank half remains my side, an empty surface, a void. I don't exist, even inside my own locket. I'm invisible, unseen, the rabbit who's not pictured on this page because her photograph is missing.

But recognizing myself is not why my father insisted I get *the book*. He intended for me to find more. He needed me to discover something.

I click on the page's revision history and scroll through the archived edits: the fight over whether *rabbitats* is a word, claims added and removed because they have no source, missing commas and unbalanced quotes repaired, contradictions resolved, edits reverted, wording clarified, descriptions expanded, and then three edits by me, TheRabbit—one from a moment ago and two I've never seen. The first of these is called simply a "minor change," the second a deletion, with no explanation at all.

I have come across my father's edits before. Usually, I'm amused to see my name beside a change I didn't make. Tonight, I feel unsettled. I can't call my father on the radio and tell him that I found his edits, or ask if I'm reading the clues he left for me correctly. I can't meet him at the dock and ask why he left me *the book* to begin with. Seeing my name in the edit history now, I have the eerie sensation that I made all three changes myself and forgot: I added a comma and then changed my mind; I changed a line of text and then decided I'd rather delete it than have to argue for it to remain.

But I did not make all these edits. The text my father added and then removed is no longer displayed in the article, but each change to the page remains tied to it. I can, and have, spent hours reviewing deleted content so that I can weigh in on disputes about it, usually late at night when I can't sleep. Missing text is often more fascinating than the words that remain, a reminder that history is both written and erased, a palimpsest with no final version.

Again, I look over my shoulder, and again, no one stands behind me. The computer screen to my left flickers. I bend forward. My chair clicks against the floor.

I pull up the old versions of the Rabbit page and read the text my father added and then removed just a day before he was meant to meet me—a reference to a book:

The Private Life of the Rabbit, R. M. Lockley, 1964. Chapter 10. ISBN 415576.

My father and I have an ongoing argument about whether the ISBN number should include hyphens, and at first, I'm surprised to see that he opted for my preference—no hyphen, more easily read by search engines. But then I see I'm wrong. Hyphenated or not, the ISBN number should have ten or thirteen digits. My father's ISBN has only six, because it's not an ISBN. It's another page ID.

My fingers are awkward on the library keyboard. I despise it for being too slow, though the typo I make as I pull up the page with the new ID is my mistake. My heart beats rapidly, as if I were on a pier that might not support my weight, not to mention the shady people I imagine are there watching me. From somewhere behind me, a man coughs.

I type the ID twice before I enter it correctly and pull up the new page: a biography for Karl Andelman, who stares back at me from the page with his lips slightly parted. The photo is clearly a screenshot from a television program. Whoever uploaded the image didn't crop out the station logo that covers the lower part of his shoulder. He looks to be in his late thirties, though I soon learn that he died in a boating accident in 1991. He's not a mathematician but a fantasy author.

My father rarely reads fiction, and when he does, only in German. I check the page ID again to make sure I typed it correctly.

Karl Andelman, author of dozens of books, none I recognize. Why this man?

I click to the edit history, where I look for TheRabbit again, but the only recent edit is from an unregistered user. Instead of a username, the editor is identified by an IP address, an account that has made only a single edit. Still, the edit could belong to my father. He may have been working on a different computer. He might not have thought to log in. He could have been moving, never remaining long in any one place.

When I look at the edit more closely, I see it is his. This time, he added a book Karl Andelman himself wrote: *Underground*, not the original, but a German translation.

I care less about the book than the ISBN, the page I should try next: 42628556. I hope my father added more to this next page: a passage, an image, a map, the name of a person who can help me. I've learned the pattern of his edits. I know how to unravel the clues, though I still don't understand why he left a puzzle and not simply a note, unless he worried someone else would discover it. He's always shied away from people, preferring his work to conversation, solitude to company, except mine and Dr. Ord's, and even then, he seemed relieved when I moved off the boat and he had no one to disturb him, no one who knew him well enough to care that he was missing. No one but me.

And yet, he was clearly thinking about someone else—someone he must hide from—when he made these edits.

I type in the new number, 42628556. At the very least, this next page will point to another Wikipedia page, and I can continue to follow my father's instructions.

But the page that should open does not.

It no longer exists.

Over five million pages—from "List of animals awarded human credentials" to "Toilet paper orientation"—and the one page I need has been deleted.

It's gone, just like my father. Missing.

I slam my palm against the keyboard. The library will close any minute, and I've found nothing.

"Excuse me, ma'am?" The voice behind me rises, as if the speaker is asking a question, but what follows is a rebuke: I must not abuse the library's equipment, I have not made a reservation, I shouldn't be using the machine at all.

"It's garbage," I say. "It's all garbage anyway."

The librarian is not much older than I am, perhaps in her midtwenties. Her gaze is stern but disingenuous, as if she's confronting me about behavior she herself indulges in. Her eyes linger on the straps of the shirt Harriet lent me. She is sizing me up, though the person she sees is not really me. I'd never choose the fitted skirt and top. I would not strike the library's keyboard, or if I did, I wouldn't get caught. The dark circles beneath my eyes belong to a stranger, someone much older, perhaps even mad. Will this librarian suggest I seek mental health services? If she asks me to leave, I won't argue, though there's no place I want to go.

As disappointing as my search through Wikipedia has been, at least I had the promise of finding something.

"Karl Andelman," she says, pointing to the browser window on my screen despite the etiquette policy on the wall just beside it: *Please respect the privacy of the current user.* "Love his work."

"I have no interest in Karl Andelman," I say.

But I think of him anyway. *Underground*, the book my father added. If my father buried something, I won't find it, not unless I can find the missing page and its clue—a map or coordinates, erased but not lost entirely. Not yet.

"The library's closing in ten minutes," the librarian says. "If you want to reserve a computer for tomorrow—"

I don't want to run into this librarian again. If I use a library computer, it will be at another branch, but I just say, "Thank you."

"You have a good night now," she says.

I nod, but I'm thinking of my father. I'm thinking of a time and a place that no longer exist, the narrow bunk where I slept, the sheets that never fit the mattress right, my father wishing me good night, the darkness of the boat, and the way it rocked, no matter how still I lay.

"You, too," I say, but she is already walking away.

13

Anton

VIENNA, 1933

That fall, the university closed often due to unrest. Several times a day, I ran to the newsstand to buy the latest extra so I could read up on the street violence and plan a safe route home. I missed Engelhardt's weekly discussions. The circle ceased to meet when he left, rather abruptly, for a stint at Harvard. Many believed he would not come back—and many others wished him gone. He was too liberal, too radical, too powerful. Among the faculty, even I was seen as too closely allied with the left, which unnerved me. For years, I'd dreamed of joining Engelhardt's circle, and now that I had, it was seen as a deviant group of dangerous thinkers.

But I had little time for politics. Between Professor Huber's classes—which Engelhardt asked me to take over before he left—and the conference on logic and the exact sciences, which Adler proposed and I'd offered to help organize, I scarcely had time to sleep. I walked from my rented room to the campus and then home again late at night, a daily routine that changed only when I noticed Haskell Gaul in the department library.

I hadn't seen him since our stay at the Popovics' estate some weeks before, when the horror of Josef's accident brought the weekend festivities to an abrupt stop. I'd ridden back to Vienna with Adler, Engelhardt, and Fräulein Popovic, while Gaul rode with Katarina Popovic and Josef to the sanatorium, and from there to wherever Gaul had come from. I thought of Gaul often but did not seek him out, nor did I know where to find him, as we'd not exchanged cards. It was best I never again saw him. Josef's confinement relieved me, but it did not erase the horror of his blackmail.

When I spotted Gaul in the library, however, I immediately felt as I had when he'd drawn me close and I'd pulled away: I wanted to hide, but in a place where I could see him; I was terrified but transfixed. I shuddered.

I considered turning back. I'd come to the library to collect Émilie du Châtelet's translation of Newton, as I'd been told it was clearer than the original text, and I was curious to see for myself. Mine was an unnecessary errand, and one I could easily abort, and yet, I did not. I stood, indecisive, until Gaul looked up and gazed at me quizzically.

"Anton," he said.

I was too nervous to approach him, but he must have sensed both my discomfort and fascination, because he came over to me. He'd made a mistake at the Popovics' estate, for which he was sorry, he said. He assured me he would respect my wishes. He was delighted to see me and had hoped, in fact, to cross paths with me here. He wanted very much to work with me, to read my latest papers, to be a colleague, perhaps a collaborator. He was, he told me, caring for Engelhardt's flat—forwarding mail to the States and seeing to repairs.

"He gave me the library key before he left," he said. "I see why you like it here. It's very conducive to work."

The department reading room was far less grand than the one in the central library, but its double-paned windows looked out over an apartment building's dull gray facade, and the room was just uncomfortable enough that I rarely encountered anyone sleeping at the wide wooden tables. The light was nearly constant, regardless of the hour, divorcing the space from passing time.

"Would you like to join me?" he asked.

My attraction to Gaul was a wilderness I would not enter, but separated by a library table, a solid oak surface with legs nearly as thick as my own, I could be near him. His knee might even bump mine accidentally.

"I was just about to sit down," I said, though I carried nothing with which to occupy myself, and I could not, at that moment, even recall which book I'd come for. I should have turned back immediately. "Not sit—" I struggled and failed to find the words to correct myself. "Perhaps tomorrow," I said, helplessly. "If you'll be here?"

"You're always welcome at my table," Gaul said with a generosity I did not question, as I sat across from him every night thereafter, sometimes arriving before him, sometimes after. I'd bring papers to review, or the lecture notes I was preparing, while he worked on his own derivations, looking up only to ask if I'd made progress in my own work, and when could he read more?

* * *

WINTER ARRIVED, AND with it the ice rink at Heumarkt, where I skated when I was a child, and the Christmas Market with its scent of mulled wine and roasted chestnuts—familiar holiday festivities against the now-familiar disquiet in the streets. I missed my father, who had died of tuberculosis on Christmas Eve over a decade before, and my mother, who followed a year later, and though I was inclined to ignore the dreadful holiday entirely, I purchased a handwoven scarf for my landlady, and she prepared carp and dumplings, which she served on a tray she used once a year for this purpose. Mostly, I was grateful for the break in teaching, which permitted me to prepare for the coming year and catch up on correspondence. The campus was peaceful, the library often empty of anyone other than Haskell Gaul and myself.

When classes began and the tables filled, I missed our quiet nights together. We were colleagues, I assured myself, though he was not with the university, and, from what I was able to glean from across the table, his own work had little to do with mine. I recognized a few lines that resembled my own derivations—earlier studies of spirals and higher dimensional spaces—but the bulk of the symbols were unfamiliar.

"It's quite complex," he said, noticing my gaze. "But if we were to go through it line by line, I'm certain you would quickly see—"

I was embarrassed to be caught studying his work, though he had offered to share his pages with me many times. I was curious, of course, but unable to spare the attention.

"Of course," he continued. "I don't mean to impose. But I'm certain you'd find it interesting. You're the only person capable of solving—"

"I can't even solve the problems in my own work."

"You just need to spend more time on them. You must spend more time—Anton?"

I blushed when he spoke my name. He must have realized that I'd made no progress, that I hadn't even opened my notebooks. Since taking over Professor Huber's classes, I spent most of my nights preparing lectures, and the conference, beginning in just two days, consumed the hours I should have been asleep. Engelhardt would be returning to Vienna to give the keynote address.

"After the conference," I said.

"That's too late."

Impatience suited him. He bent closer to me, glaring, as if my unfinished derivation were the most important in the world and my reluctance to look at it now unforgivable.

"The busywork can wait," he said.

"It cannot wait," I explained.

"You don't understand the danger."

The danger? The only real danger was around us: that Chancellor Dollfuss, without attracting international notice, had softly staged an authoritarian coup, or that the German Nazis were intent on destroying the Austrian economy by frightening away the tourists with terrorist bombs. Such concerns were valid. Such concerns had impacted the conference. Just today, seven presenters had asked that we read aloud their papers, as they were unable or unwilling to travel to Vienna. The auditorium we originally feared would not accommodate the attendees would be only half full.

"If you show me your pages, perhaps I can help," Gaul began, but I shook my head. I had nothing to show him, only pages and pages of equations and mistakes.

"But do show me, you must—unless, of course, I've ruined everything."

I've ruined everything. He spoke the words very softly, as if to himself. Was he thinking of the garden? Of how he touched me and I pushed him away? Were his thoughts, too, always tinted by that moment?

He looked deflated, consumed with regret. I wanted to hold him, to assure him that my reluctance had nothing to do with the events at the Popovics' estate, but I couldn't stroke his cheek or wipe back the curls that fell over his forehead. There were dozens of people in the library, and I refused to act on impulses that could destroy me, destroy us both should our names be added to the administrator's list of undesirable thinkers.

And so I offered him my pages—the ones I had with me, which were the most recent and raw—instead.

"Here," I said, pulling the slim portfolio from my satchel and sliding it across the table to him. Perhaps he would find the mistakes in my thinking. Perhaps he would help me move forward.

He opened the folder immediately, and only then, seeing him bent over my pages, did I realize how much I, too, wanted to be working on them.

I tore open another letter, my irritation such that I nearly mistook the invitation from the University of California at Berkeley for another cancellation.

"What is it?" Gaul asked.

I handed him the letter—an offer to serve as a visiting scholar.

"That's wonderful," he said, reading no further than the opening line. "Berkeley's a beautiful place."

His words were encouraging, and yet, I was disappointed. He should have urged me to carry on my work here, to press for a permanent appointment or to continue without one. He should have pushed me to say no, or expressed the feelings I could not bring myself to share: he would miss me too much; the ocean between us would be a wound.

"You should go," Gaul said. "Things will only get worse here. This whole country is mad."

"Come with me, then," I said.

I felt my cheeks redden. I'd not shown him the letter with the intent of inviting him, though parting from Gaul—after the obsession I'd kept secret—seemed impossible as well.

His silence felt like a blow.

"To visit," I added, but even as I tried to modify the invitation, I knew he'd heard it. He'd seen through my words to the feelings behind them. He knew the distance I kept was a lie.

The floor would not swallow me if I remained seated, and so I stood, unable to linger in the shadow of my own revelation. I was a fool! An idiot!

"Are you leaving?" Gaul asked, surprised.

"No," I said, but I was thinking of California.

I was thinking of him, of us.

Perhaps he understood this, too, as he gathered his papers and stepped around the table so as to walk beside me to the door.

* * *

THE MOON ABOVE us was a sliver, the shops closed for the night. Even the late-night cafés were beginning to shutter. I had no destination, only agitation. How could I have invited Gaul to come with me to California? I hadn't even decided to go myself.

He walked beside me as I reproached myself. My stride was not as long as his, and yet, our paces matched. He said nothing, but I felt him more strongly than I did the wind, or the chill, which snapped against us. Was he angry? Disappointed? Why had he said nothing?

"The spiral, your spiral—" he said at last, his thoughts on the pages I'd given him. "It's never been described before."

"It's more of a sketch," I said. "An idea."

"Bernoulli, Descartes, Cavalieri, and now Moritz." Gaul drew out each name as if it were a work of art he wished to stop and admire. "I can only imagine the excitement you felt when you saw it."

I could not meet his gaze, even softened by the dark. The invitation I'd spoken in the library still gnawed at me, and now his compliment did as well. My work, by its roughness, deserved no admiration.

"I can't explain the behavior," I said. "The discontinuities—whole areas that should be—that are missing."

"They're not missing," Gaul said. "We just don't understand them yet."

We reached the turn toward my apartment, and I said nothing. I did not want to return to my room. Gaul had spent no more than a few minutes reading my pages, and yet, he seemed to know them better than I. *They're not missing.* I wanted to contemplate this, but my thoughts refused to cooperate, and so I did the one thing I could. I kept walking.

Our pace was brisk, as if we had a destination and would slow only once we arrived. How could I go to California? I'd be a fool to leave Vienna, the possibility, this conversation. The city, even now, in its late-night stillness, was alive—the heart not just of Austria but of all of Europe. We passed the Burgtheater, shuttered at this hour, and City Hall with its slender windows, all dark as well. Gaul asked questions I could not answer: Assumptions in my work—must the values be constant? Why a cylindrical surface? Why constrain what you can demonstrate is boundless?

He paused. Beside us, a tree-lined pathway led into the Rathauspark. The grounds were quiet at this hour, but the peace was superficial. Men came here to find each other. They came knowing they could be arrested, jailed.

Was this where we'd been headed all along?

"Are you stopping?" I asked.

"Here?" He gazed into the park, past the reach of the streetlight. I thought he would start down the pathway, but he did not. "No," he said. "I just had a thought, but I need pen and paper."

"It's too dark to write here," I said.

"Yes," he agreed, but when he stepped forward, away, I felt there were words he left unspoken.

We passed the Volksgarten, the Burggarten, the opera house. At Kärntner Strasse, we turned, the usual bustle silent. Even Café Scheidl was closing, the last customers—a pair of college students—lingering by the door. Were they lovers? They were standing so close. Through the windows behind them the chandeliers glittered.

Gaul turned, the shop-lined street empty. He turned again.

"Here we are," he said.

We'd arrived at Engelhardt's apartment, the building a narrow stone structure with balconies at every window.

"Engelhardt won't be back until tomorrow afternoon," he said. "I'm sure he wouldn't mind if you came up."

* * *

ENGELHARDT'S APARTMENT WAS awash in patterns, the curtains a pale green floral print beside a pair of couches upholstered in the same material, the floor brightened by a pair of intricately woven Persian rugs. The throw pillows were stacked in one corner, perhaps by Gaul, and the long wall facing the window was decorated with framed paintings of unfamiliar harbors that I mistook at first for photographs. Across from me, a double door trimmed in steel led into the study, of which I could see only a part—a floor lamp and the edge of a desk that extended into the room from the wall.

Gaul removed his shoes, revealing mismatched socks, and set them in a low wooden box on the floor just beyond the swing of the door. From this box, he extracted a pair of wool slippers, which he offered me and which I accepted, though they were far too large. Engelhardt had never invited me here. Seeing his home—the built-in bar with its selection of brandies, the child's drawing of the Alps beside a portrait of the woman who must be his wife—was a stolen opportunity, and I did not want my shoes to leave a trace of my trespass.

"I have pen and paper in my room," Gaul said. He headed toward the hall across from the entryway.

I followed.

Was he hoping to finish the conversation I'd started with my invitation to Berkeley? Paper and pen were a flimsy excuse for asking me upstairs. My heart raced, but I would not turn back. Each step forward was a choice, but I did not yet know what I was deciding.

The room he led me to was—by the collection of mathematical texts on the shelf against the far wall—unmistakably Engelhardt's. From the doorway, I could see that Gaul had been using the space as his own. Piled on the bedside table were more of his papers, and the clothes on the floor—a plain white shirt much like the one I was wearing and a wool sweater—were ones I knew. The bed was unmade, but Gaul seemed only to notice when he saw me looking at it.

He straightened the cover.

"You sleep here? In Engelhardt's room?" I asked.

"Where else would I sleep?"

"The guest room."

"Why? It's not nearly as comfortable. Sit," he said, tapping the mattress beside him. "See for yourself. It's perfect—firm, but not hard."

I sat down beside him. Pen and paper were indeed a ruse. He had lured me here, and I'd come willingly.

"See?" he said, smiling. "Imagine sleeping here every night."

I could not imagine. Even thinking about Engelhardt's bed was inappropriate. I should not be sitting on this mattress, and yet, I was.

Gaul pulled my pages from his satchel and thumbed through the sheets, pausing only to jot a note in the margin. I wanted to stop him, to tell him to set the work aside, but I was too anxious.

"Here," he said. "Did you really mean to imply these are equivalent?"

I ran a finger under the line he'd indicated, but I could not remember what I'd thought when I wrote it.

"Anton?" he asked, and I became self-conscious, as I often did when he spoke my name: I'd spilled coffee on my jacket or gained weight or lost hair, though he did not appear dissatisfied or even concerned with my appearance. My shoulder touched his. Our thighs pressed against each other. We were sitting close, but I wanted him closer. I wanted him to mark me as he had my page, to be forever altered by his touch.

I reached for his shoulder. My hand trembled, but I traced the line from his neck to his cheek, wrapped my fingers in his curls.

"Oh," he said.

And then my papers were on the floor and his hands beneath my shirt, and I felt his body over me, his hands on the small of my back. His skin was impossibly soft. I could make out the lines of veins beneath it. I heard his heartbeat in his throat. I felt the air leave his chest. He was taller than I, his muscles as firm as bone. I was terrified, but also excited, a boy jumping from the high rocks into the water. I pulled him closer.

His lips were warm, his tongue forceful.

He closed his eyes, but mine remained open. I heard his heart, his lungs, the slap of his flesh against mine. My fears became desire and desire consumed me. I felt powerful, but also knew that had he let go of me in that moment, I would disappear. The world would collapse around me.

* * *

I THOUGHT I would never sleep, but I woke beneath the covers, the bedside table upended beside me. I didn't remember sliding under the blankets. I'd not heard the table fall.

Haskell was awake beside me, reading my papers, which he'd collected from the floor. He wore a robe, which hung open over pajama bottoms, both too large and likely Engelhardt's. My eye fell on the green-brown bruise above his clavicle. He bent to kiss my forehead.

"I think that was your elbow," he said. "Perhaps your chin."

I hadn't realized how awkward I was. "I'm sorry," I said.

"Sorry? Don't be absurd."

The early morning sun lit the space between us. I felt hesitant. I didn't want to misspeak, nor did I wish to remain silent. I was in bed beside Haskell Gaul. I had expressed myself in ways I'd never known before. Words, silence, touch. I laughed at the newness of my confusion.

He handed me the page he'd shown me last night, as if we'd only stepped away for a moment, though the margins were now filled with his writing. "So," he said. "Equivalent? Or not?"

"Do you always start so early?" I asked.

"I don't have much time—"

"Do you need to be somewhere?"

It was I who always had to be somewhere: the lecture hall, my office, a committee meeting. In just under an hour, I had to meet with Adler to finalize the preparations for tomorrow's conference.

Haskell, on the other hand, had nothing but time. Other than caring for Engelhardt's flat, he had no commitments.

He nodded. Beneath the soft light that slipped in through the curtained window, he seemed almost ghostlike.

"Where?" I said. "For what?"

"What matters is that you remain here, in Vienna," he said. "Or go to Berkeley, like you planned."

"I have no plan to go to Berkeley."

"Anton—"

We'd just spent the night together. I'd shown him how I felt. Was he rejecting me? Did he take my feelings so lightly? It was I who was worried about my job, my standing. He never cared. He'd said as much to me.

I pulled my clothes from the floor. My thoughts spun.

"I promised you I'd undo everything," he said. "I'd end this all before it starts."

"But it did start," I said. How could he deny this?

He pulled Engelhardt's robe closed around him and folded his arms across his chest. For several moments he thought, and I waited, like a fool, hoping he'd agree with me.

"There are books about us. I've studied them. I came here knowing all that's been documented. But I didn't know about this. About us."

In the light, his eyes looked more gray than green or blue, though I could see all of these colors in the narrow lines that ran like streams between each pupil and the curved edge of iris.

"What books?" I asked.

"They haven't been written."

"You cannot travel through time."

"I did. You, too. You wrote to me—you will write to me—pages and pages." He squinted at me, as if trying to more clearly see a mountain from a distance. "Our lives are like the spiral you've described—only ours are entangled. We've made a mess—much bigger than either one of us. I came here to undo that.

"I can't expect you to understand this, but you are in my past and I'm in your future. To this day, I don't know where my thoughts end and yours begin."

He laughed, but he sounded tired, perhaps from his own nonsense—a life I knew nothing about, a time that did not exist and had not been proven.

"We have a choice," he said. "We can change our circumstance. We can erase my mistakes, release you from their consequence. We just need to finish."

He held up my work.

"This is why you sought me out?" I pointed to my pages. "Only this?"

Either what he said was true, and he'd found me only so he might leave me again, or his words were false, and he was a madman. Either way, I was stunned. How naive I'd been! To think he loved me.

I dressed as quickly as I could, my back to him.

"Please," he said. "Stay. We can finish this."

"I'm late," I said.

"Take the pages, at least. You can look at them on the tram—whenever you have a moment."

He extended the pages that had excited me only hours ago. Now I cringed.

"I want nothing to do with your notes." I turned to the door.

I expected him to argue, but he looked away, past me, to the hall. He spoke next in a general sense, but I believe he was referring to himself. "Ultimately, men must do what they think right, but what is right is wretchedly complicated."

I took my shoes from the box and ran down the stairs to the street, which I'd walked hundreds of times, but never when the sun was so low or the sky such a chill gray.

* * *

I DID NOT see Haskell again that day, nor did I open the letter he left for me at my office while I was at the conference hall preparing for the next day's opening. I recognized his handwriting on the thin white envelope and set it aside. I resolved not to dwell on the night we shared or the morning that rendered it meaningless, but I returned to those moments again and again. I was angry. Embarrassed. I did not want to see him. In a day, or a week, our paths would cross, and I'd be forced to confront him, but not now. The conference would begin the next morning and required all that remained of my tattered attention.

I tried to sleep that night, but alone in my bed, Gaul might as well have been with me, so present was he in my thoughts.

* * *

THE OPENING DAY of the conference was chilly but clear, the sky a pale blue that might easily fade to white. Adler and I decided to proceed as scheduled despite news from Linz, where the militias of the left and right had clashed very early that morning, raising concerns about wider skirmishes and martial law. Like Adler, I was worried, but we were also accustomed to political strife. It was too late to reschedule. Engelhardt had traveled from America. Violence would not force us to cancel.

I arrived early to get a seat near the front of the room, and no doubt would have done so had I not noticed Engelhardt just outside the hall.

He'd returned to Vienna the day before, he said, and I did not admit that I knew this or that I was, as he spoke, envisioning his bed. He'd come to Vienna by way of Paris so as to visit his wife and son. He'd not seen them in many months because the trip to the States was deemed unsuitable for the boy. Evidently, the cure the child had undergone in Paris had done nothing more than prevent his epilepsy from growing worse. With time and continued treatment, the doctors hoped to effect improvement, though even Engelhardt shook his head when he spoke of it. He stood now with a dark-haired man, a giant. I wondered how I failed to know of this tremendous man and was about to ask him about his work when Engelhardt explained.

"He's my bodyguard."

"Your bodyguard?"

I was in a hurry to get a seat, but I stepped closer so that we could speak in confidence. I wanted very much to ask Engelhardt about his plans for the coming year, particularly in light of my offer from California and my urge to flee my own demons, but first to hear why he had need of a bodyguard.

The giant, meanwhile, busied himself by pacing the perimeter of the wide porch where we stood, his gaze fixed on the horizon, as if he might find ill intent in the sky itself.

"My wife insisted I hire him," Engelhardt said. "I've been receiving some very troubling letters."

He did, in fact, appear gaunt and troubled, though I'd assumed he'd been concerned about his son and exhausted from his long journey. He was no longer young, and the New England winters—at least as I'd heard—could take a toll on even a hearty man.

"Threats?" I asked.

He nodded. "Gaul forwarded me several letters, and there was another waiting for me when I arrived. Whoever wrote them is deranged. In addition to some horrible threats to my person, the letter contained 'a mathematical proof of love.'"

"That's terrible," I said, but I was thinking of Haskell Gaul and the love I'd imagined. Logic and love were incompatible.

"So, yes, I've hired a guard to accompany me while I'm here. He's the best, they say. They also say he was shot through the head, and the bullet passed through without causing harm. I've looked for the scar"—Engelhardt smiled, a ghost of his hearty laugh—"and seen no sign of a hole. There would be two, wouldn't you think?"

I could come up with no response, and so Engelhardt was forced to change the subject himself. He gestured to the city—the square beneath us, the row of little shops with their hopeful awnings and window displays: bolts of fancy cloth, fresh-baked pastries, wooden dollhouses.

"Have you ever seen such beauty?" he asked. "The magnitude of human endeavor."

I realized that I, like the bodyguard, was staring out over the surrounding landscape—a cobbled square, a narrow strip of grass, several bare trees that afforded no privacy, a handful of shops. I, too, was searching for the letter-writing madman.

"We should go inside," I said.

The bodyguard opened the door for us, and we all three passed through the opening, the overhead lights announcing themselves by drawing circles on Engelhardt's head. He did not look behind him to see if he was followed. The news he'd just shared with me did not appear in his confident gait. He must have made a joke, as the bodyguard laughed.

I stepped forward, intending to follow, but Adler stopped me. Dr. Kaminski could not attend, he said. The violence in Linz was, in his view, an unfolding civil war, and he would not risk travel. Would I be willing to read his paper? Also, two of our colleagues from Paris were quite upset about the schedule, or their place in it, or perhaps the place of someone else.

"They have a complaint," Adler told me, his patience frayed. "Please handle that as well."

* * *

I MISSED THE morning talks while tending to the needs of the two colleagues from Paris and would likely have missed lunch as well had not the applause alerted me that Engelhardt's lecture was done. I'd been looking forward to hearing his thoughts, and my best hope for that now was to catch up with him, at least briefly, over the noontime meal.

I searched for him as I exchanged pleasantries with several acquaintances and agreed that the art—landscapes that were overly bright and large—was striking. Excusing myself, I pressed through the crowds until I stood with Engelhardt and Adler, who were the last men in the lecture hall.

"We must do this every year," Engelhardt said. He seemed in much brighter spirits than he'd been in that morning. His bodyguard remained beside him, but the man now seemed like a shadow.

"Absolutely," Adler agreed. He led the way to the hallway, and I suggested we adjourn to a nearby café, though I could not recall the name. I believed it belonged to a woman or flower: Edelweiss, Rose, Hyacinth. These were my thoughts when I saw Josef approaching in his black waiter's costume.

I wanted to run, but Josef was standing between me and the exit, his eyes red from want of sleep. His teeth were set as if against cold. He looked unwell, even to me, and I was not in a frame of mind to notice much more than my own despair.

I did not at first understand that he had pulled a pistol from his pocket. The gun was trained in my direction, and still I did not feel its threat, or, rather, the threat that consumed me was of another nature. I was thinking of myself and the blackmail note. I was thinking of my career, and of Haskell Gaul, and of our night together.

The bodyguard pushed past me. I should have stepped aside. Had I stepped aside, he might have reached Engelhardt, but I did not step aside because I did not yet understand what was happening.

The gun sounded.

Engelhardt drew a hand to his chest. By his expression, he looked pleased in the way he was when a terrible student said something brilliant, but we were not in a classroom. Engelhardt was not, as he always was when he lectured, in control.

The gun fired again. Again. Again.

I should have rushed Josef, forced the gun from his hand. I should have thrown my body in front of Engelhardt's. But these thoughts are only possible in retrospect, and were it all to happen again, I know I would still drop to the floor. I would cover my head with my arms.

I am, and have always been, a coward.

* * *

THAT NIGHT, I lay in bed unable to sleep. Again and again my thoughts returned to the conference hall, Engelhardt bleeding on the floor, Josef falling—too late—beneath the weight of the bodyguard, and Haskell, whom I tried to push from my thoughts but could not. When I closed my eyes, I saw Engelhardt's bedroom, Haskell lying beside me. *We can erase my mistakes, release you from their consequence.*

I wanted the morning sun to wipe clean the darkness. I wanted dawn to promise a new start, but I rose, exhausted, dressed in my best suit, and with a heavy heart, set off for what was now a symposium to honor Engelhardt's memory.

The event had been hastily organized by Adler and several conference attendees who wished to publicly acknowledge Engelhardt's life and work before returning to their respective countries. My feelings remained raw, and I shuddered at the ill-conceived decision to hold the event at the same venue where Engelhardt had been murdered and in the midst of what was indeed an evolving civil war. I'd had no energy to read the paper, but Inge informed me that our city mayor was now in prison, having been forcibly dragged there, and the Social Democrats dismantled along with all institutions bearing the party name—from public housing to recreational clubs. The socialist presses had been silenced and the public libraries shut until cleansed of inappropriate materials, from Bertha von Suttner to Karl Kraus.

Crossing the square to the conference hall entrance, I felt the entire world was collapsing, though I was startled from my dismay by Engelhardt's hired bodyguard. He'd come, along with several dozen students and faculty—far too few for so great a man—to pay respects.

I chose a seat near the back of the auditorium and listened to my colleagues speak their memories of Engelhardt. Adler had invited me to share comments, but I'd declined, as I did not trust myself to deliver a coherent speech. This decision haunted me as well, and I felt not only devastated by the loss of the chair but appalled by my own inadequacy in the face of the tragedy.

At last, the service closed, and I rose with the others, planning to slip out before the reception and the awkward conversation, only Adler stopped me. His face was drawn, his eyes tired.

We spoke until I was able to excuse myself and hurry past the painted landscapes along the hallways to the exit. I was tired, not just from lack of sleep. I was tired of being afraid. I was tired of Vienna, of political parades and demonstrations, of the feathered caps of the Heimwehr, of the bright red socialist flowers, and of the neat military uniforms the men on all sides seemed to think validated their positions. I detested the rallies and the reports that followed: men fighting, men wounded, men dead.

I wanted to depart as soon as possible, to leave behind the feelings that throbbed inside me and the horror of the last few days. I would go to Berkeley. I would accept at once. I ran across the square to the station, intending to take the tram to the telegraph office. Only the station was closed, the workers striking.

I had nowhere to go but my apartment, where I would pace like a prisoner, or campus—where I was haunted by ghosts. I chose my office, not the library, where I feared I might cross paths with Haskell, though alone in my office, I still found him or, at least, his letter. I tore open the envelope.

Inside was a rectangle of paper ripped from a book—an article bearing that day's date, though the letter had been left for me two days before:

> **Vienna, February 13, 1934.** Yesterday, police entered the Hotel Schiff in Linz, where there was rumored to be a large stash of weapons concealed by the Schutzbund, the workers' defense organization. Police were ambushed by armed revolutionaries, several of whom were killed, sparking similar clashes throughout the country. Fighting has been particularly intense in Vienna, where three men were fatally wounded in the crossfire. To date, the only victim identified is Haskell Gaul, who had been residing in the home of Dr. Walfried Engelhardt, now deceased.

In the margin, he'd written: *Please meet me in the library—before this unfolds. Everything I've told you is true.*

What madness was this? How could this be true? He couldn't have known he would die, and if he had, why would he allow it? He was toying with me, and yet, the day's newspaper, which I found in the lobby, confirmed he was not. The story appeared on the front page.

I read it again, then again. There must be an explanation. He could not be dead. Not in this way. I would find him in the library at our usual table. We would apologize. I'd tell him about the conference, and Engelhardt, and the telegram I'd planned to send to Berkeley but could not because the trams weren't running.

I raced from the lobby and up two flights of stairs to the library. In the silence, I could hear my heart. Haskell was not at our usual table. He was not collecting a book from the shelves at the back or returning from the lavatory. He must have stepped out for a coffee. He would be back in a minute or an hour. When he walked through the doorway I'd tell him about my day and he'd listen, just like always. *There were very few people at the memorial*, I would say. *I should have spoken in his memory, but I did not.* And Haskell would tell me—what would he tell me? He was in my head, only I could not hear his voice.

14

Hase

SAN FRANCISCO, 2016

I decide to walk the half mile home from the library. Maybe I'll pass an internet café, where I'd rent a computer if I had cash, though I emptied my pockets at Harriet's house and now don't even have change.

It's night, but still light, June's distortion of my wintry expectations. I don't see the moon. Beside me, traffic is slow. I outpace the cars, though I have no reason to hurry. I won't sleep. If I close my eyes, I'll feel only the ocean, the tide receding as it did this afternoon on my father's boat. My thoughts race between voids: the empty cabin, the missing letters, the missing Wikipedia page. My father is lost, not me, but I feel lost, too.

What is he trying to tell me? I want him to explain that this is a terrible joke—a mystery he thought would be an exciting birthday adventure. He never meant it to go this wrong. He never meant for me to feel so desperate.

I know it's not a joke. My father would never involve someone like Dr. Fury. He was disgusted by the Zedlacher Institute, the student who died.

Fury's business card remains in my jacket pocket. If I call him to see what more he's found out about my father, would he tell me?

I doubt it.

I pull his business card out anyway. The logo, a bold *Z* drawn in gold foil, reminds me of cheap costume jewelry. Why would Dr. Fury care about my father?

I turn the card over. The back is blank.

If I had my laptop, I'd search for Dr. Peter R. R. Fury. I'd look at online photos, find his résumé, where he went to school and everything he's done to bring him to where he is now, Director of Crazy People, though the card describes him as "Author and Translator."

I wonder what sort of books he writes. I should have checked while I was at the library. Now it's closed, but the bookstore's open until ten, and it's only a few blocks away. If I stop there, I'll have to walk home in darkness, but that doesn't matter. I've never been afraid of walking at night, despite my father's warnings. I hear his voice in my head: *Hase, you will be mugged. Hase, you might be kidnapped.*

Kidnapped, he says, not *raped*. I don't know if he means the latter but his translation is off, or if he can't bear to speak the word *raped* aloud, or if he truly believes kidnapping is the greater threat. Whatever the reason, he spoke the word so often that when I was a child, I began to think my mother had been kidnapped.

I was six, maybe seven, but once the idea of a kidnapping occurred to me, I felt foolish for not realizing it earlier. Of course my mother was kidnapped. That's why my father is so concerned about this possibility. She wanted to be with us, but horrific criminals held her prisoner; she was trying to contact us, but her messages couldn't get through. I even considered the possibility that she had written and my father had hidden her letter, which is absurd, but then, his stories were inconsistent. For one, he doesn't know where she is buried, and he must have been at her funeral. *Unless there never was one.*

And he did not remarry. He never even dated, which also implies that my mother is alive. He, too, is waiting for her to find her way home. He doesn't speak about her only because the memory is too painful.

* * *

For my eleventh birthday, my father gave me the silver locket with my mother's picture inside. I still believed she was alive, mostly because I refused to accept that she was not. She, like Harriet's father, who walked out before Harriet was born, was subject to the same possibility: returning.

My father and I celebrated my eleventh on June 11 in the Rose Garden in Golden Gate Park, where we used to go twice a week because he volunteered there. The roses were in full bloom, the air heavy with their sweetness, and we had all my favorite foods: baked spaghetti, tangerines, almond croissants, and the traditional Jell-O, lemon that year and formed in the shape of a bird.

After we ate, he extracted the locket from the inside pocket of his corduroy jacket and extended it to me, the thick cable chain dangling from his fingertips.

"Happy birthday," he said, and I said nothing because the piece was dazzling.

The locket was engraved with interlocking roses, the design filling both positive and negative space like an Escher, only in miniature. On the back was a sideways eight, for infinity, my father explained, though the symbol has worn away over the years.

"Your mother would want you to have this," he said.

At first, I couldn't open it. The latch—a small onion of scalloped metal at the top of the locket—was as intricate as the engraved roses, requiring a combination of presses and turns, which my father showed me, and then it opened with a click that made me worry I'd broken it. Inside was my photograph and, across from it, my mother's portrait. The reds and golds and blues of her skin are at once alien and electric.

"She looks like you," my father said, though in my photograph, I had neither hair nor neck because my face filled the entire circle. My skin looked like wax, and I was looking the wrong way—toward the left, away from my mother.

Whenever I went with Dr. Ord and Harriet to the San Francisco Museum of Modern Art or the de Young Museum, I looked for the original painting. I didn't tell the Ords—they are my oldest friends, but they never met my mother. I didn't even show Harriet the portrait. But I imagined the artist was famous, and I was sure I'd find a picture—if not of my mother, at least a painting by the same hand. The artist would know more about her.

I never found the painting, but I did, by chance, come across my locket. I recognized its clasp on the front of *Handcrafted Magazine*, which I would never otherwise have picked up. The cover story featured the jeweler, who was based in Portland and had been designing lockets for nearly half a century. It was a family business, she said, which she took over from her parents.

I found no email contact, so I wrote a letter to the shop's address and enclosed a photograph of the locket and the portrait. I explained that my father told me my mother is dead, and I used to believe she was kidnapped. I admitted that I still thought this sometimes, but I was older now—thirteen—and just wanted to find out everything I could. I wrote more about myself, too: That I lived in a house behind a much larger one where my best friend lived. The last book I read was *Jane Eyre*, which gave me nightmares. I loved my locket and wore it every day.

All told, the letter covered four pages and took the better part of the day to write.

Two weeks later, it was returned unopened, and I was outraged. The store had closed—after nearly fifty years and the magazine feature.

Still, I remained determined to contact the jeweler. That I stumbled across the magazine with her interview could not be a simple coincidence. We were meant to meet in person.

* * *

I TOOK THE bus to Portland, packing only the cash I saved from helping Dr. Ord with Harriet's chores—sweeping the sidewalk, taking out the trash, folding laundry. I didn't ask my father's permission because he'd say no. Instead, I left a note, which he'd find when he returned from campus. By then, I'd be in Portland.

Except I was not. I spent four hours in Sacramento waiting for a connection and another four at various highway stops where I could buy a sandwich but was afraid I'd miss the bus. On board, I read until I got a headache, and by then it was too dark to see out the window.

I reached Portland after the late-night spots closed and before the cafés opened and sat in the station with a bottle of orange Gatorade, which was all the vending machines had in stock. Once the day grew light enough that I could read the city map, I found my way to the jeweler's store. It might be shuttered, but someone in the neighborhood would know where to find the owner.

The walk from the bus station to the shop took about an hour, but

I reached the storefront without getting lost, and I found the jeweler or, rather, the note taped to the front door that explained that she was dead. I'd come all this way to discover a bolted door with its sad report. I must have looked terrible, because a middle-aged woman stopped to ask if I was okay and if anyone had hurt me. She ran away from home when she was about my age, too, she told me.

"I'm fine," I lied.

She offered to drive me to school, or back to my house, and I considered asking if she'd take me to the bus station but decided that might alarm her. Had I gotten a ride, I might have caught the 9:00 a.m. bus. I might not have spent another two hours at the bus station or called Dr. Ord collect because my father and I didn't have a telephone.

"Hase?" Dr. Ord said. "Where are you?"

"Is my dad there?"

"Hang on," she said. She had to run outside and across the backyard to knock on the cottage door to fetch him. We would move to the boat in just a few months, but I did not know this yet.

I counted to one hundred, then began counting again. I imagined my father's song, the sad melody that always brought me comfort. Even inside me, the notes felt distant, more like the sheet music that hung on my wall, which I could see but not hear. My father would come to the phone any moment. He would be angry or, worse, disappointed. But he would come. If my mother were alive, if she loved me, she would find me, too. She would call or visit. She would find a way. Either she really was dead, as my father said, or she was alive and hadn't bothered.

Funny how I only realized this in Portland, that either way, she would never be part of my life.

* * *

THE BOOKSTORE IS open but nearly empty. Aside from me and the woman behind the register, I count only four people: an older couple browsing the travel section, a man who might be in college, and another man who might be his friend, only he looks like the drug dealer who hangs out across from my apartment. He's looking at a book on the Spanish-American War, which he's opened to the index.

I'd rather watch a stranger read an index than go back to my apartment, but I came to the bookstore to look for books by Peter R. R. Fury. I don't know what he writes, or even if he's published anything, so I ask the woman at the register.

"If we have any, they'll be over here," she says, leading me past the cookbooks and philosophy texts to the cult section. "I know we had some—people have been asking for stuff on the Zedlacher Institute ever since that movie came out."

She tells me the movie was playing across the street. "The line went around the block. Apparently, the actor who plays Zedlacher is some sort of heartthrob. Honestly, I can't even remember the name of the movie, and it was up on the marquee for months.

"Have you seen it?" she asks.

I shake my head. I almost never watch movies in theaters, because it's too expensive. The last one I saw was with Jake, who chose a silent foreign adaptation of *Macbeth* and then insisted on translating the intertitles from the French, disturbing all the people around us.

"*The Music Box*," she says. "That's it. I haven't seen it, either, but it brought a whole new crowd to the bookstore.

"Looks like we don't have any of Fury's work," she continues. "Want me to order it for you?"

"That's okay," I say.

She pulls a book from the shelf and extends it toward me. "This one was a finalist for the Pulitzer. I mean, if you're just interested in learning more about Zedlacher."

The book, *Genius or Madness*, is a paperback and large enough that it can only be shelved sideways. Across the cover is a photograph of Josef Zedlacher, probably from the 1950s. He's wearing a striped sweater and scarf, which together completely cover his neck and torso but fail to conceal his gauntness. He appears to be about fifty, but his hair has no gray, so he might simply look older than he is. His smirk reminds me of the men who explain Wikipedia to me, but there's something about him that's compelling as well—the confidence in the way he carries himself, the intensity of his gaze. I turn to the back cover, a cornucopia of praise for the journalist author who unearthed this "story of insanity" and "brought it to life with a sure hand and vivid detail."

Maybe Peter R. R. Fury is mentioned, I think, but when I open the book, I flip to the glossy pages in the middle to look at more photographs: Josef Zedlacher as a pudgy infant in a collared nightshirt; as a schoolboy in uniform, standing proudly between his twin brothers; as a student at the University of Vienna, in what appears to be a lecture hall. Josef with his mother at Café Central—she looks at him, but he stares into the camera with the intensity I recognize from the cover photo; Josef in front of his institute, an old stone building on what must be a narrow alley, as the photograph captures him at an angle and not full-on from across the street.

The final photograph is spread across two facing pages and depicts Josef in his office at the institute. His desk is covered in papers, so neatly arranged that I wonder if he used a ruler. The desk lamp casts light on only half his face and the wall behind him, which is covered in silk and paintings that send a chill through me. The photograph is in black-and-white, but in the framed work behind Josef, I can still discern the wild brushstrokes I recognize: the artist who did my mother's portrait.

I bend closer. All of the paintings are portraits, each framed in an ornate rectangle of silver or gold—something that reflects the light. I recognize Emperor Franz Joseph I and a man in dark round-framed glasses who could be Gödel or Schrödinger. I can't identify the others. By the cut of their clothing, three-piece suits and high-collared dresses, I imagine they are all dead, and yet they look so alive I feel we might have just passed each other on the sidewalk.

And then I startle. Hanging on the shadowed side of Josef's desk, where at first I didn't see it, is my mother's portrait. I know it, though I only own the circle cut to fit inside my locket. Her hair is pulled back from her face, and I can now see that it's tied with a ribbon. Beneath the lace band at her neck is a gown that must be silk, though I don't understand how the artist captured its shimmer. She's seated at a desk before an open notebook, and her hand rests on her pen as if she's just set it down. I realize she is thinking about what to write next. Behind her stands a coatrack with a man's hat and overcoat, but otherwise the background is dark.

How is her portrait hanging in Josef Zedlacher's office? She would have been no more than a child, perhaps not even born. And yet, there she sits, the young woman I know as my mother.

It makes no sense.

I want to take *Genius and Madness* with me so I can look through the images again more closely, but it's far too large to conceal beneath my jacket. Even if I were to try, the salesperson still stands beside me in the cult section, waiting for me to look up.

"What do you think?" she says. "Pretty crazy, huh?"

"Yes," I say, handing the book back to her. I reach for my locket but do not open it. Not here, where the light suddenly feels harsh.

15

Josef

VIENNA, 1934

Josef is to stand trial today, the fifteenth of May, a Tuesday.

Tuesday. Why must the court see him now? He's been in prison for several months, where he's fed three meals a day, with coffee. He needn't worry about money and groceries, or his horrid café customers. The night guard gives him cigarettes, which Josef lays out in a line on the narrow ledge that runs around the cell's perimeter. The guards call him "Professor." They complain that their backs smart from the weight of the texts they bring for him so that he might work.

Professor. He listens to the word but hears only the one unsaid: *murderer.*

He is a murderer. He remembers the bright lights of the conference hall. He imagines Engelhardt with the others: Adler, Moritz, the towering bodyguard. He again feels the force of his gun press back against his body. His arm tingles from the thrill. He can still hear Engelhardt falling. Death has a sound, the flutter of silk. What was it the cloth merchant said? *See how it holds its form?*

Since killing Engelhardt, Josef has felt a hollowness in which a single thought resounds: *I am a murderer. I am a murderer. I am a murderer.* For weeks, these words have commanded him. He is imprisoned by their syllables. He has murdered Engelhardt, but he does not feel satisfaction. He does not feel vindicated. He does not feel powerful. He has not rid himself of the anguish he felt upon seeing the chair of philosophy returned from Harvard, while Josef stood beside him in his waiter's costume and served his coffee.

I am a murderer.

Were a bird to fly through Josef's imagination, he would trap it between his bare hands and twist its neck so that it would not disrupt his contemplation: *I am a murderer. I am a murderer.* There is peace in that, he thinks, though he does not feel restful. He is falling. He has jumped but not yet landed. In the air is possibility: that his body will break against rock, or that he will grow wings and fly. Today, this peace will be stolen from him with the verdict that will forever describe him to the world. The word, *murderer*, will at last be spoken. History will trap him as he would his imagined bird. He will never disturb the peace again. Or perhaps, like a bird, he will soar, free.

The guards gather around his cell and regale him with stories—of press censorship and bans on assembly and protest; how Chancellor Dollfuss announced a new constitution; how the leaders of the Social Democrats have also been imprisoned and their miserable party disbanded.

Another guard is approaching, Josef's mother behind him. Josef cannot yet see them fully, but he's been told she's bringing him a suit for the trial. Josef recognizes the guard, a Heimwehr man who boasted of killing three men the day of the socialist uprising at the Palace of Justice. Josef does not admit he was at the riots that day as well, and that all he recalls is Sophia. Will she be at the trial? She hadn't come to the conference, but now that Engelhardt is dead, she has no reason to remain in America. Which side will she take? Josef's? Or her dead lover's? Surely, she must realize that Engelhardt swore an oath to his wife. Or are such vows also meaningless?

"Josef," his mother says. He can tell by the way she looks at him that she finds him abhorrent. Her lips are pressed together tightly. Her eyes will not meet his. This is why she has not visited. She cannot bear the sight of him.

He says nothing. The woman who cries before him could be a street whore or a seamstress. She could love or detest him. He is her son or a stranger. Either way, Josef feels nothing. She would have been kinder to stay home and spare him her disgust.

"Did you bring the clothing?" he asks.

She nods. She wears a dress he recognizes from his childhood, one patterned with intersecting lines that wrap so that they have neither end nor beginning. The fabric has faded, and she looks old, her hair, fine and thin, a translucent veil. From the circles beneath her eyes, he can tell that she has not slept. Her lips have no warmth in their color. She has come to preserve what remains of the family's honor. Her son will not be condemned in a waiter's costume.

"Put them on," she says.

Josef dresses beneath his mother's red stare, while the guards, kinder than she is, avert their eyes. The new clothes are crisp, expensive. The jacket, vest, and trousers are cut of the same fabric, a gray closer to silver than to black. Folded in a handkerchief is a pair of cuff links, silver, inset with a gem that appears blue in the low light, with more facets than he can count.

"Where did you get them?" he asks.

"You have many friends," she answers, and Josef laughs, because he has no friends, only his mother, who must have sold her necklaces and rings to procure these garments. She hands Josef a pair of shoes. These, too, are new and polished. Josef sees his reflection in the leather, the sharp line of his chin, the dark hair, neatly brushed.

"I am a murderer," he says.

"Engelhardt was no friend to Austria," one of the guards says. He inspects Josef's outfit, nods approvingly.

* * *

JOSEF IS NOT prepared for the crowded courtroom. The seats are full, the standing room overflowing. Who are these men? Friends of Engelhardt? Not Josef's friends, certainly. He feels the stiffness of his new shirt against his skin, hears the rub of his trouser legs against each other. He does not see Sophia in the audience, or his mother. He recognizes no one aside from Adler, who has made a statement against him and now sits among the witnesses. He does not meet Adler's gaze but feels he is watching him.

Josef hears the crowd but can make out neither words nor sentiment. The man beside the judge's bench is calling the room to order.

Surely, he is too young to be a judge. He looks no older than a student. A clerk directs Josef to his place, directly across from Adler.

The statements of the witnesses and the evidence correspond: Engelhardt was killed. Josef held the gun.

But is Josef guilty?

Josef's counsel speaks on his behalf. Should a man be punished for killing a burglar who breaks into his house? Or for striking a soldier invading his homeland? Right and wrong are not as simple as who is shot and who pulls the trigger. Right is the man who protects us from those who would tear the ground from beneath our feet. Is it not right to stand between society and danger? Right is a man who sacrifices himself for the good of all.

As the counsel speaks, Josef feels Adler studying him. Can he see motivation in Josef's new suit? Can he measure the anger that forced Josef's hand? Adler was never Engelhardt's student. He was never asked to upend his beliefs or endure the agony of a broken heart. Whatever his judgment, it has no basis. Josef feels contempt, almost pity. The old man's face is a red knot of fury.

Josef closes his eyes. In his mind, he sees a landscape, marred by poorly wrought lines and garish colors: mountains, a lake, a riverbank. He knows this place. He saw it first in the paintings on the walls of the conference hall. No one lives in these landscapes. The unnatural symmetry of branches and shadows do not match the sun. The ground is snow covered, the leaves full and green. The world has no such season.

He knows he murdered Engelhardt, but the word has lost its meaning.

"Look," the counsel for defense says, "Josef is an intellectual, a former student of mathematics at the University of Vienna, where he had the misfortune of falling under the influence of Dr. Engelhardt, an unsuitable educator whose name appears on the yellow list of tendentious professors. Engelhardt questioned even the Catholic faith! The natural sciences do not explain the world, not alone. One cannot dismiss God and the soul."

Yes, Josef nods, his eyes closed, the words pouring down upon him. Josef has rid Vienna of its sweet-speaking poisoner. Never again will students learn that the only truth is verifiable. No! The heart is a sense.

The soul is wise. God exists, and man has a spirit, which Maria Campioni, the great medium, can contact once the body has passed on.

"Who among us can disagree?" the counsel asks. "Who but a Jew or a freemason? Our chair, Vienna's chair of philosophy, should be a Catholic philosopher, aligned with our values and culture."

From the courtroom comes a rush of assent.

The counsel pauses to let the voices sound.

"Dozens have filed petitions for clemency, for pardon." The counsel raises a stack of papers toward the crowd, as if to acknowledge and thank them. "For far too long, we've permitted the wounds Engelhardt inflicted upon us to fester. We are to blame, not Josef."

* * *

THE SENTENCE, WHEN it is read, is for five years' imprisonment. Josef's eyes are closed when the judge speaks. He hears the words but does not feel their impact. A stranger could have wished him a good day or asked him to step out of the way.

I am an intellectual, Josef thinks, the counsel's words running through him like the tremble of fever. *I am an intellectual. I am an intellectual.*

The counsel bends close to whisper, "Don't worry. We'll get you a pardon. This will soon be expunged from your record entirely. I'm only sorry you must wait at all."

"I forgive you," Josef says.

The prison might hold his body, but his thoughts are free. He is not a man who must be forgiven, but a man who forgives.

16

Hase

SAN FRANCISCO, 2016

Harriet must have risen early, because she arrives at my apartment before eight with a box of pastries and two coffees. Normally, I would be asleep, but I slept fitfully, and not at all since about 3:00 a.m.

Only as I buzz her in do I realize I'm still wearing her clothes.

"Nice outfit," Jake says, his gaze dropping from the spaghetti-strap top to the lavender skirt. Both baffle him, much like an unexpected rain from a clear blue sky. He's fixing his own breakfast, a vegetable shake he likes because he believes it will extend his life. His diet is more about control than health, but I understand this. I like to be in control, too.

I unlatch the front door of the apartment and hurry back into my bedroom, hoping to change into jeans and one of my thrift-store sweaters before Harriet ascends the steps and confronts me about the importance of pajamas or the proper way to take care of her clothing.

She must take the steps two at a time because as I finish dressing, I hear Jake introduce himself. Just a few months ago, at Dr. Ord's memorial, he spent at least ten minutes talking to Harriet. He's met her many times over the years as well, but he never remembers.

"Harriet," she says patiently.

"I have something to show you," I say to her. I don't feel like engaging in small talk or explaining what's going on to Jake, so I turn to him and add, "Excuse us."

"Excused," he says. He raises his glass of health shake as if toasting us.

* * *

I CAN SEE the mess in my room via Harriet's gaze, which she keeps fixed on the wall, as if no other place is safe: the unmade bed; the clothes on the floor along with the loose change I brushed from the mattress; the shards of broken frame, swept into a pile but not yet picked up. The only things folded are her skirt and top, which now sit on my desk beside the ham radio and the crumpled sheet music.

There's no place to sit aside from the single chair and the unmade bed. Neither of us wants to take the chair, because it's the only good option, and not even I find the bed appealing, so we remain standing by my desk, Harriet's gaze on the wall, mine on the sheet music.

"Did you find anything at the library?" Harriet asks. She hands me a coffee and sets the box of pastries on the bedside table beside my lamp.

I tell her about the Wikipedia pages, and she seems unimpressed.

"Why would he go to all that trouble?"

"It's not hard to edit Wikipedia pages," I say.

"I mean, he could have just told you he buried something and where, if that's what he did. Why send you on a treasure hunt?"

"I've been thinking about that," I say. "Here's the thing. He told me about *the book* years ago—before we even moved onto the boat—but the Wikipedia edits were all made just a few days ago."

Harriet selects what looks like a jelly donut from the box, though I know it can't be a donut because she doesn't eat fried food. "You should try these," she says, offering me the box. "They're vegan pastries."

I shake my head. I don't even want the coffee, though I sip it, hoping it might help me remain alert.

"In other words," I continue, "he didn't tell me he'd buried something, because he hadn't buried anything yet. He didn't know where, or what, or when. Right? He just wanted a way to reach me—a very secret way—"

"The book," Harriet says.

"Right," I say.

"But the Wikipedia page you need is gone."

"Yes, but nothing is ever deleted completely. The page is archived somewhere. There's no good way to search deleted pages by ID that I know of."

"Well, if anyone can figure it out, it's you," she says. "I should have brought my laptop—I'm sorry. I was rattled. Three of my mom's old graduate students were front-page news this morning. One was practically family. He had dinner at our house most every Sunday—"

"Bruce?" I say. I know him, not from dinner at the Ords' but because my dad used to tutor him. Whenever he saw me, he boasted about his meals with the department head, like that made him somehow smarter. "Is he okay?"

Harriet flicks her wrist, as if shooing away a mosquito before it bites. She's already finished the vegan pastry, but I can still smell cinnamon and orange. She'll probably leave the box with the remaining pastries behind, and I'll toss the stale leftovers in a few days or weeks. I am impressed that she thought to stop at the bakery, even when rattled.

"There's some wacko breaking into apartments," she says. "The burglaries all happened over the last couple days, but now that the cops figured out the victims are all mathematicians, it makes the front page of the news."

"My apartment, too," I say. I'm standing between the piled-up sheets the thieves tore off my bed and the drawers the same strangers rummaged through, and yet, Harriet seems to have missed that I'm also a victim.

"Yeah, but you're not a mathematician."

"No, but Jake is—was. I mean, he went to school for math."

Harriet raises an eyebrow.

"You know that weird math you showed me?" I ask. "The stuff the Zedlacher people asked you about?"

"That wasn't really math," she says. "The Zedlacher people are basically insane."

I step over the bedsheets and reach under my pillow, where I slipped the letter I'd retrieved from my father's P.O. box, not to conceal it but so that it wouldn't get lost.

"What do you think of this?" I ask.

Harriet unfolds the pages and sits down in the one open chair, her attention fully consumed by the letter. Her expression reveals nothing. She could be reading a novel or a newspaper, a movie review or a fashion spread.

"Huh," she says, setting the pages in her lap.

"And?" I expect she'll point out a line or a symbol, like she did with the Engelhardt book, but when I move closer to see, she shakes her head.

"I can't read it. If I had the whole thing . . . maybe I could figure out more."

"My dad has the rest," I say. "Had the rest. On the boat."

As a child, I never once questioned my father's behavior; as an adult, I always thought his obsession with solitude and privacy extreme, but then, so many mathematicians are a little mad. My father would never harm anyone, and he was always able to care for himself. He would not have fallen overboard. He would not have missed my birthday. He would never lie to me.

And yet, in his mailbox was a letter with the same symbols that are on the Wikipedia page that the librarian from the Zedlacher Institute grilled Harriet about. My apartment has been ransacked, as have those of my father's other math students, and I've had my own peculiar visit with Peter R. R. Fury. The envelope he gave me for my father still sits where my laptop used to.

I reach over Harriet's shoulder to take the Zedlacher envelope from beneath the crumpled sheet music. For the second time, I tear open a letter meant for my father.

Inside is a sheet of paper: a printout of the Wikipedia page I first saw at Harriet's house. Circled in red ink are the strange symbols the editor Manifold added. A hand-drawn arrow points to this line with a single word:

Gotcha.

* * *

NORMALLY, I WOULD never meet anyone from online in the physical world, but Manifold is the one person who might know something more about the work my father's doing and that I'm increasingly certain is related to his disappearance.

"You brought your phone?" I ask Harriet. I don't like cell phones, and I detest the small keyboards, but if Harriet has her phone, at least I can get online.

"I had to turn it off," she says. "Some journalist keeps calling, wanting to interview me about the burglaries—"

"Can I use it?"

She looks over my shoulder as I bring up the user page that lists Manifold's Wikipedia contributions. Scrolling through his archived list of edits reveals that he rarely sleeps—his contributions are frequent and logged at all hours—and that his interests include gardening, history, and classical music in addition to mathematics. He has created more than eight hundred pages, and he must keep them on a watchlist, as he often drops by to correct typos and grammar.

Although his bio reads "don't contact me," and his user talk page (where anyone is free to post a public-facing message to him) contains dozens of notes, all unacknowledged, I know exactly how to reach him. I must say this aloud because Harriet asks, "How?"

She's staring at a page Manifold dotes on, Darwin's Garden, which I've pulled up on the screen. By the edit history, I can see he visited it less than an hour ago to add an Oxford comma to a line contributed by a user named SirenOfSinsare.

Harriet bends closer. "What is it with the weird names?"

I'm not in the mood to discuss usernames, especially as I'm logged in as TheRabbit. As soon as I commit my change, anyone coming to the page will be able to see that I, TheRabbit, have selected every word in this article and deleted it. I will remove the work of dozens of editors in a single bold act and explain my change in the history simply by typing:

Urgent. I need to see you regarding your letter. "Is it hopeless?"

That Manifold wrote the letter to my father is a leap of faith, but it seems likely enough that I mention the handwritten note from the margin, the one thing I could decipher. If Manifold didn't write the letter, he'll find some other way to interpret my comment—or will simply ignore it.

I hate using TheRabbit to vandalize the page, but Manifold will probably recognize the handle from my father's work on the math pages. If not, he will check my contribution history before he responds, but I'm certain that he will respond, if only to chastise me for blanking his favorite page.

He restores the page content within a minute, and within ten I receive a private note with his phone number and instructions to text.

"Who is this guy?" Harriet asks.

"My dad's pen pal," I say.

Manifold did, at least, confirm that much.

* * *

THE SUN IS bright and the streets crowded when Harriet and I leave my apartment. It's too late for breakfast and too early for lunch. Two unkempt men sit in front of my apartment building beside a sidewalk tent. They must have set it up late last night, as it wasn't there when I returned home from the bookstore. Now they share a sleeping bag as a makeshift couch, an old radio before them. Propped on the sidewalk beside them is a cardboard sign reading, "Money for Food."

"Don't. They just buy booze," I say, nearly whisper, as Harriet pulls out her wallet.

"I like to help people," she says, her voice as soft as mine, though the men probably heard us both. I forget sometimes that people can hear me.

She bends down to place a ten-dollar bill on top of the broken radio, and the men stare up at her, surprise slowing the expression of gratitude.

Harriet does like to help people. I admire this about her. I think of the piled papers and the book she hopes to finish—and yet, here she is, helping me, too. If she hadn't come this morning, I'd be heading toward the library, or maybe still in my room. Instead, I'm standing with my thumbs hooked into the back pockets of my jeans, my sweater coffee-stained, my hair unbrushed, about to meet Manifold.

"I'm parked just up the street," Harriet says, and I follow her to her car, where she plucks a parking ticket from her windshield.

"You need a neighborhood permit to park here?" she says. "Here?"

I would offer to pay the ticket, but I don't have the money. I still owe Jake rent. I have no income coming in and probably lost half my tutoring clients because I missed their sessions. I resist the urge to take the ticket from Harriet and simply tear it up.

She tosses it into the back seat.

"What's the address?" she asks.

* * *

THE INTERSECTION MANIFOLD chose is in a residential neighborhood with driveways that blend into sidewalk because all are the same gray concrete. We pass rows of houses, most without trim or any of the charm the city is known for, but find no stretch of curb large enough to park until we're several blocks from the meeting spot. Harriet offers to drop me off, but I tell her we should stick together. I'm not afraid to meet Manifold, but as he's a math person and she's a math person, I think it's best that I have a translator.

I see him as we approach the intersection, the only other pedestrian on the sidewalk, his hair a mess of curls, his body shrouded in a long dark coat that makes him appear a choirboy. His face is beautiful, intelligent but also strained, as if he plans to carry out some act of violence but has concerns or reservations. I take him for thirty, give or take a few years.

He looks Harriet and me up and down, like we're an unknown species, rare birds that have appeared on his front stoop.

"Which one of you is TheRabbit?" he asks.

"That's me," I say.

The intensity of his blue-green eyes subdues even the garish turquoise of his shirt. "And this is Harriet," I add.

Harriet pulls at the hem of her scoop-neck T-shirt. She runs her fingers through her hair, which appears wine-colored in the bright daylight. She is nervous, I realize.

"You're not from the Zedlacher Institute," Manifold says, a statement, not a question, though I feel he expects an answer all the same.

"No," I say.

I think of how my father snapped when Dr. Ord mentioned Zedlacher that long ago Fourth of July. We celebrated the holiday each year and then stopped—probably because we moved to the sailboat.

My father never liked fireworks. They reminded him of war: air raids, sheltering, rations, hardship. He would point to the smoke, the shadow.

Manifold is studying me. His lashes—very long, even for a man—make his eyes seem larger. I'm aware of both my body and the silent street. No one drives by. The sidewalks are empty. A dog barks from a backyard nearby. "Those people have been hounding me ever since they figured out how to read a Wikipedia page history."

"Well," I say, "you did edit Haskell Gaul's Wikipedia page."

"I am Haskell Gaul," Manifold says.

Harriet meets my eyes, and I remember the hours we spent browsing through the men who claimed this dubious distinction. The possibility of a mythical music box that permits men to travel through time was enough to make us laugh even then, and we were just kids.

Already, my conversation with Manifold is not going as I imagined, though I'm not sure what I'd imagined—that he'd know where my father is and what happened? That a stranger could explain everything?

"After I edited the page, the Zedlacher people gave me no peace," Manifold says. "They are, in fact, why I tell people not to contact me at all."

"Why edit the page, then?" I ask. "You must have known that would attract their attention."

"I can't help that."

He folds his arms across his chest, then unfolds them, as if he's trying to appear approachable but has forgotten how to best hold himself. My fingers find my locket, and I tug it back and forth on its chain, like a rocking boat. Harriet's cell phone rings, but she doesn't pick up.

"Anyway," Manifold says. "In light of how time travel could be abused, publishing the full work would be irresponsible. But I edited the Wikipedia page because I wanted to make sure that Anton got credit. It's his work, too. How is it you have the letter I sent him?"

17

Anton

BERKELEY, 1934–1936

I took a train to Le Havre, and from there a passenger ship to New York. The seas were rough, but I was surprised to discover myself suited for such travel. I slept soundly. I was never too ill to miss a meal, and I made good progress on my lectures. I was to begin teaching as soon as I arrived, and I looked forward to the challenges of working in a foreign tongue, of having a new circle of colleagues, of starting afresh.

The food on board was surprisingly good—roast beef, lamb, grilled steak—and I was embarrassed by the sack of dry sausage I'd packed as a precaution. Engelhardt once told me he always lost weight when he voyaged. Only now did I realize that he did not mean the food was horrid, but that his constitution was not strong. I thought of him often on my journey, imagining how he must have stood staring out at the sea, unaware that he'd never again travel over it. I thought of the work he'd left unfinished, and of his wife and child, neither of whom I'd met, though I'd been in their apartment, an uninvited guest.

I thought of Haskell, too, of course.

For weeks, I kept the unnerving note he'd left in my pocket. At night, it would turn in my thoughts: Had he snuck into my office and replaced his original envelope with a new one? Was his death staged and the news article one he himself gave the paper? Was he a spy? Was he toying with me? And if so, for what reason? Because I was gullible? Naive?

Or was what he told me true? If I'd opened his note one day earlier, would he still be alive? Everything about him was a contradiction: his friendship, his death, his parting words to me.

I wished we could mend the rift I'd left gaping when I fled Engelhardt's apartment. I wanted closure, certainty, resolution, but had nothing but questions. Had I only taken the pages with his margin notes! I could at least read his thoughts. But they, too, were gone.

Dear Haskell, I began, a letter I would never send. *I don't understand why you left this way. I know you are gone, but I still imagine I'm with you. I'm explaining how foolish I feel for writing this letter. I love you. I have from the moment I first saw you.*

The letter was ridiculous, but I could not bring myself to tear it up. I slid the sheet between the pages of my journal, beside the discarded sheet of Katarina Popovic's symphony and the charcoal sketch Josef had drawn of me, the beautiful and the terrible, and then this, which was both.

* * *

THE DAY I gave my first lecture at Berkeley was warm, and the students constantly asked me to repeat myself. "What?" they'd say, or, "I don't understand." I got through a quarter of a lecture that would have taken an hour in Vienna.

The students were eager but poorly prepared. They liked to come by my office with unfinished work, and they expected me to review it then and there. Their questions had to do with grades, not math.

There had been a miscommunication about my employment status, and correcting the mistake required some months. The dean apologized for the oversight. He told me administrative matters were always handled poorly, as no one wished to deal with them. I laughed, but he didn't smile, and I wondered if he hadn't meant the remark as a joke.

I found a two-story house, far too much space for a single man, but affordable and close to the university, which was what I desired most. I bought a bed and a desk and a table, chairs, a sofa, and floor lamps, but the place remained mostly bare. Two of the rooms had no furniture at all. I never went into them unless I was stuck in my work and needed space for pacing.

I had no art aside from the picture Josef had drawn of me. I hung it up to break the emptiness but soon took it down. Each time I looked at it, I was reminded of Engelhardt's murder, of Vienna, of Haskell. On campus, I mistook passing strangers for him. In the library, I looked up, still expecting he sat across from me. At the grocery store, I often heard his voice. But it wasn't his voice.

I stuck the likeness in a desk drawer, where I'd never have to see it. I could not, despite my impulse, tear it up, erase the past, start over.

My life was solitary, my time consumed by work. I went to department meetings. I attended public lectures. I spent my first summer alone, preparing for classes. In the fall, I was invited to write a book chapter, which was never published. I spoke at conferences, though none appealed to me as much as the ones I'd left behind in Vienna. Occasionally, my department gathered for lunch, and my colleagues spoke of children and vacations, awards, promotions, retirements. My English improved, but my accent did not. I was always a foreigner.

After my second lonely summer in Berkeley, I proposed a conference on language and logic, to be held in February, the second anniversary of Engelhardt's death. Planning the event took most of my time, as I wanted it to be worthy of Engelhardt's memory. Adler offered to write a tribute, and I volunteered to collect funds to support a scholarship in Engelhardt's name.

Of my colleagues in Vienna, I remained in touch only with Adler, who had—after Chancellor Dollfuss was killed in a failed Nazi putsch—moved to London. He sent the first contribution to the scholarship fund, but he died two months before the conference. I know my hands turned cold when I learned this news, because I pressed them to my face and shuddered from the chill.

I would have canceled the conference, but I'd already begun to accept papers.

* * *

February arrived, and with it the familiar press of correspondence. Between the administrative work for the conference and the Engelhardt tribute that now fell to me to write, I scarcely slept. I left the house only to teach and pick up mail, and on those occasions, I was so intent on saving time that I ran to campus and arrived out of breath.

I began to carry my journal everywhere, hoping I might have a moment between lectures to flip through the pages and find details for my Engelhardt piece, though most days I brought my satchel home again unopened.

By the time the conference arrived, I was exhausted, then dismayed. I'd made no plans for a formal luncheon before the proceedings, and yet, an alarming number of attendees arrived on campus with this expectation.

I tacked a list of local restaurants to the door of the department lobby and fled to my office, where I hoped to hide from the collective disappointment. I'd not yet completed my opening remarks. I needed to shut out students and faculty alike, but my door was already open.

I must have forgotten to lock it, though when I reached the threshold, I saw my trash bin emptied, papers tossed across the floor. An intruder had gone through my desk drawers and file cabinets and kicked the library books I'd left on my desk into one corner.

I sat down at my desk and stared at last year's wall calendar. Who would go through my office? A student? I hadn't graded the exams. No one had reason to be angry.

"Anton Moritz?"

I recognized the voice but did not at first place it. A woman, but not the wife of the department head, who sometimes helped organize events, or the department secretary, who'd handled most of the conference's administrative work with great competence.

"Yes?" I said.

In the doorway stood Fräulein Popovic. Her dress, a plain cut in rich cloth, made her eyes more gold than brown, and she looked radiant when she met my gaze and smiled. Beside her was a child's pram. The canopy concealed all but the child's legs and feet, snug in embroidered stockings.

I managed to stand and make a small bow in greeting.

"I hoped I might find you here," Fräulein Popovic said. Her eyes moved from the papers on the floor to the drawer fully pulled from its mooring, but she made no mention of the disarray.

Seeing her, I felt that Engelhardt, too, was on his way. He was just running late, dealing with the administrator or answering a student's question. Fräulein Popovic had come to apologize for his tardiness, to assure me he was coming, even though this was impossible. That Fräulein Popovic was here seemed impossible as well. I'd sent an invitation to her, of course, but had received no reply. I assumed the event was too painful, or that she was unwilling to travel from Vienna to Berkeley.

I was about to ask what brought her to my office when the child interrupted, her voice surprisingly loud. "Mama!"

"Ah, Hase." Fräulein Popovic lifted the girl from the pram, a dark-haired child in a formal dress that ballooned beneath her torso. "If I never finish my textbook, she's the reason."

"She looks just like you," I observed.

"Mmm, her father, too. He died before he met her." Fräulein Popovic stepped into my office, and I smelled her perfume—not lavender, but a field of wildflowers. "It's wonderful you're remembering him at the conference."

"He was a great man," I said. "I am very happy you could make it."

She laughed. "Of course I made it. I'm speaking tomorrow."

The shock must have shown on my face, because she added, "Wellesley isn't across the ocean, you know."

From the scattered papers that remained on my desk, I selected the conference program and found her: Dr. S. L. Popovic, On the Nature of Inconsistency, scheduled for 11:00 a.m. the next day. The department secretary had put together the schedule, and I'd been so busy with the preparations that I hadn't read it closely or noticed Fräulein Popovic's session.

"Could you hold her for a moment?" Fräulein Popovic asked, extending the child toward me. "I have something for you."

I'd never held a child so young and thought to decline. However, the girl was already in my arms, surprisingly heavy and quite warm. She rested her head against my chest, as if I were no more threatening than a pillow. My satchel—or at least its leather strap—became a toy she snapped against me.

Fräulein Popovic knelt and from beneath the pram and a pile of blankets extracted a paper-wrapped parcel, about the size of half a loaf of bread. I could not accept the gift with the child in my arms, and so I stood awkwardly while she held it, waiting.

"You can put her down." She laughed.

I set the child down on my chair, where I assumed she would sit, and she did.

"This was in Engelhardt's apartment," Fräulein Popovic said. "I'm sorry it took so long to reach you."

The box was a gift, but I'd initially mistaken its origin. Written across the top of the package in Haskell's hand, not Engelhardt's, was my name, and the following note:

We will figure this out.

I wondered what sense Fräulein Popovic had made of it. Did she suspect we were lovers?

As if to prove I had nothing to hide, I tore open the package.

Beneath the paper was a wooden box carved with an intricate pattern of night sky. I recognized several constellations, though something about the arrangement of stars seemed foreign, not quite right. The finish was chipped, but the box was still beautiful. I ran my hand over the crescent moon carved into the lid. On the bottom, I felt a metal key.

"It's lovely," Fräulein Popovic said.

I opened the lid and saw inside, beneath glass, the metal workings, a universe of interlocking gears and coils.

Fräulein Popovic looked at me expectantly. "Are you going to wind it?"

18

Josef

VIENNA, 1934

The morning Josef becomes a free man is cold. He expects to see a crowd outside the prison, but the streets are empty. The moment is nothing like the courtroom, where his innocence was proven—just six months ago—and all of Vienna cheered.

"Ready?" the night guard asks.

Josef nods. He will stay with the night guard until he finds permanent lodging. His mother, who moved to Paris to live with her cousin, relinquished the apartment in Vienna, but Josef would not choose to live with her, regardless. The guards have taken up a collection to help with his expenses. Josef feels the thick wallet in his pocket and knows it portends greater wealth to come. The emptiness inside him is like a song.

The night guard introduces Josef to his wife, who glares at Josef's one small bag each time she passes by it. She cuts Josef's hair and chooses an outfit for him from her husband's closet. From the roughness of the fabric, Josef feels she must despise him.

"Good," the night guard says, admiring the transformation. "Herr Eckhel will like you."

Herr Eckhel is the editor of a local newspaper. He has need of a bookkeeper, and the night guard has arranged an introduction. Over the years, the night guard has provided the newspaper with much information. Herr Eckhel and he are old friends, and friends look out for one another.

At dinner, Herr Eckhel offers Josef the bookkeeping job.

"You'll have to travel to Bad Vöslau once a month," he says. "Our publisher lives there, and he likes to review the books in person. We will reimburse you for expenses, of course."

Josef nods.

"Travel gives me time for my studies," he says.

* * *

FOR HIS FIRST day with the newspaper, Josef wears his trial suit—he has that or his waiter's costume, or the night guard's tremendous shirt and trousers. He will have to buy new clothing. The suit is too expensive for his station, but he would appear foolish in anything else. He combs his hair with the night guard's comb and scrubs his face with a washcloth. His skin is sallow from the months in prison, but his face has filled out. He has put on weight. When he examines himself in the glass, he sees the ghost of the Josef who abandoned art in favor of mathematics, the Josef who was in love with Sophia, the Josef who thought he would find his father's fortune buried in the floorboards. A fool.

"You look nice enough," the night guard's wife says to him. She still wears her nightgown, a sack-like gray garment that covers her "well enough," though Josef does not say this aloud.

"I won't be home for dinner," he says. Surely, his coworkers will invite him out. They'll want to know him. Josef read the newspapers in prison. Not everyone in Vienna thinks his release is just, but this newspaper campaigned for his pardon.

When he arrives, the office is bustling, but no one is expecting him. The editor is out. The man at reception tells Josef he is welcome to wait in the lobby.

"You expect me to sit? When you're paying me? Show me the books. I'll get started."

"That's not how things work."

Josef waits until the editor arrives an hour later, a full hour for which Josef is paid. Money falls from the sky! All he must do is reach out and grab it.

"Have you been waiting long?" the editor asks. "I'm sorry. Let me show you your desk."

Josef's desk is in a converted storeroom. The room smells of ink and musty paper. The editor explains that a leak rendered the space useless as a closet and destroyed years of archives.

"It does, however, suffice for an office. The last bookkeeper left his photographs. You can throw those away if you like."

The photographs are of burlesque girls, who leer at him from the wall.

Josef nods. "And if there's another storm?"

"You may need to move temporarily."

"Not I. The books."

"The books, of course. We keep those locked in the publisher's office."

"The publisher in Bad Vöslau?"

"The publisher in Bad Vöslau. The books we keep in his office. Come. I'll show you."

The publisher's office is as large as the night guard's apartment. Four windows look out over the well-trafficked street. Framed photographs of the publisher with Europe's great leaders cover the walls. In each, the publisher looks past the camera, as if searching for his next opportunity. His desk is made of glass and wood, and the top is empty. His chair is a throne of dark wood upholstered in green velvet. Josef runs his fingers over the fabric. The cushion shows no sign of wear.

Against the wall is a large cabinet. The editor unlocks it and, from the bottom shelf, extracts two ledger books tied with red cloth. He sets this bundle on the desk, where the daylight best strikes it.

"The older logs are there as well," the editor says, gesturing toward the cabinet. "If you need to refer—"

"You don't need to show me." Josef sits down in the publisher's chair and reaches to pull the ledger books closer. Not even Engelhardt had so fine an office. "You'll want a report at the end of the day?"

"When it's ready," the editor says.

"The end of the day," Josef says. He's no longer a man who waits—either for Engelhardt's favor or the verdict of peers.

With a nod and a wave of a half-turned hand, he dismisses the editor from the office.

* * *

KEEPING BOOKS COMES easily to Josef. He has done this work for many years in other contexts. A lesser man would get lost in the tight columns, unable to see the discrepancies, but Josef notices them as clearly as the moon in the night sky. Never once does he fail to reconcile the books. He thrives on systems and organization. On the publisher's desk he places boxes for receipts, and colored pencils to categorize each: blue for travel, green for distribution, red for printing costs. He writes his name across the top of each receipt to indicate that he's processed it. His name is everywhere, and yet, the work requires only a portion of his time. He spends most of his days doing math.

The editor, when he tires of his own work, enjoys looking at Josef's pages of symbols. He says there is no logic to it, and Josef always laughs, though he despises the editor's ignorance. Josef plans to solve every one of Hilbert's open problems. He resents the time he must take to chat with the editor. He will install a lock on the inside of the office door, though this will also take time, and so he has not done so.

He is working on his proof of Cantor's continuum hypothesis when the editor disturbs him again.

"Josef," he says from the hallway. "I've brought someone to meet you."

Josef never receives visitors. For a moment, he thinks the visitor has come to return him to prison, that his pardon has been revoked or his case reconsidered. Another witness has spoken, or the law has changed, as it seems to do hourly. Yet arrest is impossible. The editor knocked.

Josef reaches under the desk to button his trousers, which he's taken to unfastening for comfort. Over the months he's worked for the paper, they have become tight. He spends too much time sitting. He eats out too often. He hires a taxi when he might once have walked.

He opens the door.

The administrator extends a hand to shake Josef's.

"Josef Zedlacher," he says. "It's been too long."

The administrator is no taller than Josef. When he looks at Josef, their eyes are level.

"Can I count on your discretion?" he says.

Josef's eyes fall to the leather portfolio the administrator carries, its sides discolored with scratches. The clasp is worn smooth.

For a moment, he feels anger. The administrator had not met him when he, just released from the sanatorium, needed help. And now here the man stands, expecting a favor. Yet, the fact that the administrator has come to Josef—that Josef is now in a position to bequeath a favor—brings satisfaction.

"Of course," Josef says.

The administrator steps past him to the desk. When he rearranges Josef's papers to make space, Josef tries not to let his irritation show. He laid out his work with care and much thought, and the administrator has destroyed this order.

"We need an expert to review this work," the administrator says. "A trustworthy expert. A sympathetic expert. There's something coded here, and we need to know what it is."

Josef watches as the administrator pulls a dog-eared stack of sheets from the portfolio, each covered in symbols Josef knows, as well as ones he doesn't recognize, written in pencil with annotations in black ink—lines struck, symbols added and changed, cryptic notes (*you do this again* or *watch this*). At the top of the first page is a single line of text: *I assume you can figure out the rest.*

Josef thumbs through the stack of papers. The work is not so dissimilar from his own that he can't follow it—the original lines in pencil, and the comments, clearly another hand, in ink.

"Where did you get these?" Josef asks.

"From what we can tell, they're instructions, but no one's been able to decipher them. Haskell Gaul was carrying the pages, and we strongly suspect he was a foreign agitator."

Josef runs his finger beneath the first line. A proof, he thinks, though it appears to start in the middle. "Were there other pages?"

"This is all we have," the administrator says. "It's a code. It must be.

"You will help us?" he adds, but his question sounds like a demand.

Josef rubs the paper between his thumb and index finger. Gaul is dead, and of all the scholars in Vienna, the administrator chose Josef to examine his work.

"It will be an honor to break his code," Josef says.

"I'll see you are well compensated," the administrator says.

Again, money rains upon him. Josef nods.

* * *

I ASSUME YOU *can figure out the rest.* Ha! Josef tries for nearly two weeks, but he is unable to find a quick answer, an actionable result. His failure will no doubt disappoint the administrator, who looks back at him from the far side of the publisher's desk.

Josef offers brandy from the publisher's closet. The administrator declines. All Josef can do is unfold his notes, fastened with a metal clip stolen from the newspaper office, and report his findings.

"Here, to be correct, the sign should be greater than, not equal," he says. "One cannot make this inference"—Josef runs a finger beneath the line he copied—"without first noting that the two sets are disjoint."

"There are hidden troves of weapons," the administrator suggests, pointing to the lines. "Concealed here is the address of their location."

Josef shakes his head. "Are you certain there were no other pages? Did you search Engelhardt's apartment?"

"This is all," the administrator says. "You found nothing?"

"There are two hands here, Gaul's and another," Josef insists, but the administrator hears only what Josef has not yet admitted: that he's found nothing.

"I see no reason to continue," the administrator says, rising.

"Don't be hasty," Josef says. "There must be more pages."

Josef does not yet understand the lines, but he knows they have meaning. If he had the full text, he'd see it. The original author's description of a baffling spiral is alone interesting, but in the context of the second annotator, the work is breathtaking. There's something profound in the thinking, perhaps revolutionary. Josef recognizes Einstein's field equations among the margin notes, but the rest is entirely novel. He's never seen space and time described in this way.

This work, should he complete it, will assure him a place in history.

* * *

THE HOURS BECOME weeks, the weeks months. At night, when Josef tries to sleep, he closes his eyes and is haunted by the lines of Haskell Gaul's pages: the strikes through the stems of the sevens and the center of each zero, the twist at the base of the threes. The inked letters, all curls and flourishes, are even more vexing. The two authors are alive in this work, and Josef feels he is fighting with them.

He's angry when he sits down each morning to work. His mind reels through the worn cycle of his previous observations. At meals, he eats enough for two men and does not feel satisfied. He arrives late to work. Some days, he does not leave for the office at all. The night guard's wife tells him he has begun to reek. She wants him out of the house.

Josef will not be redirected. He will complete Gaul's unfinished work. He's already expanded it, building upon the pages as if they were a conversation he's entered and now commands. To finish, he requires the sound of only one other voice.

Josef does not know this man's name, but he knows his handwriting, and he will not stop looking until he finds the man himself.

* * *

JOSEF SEARCHES THROUGH the library's special collections—letters and notebooks catalogued and shelved in boxes. Most come from personal estates on topics that bore him, but he need only read far enough to confirm the handwriting is not the one he seeks. Months pass in tedious study.

When Adler dies and his correspondence is donated to the university, Josef examines it, too. He hates the attention he must dedicate to the drivel, but in the fourth box he discovers the writing that haunts him, the man he seeks: Anton Moritz.

Josef remembers Anton Moritz, of course. He remembers the séance, the unmet demands, the teaching position that should have belonged to him. But this is where Moritz's story ends. The man has left Vienna. The library holds no recent work.

Is he, too, dead?

Josef worries that the pages he needs no longer exist, that Moritz never achieved the stature that permits unpublished work to survive. But these fears are unwarranted. Anton Moritz, like Engelhardt before him, left for America.

Josef does not know the man's address, but he learns his institution: the University of California in Berkeley.

19

Hase

SAN FRANCISCO, 2016

Manifold looks at me as if he expects an answer, even though his question is absurd. How is it I have Anton Moritz's letter? The letter I have is not Anton Moritz's. It was sent to my father. I collected it myself. At this point, I'm not sure if Wikipedia's most esteemed math contributor has a warped sense of humor or is outright mad. Even the corner he chose as a meeting spot is ridiculous, the point where Angelou Way intersects itself.

"I got the letter from my dad's P.O. box," I say. The wind has picked up, bringing an ocean chill. I pull my arms across my chest for warmth, but neither Harriet nor Manifold appears bothered. "How do you know him?"

"He wrote to me on Wikipedia," Manifold says. "Actually, when you wrote today, I thought you were him."

"He always uses my account," I say.

"Mmm . . ." Manifold doesn't move, but I can feel him draw back. I want someone to pass—a bicycle or pedestrian, even a school bus—just so our attention is once again pulled the same way. But the streets are silent.

"I should have known you weren't him," he continues. "I've asked him many times to meet in person, and every time, he refuses. The Zedlacher people are horrifyingly obsessed with finding him. Did you know they surveilled the pure mathematics committee chair at Harvard because her work on high-dimensional topology reminded them of Moritz? She knew nothing of his whereabouts, but that didn't stop them from tapping her phone and tracking her every move."

"They're after you, too," I say.

"And possibly a whole bunch of old Berkeley math students," Harriet adds. Her phone has finally stopped ringing, but she's gazing at it now to see who called. "Did you see the story in the paper this morning?"

"No, but I have no doubt it was the work of the Zedlacher people. So many people announce they're Haskell Gaul, it's been fairly easy to avoid attention, and I only discovered the institute a few years ago. My paranoia hasn't had time to consume me entirely. Is Anton okay? I've been worried about him ever since that story about the mothers' group went viral."

"What story?" I say.

"The one in the *Chronicle*. The moms' group identified him."

Manifold must note my confusion, because he adds, "It ran a few months ago."

"How the hell would a moms' group know Anton Moritz?" Harriet says. "Or any long-dead mathematician, for—"

"Because Anton Moritz isn't long dead," Manifold says. "The film showed his portrait at the end, and the moms' group recognized it."

I realize that I'm nodding. I know exactly how it feels to recognize a portrait, like the image of my mother on Zedlacher's wall: haunting, even terrible.

Harriet holds up her cell phone, where she must have searched for the story, because she reads, "*Time-traveling legend spotted in Golden Gate Park.*"

I step closer so I can read over her shoulder.

According to the piece, the witnesses watched the blockbuster *The Music Box* together—their children were grown, but the women had remained "fast friends"—and all had recognized Anton Moritz from the drawing displayed at the end of the movie. Although the mothers explained that they had encountered the alleged Anton Moritz many years ago, long before they saw him in the movie, their meeting had been "very disturbing" and they "remembered it clearly."

"It was the guy," one said. "We all recognized him. You don't forget a face after something like that."

They testified that Moritz had appeared disoriented and "wild-eyed" at the time of the encounter. He seemed "totally out of it." With him was a toddler, who was red-faced and screaming, but all he carried was a worn leather briefcase slung purselike over one shoulder.

"He didn't have a sippy cup or snacks. No diapers."

The women had been "extremely concerned" and, fearing he'd kidnapped the child, had alerted the police. "The cops did nothing. Nothing!"

"Nineteen ninety-six . . ." Harriet does a calculation in her head as she returns the phone to her purse. "You would have been a toddler."

"It's someone else," I say. I feel my muscles tighten, my body rejecting even the thought. The toddler the moms saw might have been my age, but that toddler could not have been me. My father would have told me. If he were Anton Moritz, I'd know this already. Besides, the Wikipedia pages about the Zedlacher Institute make no mention of a young girl. Shouldn't I be there? Wouldn't the history of Anton Moritz note the existence of his child?

Or is the story of a little girl trivial, unworthy of note?

Harriet squints. Manifold looks from her to me and then back again. We've been standing at the intersection for nearly twenty minutes and not a single car has passed.

"Have you seen the film?" Manifold asks me. When I shake my head, he continues. "Why don't you come up to my place? I have a copy of the Zedlacher book. You really should see it."

* * *

MANIFOLD'S HOUSE IS a corner Victorian on a hilly street shrouded in fog and devoid of trees. From the sidewalk, I can see the ocean, gray as the sky and clearly violent, though silent from this distance. Above me, a seagull circles like a bird of prey. The house itself is two stories, the exterior painted a violet blue that makes my eyes ache. The windows and doors are gated. Peering through the bars, I see the curtains are drawn.

We climb stairs leading to the door, and he types a combination into the lock mounted into the wall. A small metal plate pops open, revealing a key that he inserts into a second lock, and we go inside.

"I kept losing the key," he explains as he opens what appears to be the hall closet but is actually a staircase leading down. "The owner was getting frustrated, so I installed the lockbox."

Manifold waits for me and Harriet to pass before following us down the stairs. The lock clicks, and I fear he plans to trap us in the basement, though the room that opens at the base of the stairs is not an unlit concrete box but a finished living room. The walls are decorated with hanging whiteboards, each covered in calculations drawn in red, green, blue, black—the four primary colors of erasable pen. The ceiling is high, even for a Victorian, and especially for a basement. Where the paint shows, mostly around the molding, it has the dirty yellow cast of age. Stacked in the center of the room, directly on the floorboards, are thousands of old records, one of which Manifold selects and sets on an old-fashioned player encased in wood. The music is striking, without clear direction or resolving note, and yet, pleasant, even mesmerizing. It reminds me of my father and the song he used to hum, only fully orchestrated. I think of the sheet music, ripped from its frame and crumpled, and how little the stranger who tore through my room knew or cared about it. I think about how the things I treasure can mean nothing to someone else.

Harriet studies the mess of symbols scrawled across the whiteboards. "This your work?" she asks.

"It's more of a hobby. I'm a landscape designer."

"Must pay pretty well," she says. She's never been one to hold back an observation for fear of crossing a line.

Manifold laughs. "It's not a legal unit. I don't have a kitchen."

Harriet points to a whiteboard. "Where did you learn the field equations?"

Manifold shrugs.

He leads us through a narrow hall to the back parlor, lined with bookshelves. Above them, the walls meet the high ceiling in an arch. Below, the floor is tiled. I feel its chill through my plastic sandals. At the end of the room is a bench broad enough to accommodate the three of us, though when Harriet and I sit, Manifold chooses to stand, facing us.

The arrangement is odd, and slightly uncomfortable, but when Harriet rises, Manifold insists she relax.

What follows should be awkward silence, only it's more comfortable than anything I can think to say.

"Okay then," Manifold says, "I'll get the book."

He walks to the tallest bookshelf, a floor-to-ceiling structure with a sliding ladder to access the top shelves, and extracts a thick volume. From where I sit, I can read the bold text on the front cover:

Zedlacher's Conjecture

By Josef Zedlacher

Translated from the original German by Peter R. R. Fury.
Zedlacher Press, 2010

He flips to a page that he must look at often, as the book opens naturally to it, and returns to where we're seated.

"This one," he says, extending the book so both Harriet and I can see.

Staring up at me is a photocopy of a charcoal drawing: a picture of a young man I recognize at once, though I've never seen a photograph of my father at that age. He appears to be gazing at me from the paper, his lips slightly apart, his hair in need of a trim. His expression is one I know well, the look he fixes upon me whenever I surprise him, usually with my stupidity—I left the burner on or forgot my multiplication tables—or sometimes when I've been especially good. The artist blacked out the background around the head, and its paleness, along with the low quality of the reproduction, makes the man in the image look ghostlike.

I stare at the image, eerie in both its familiarity and foreignness.

"Hase?" Harriet says, placing a hand on my arm.

I push her hand away. This is my dad, clearly my dad, not Anton Moritz. My father could not be Anton Moritz. My father would not have kept such a thing from me, and I cannot bear to think that my father lied to me all these years.

"Anton Moritz," Manifold says. "When I told him I knew his name, he admitted it eventually."

He releases the book to me, somewhat reluctantly, and my eyes drop to the caption beneath the image: *Anton Moritz by Josef Zedlacher*. That Zedlacher rendered an image that resembles my father, that might actually be my father, makes me feel I've witnessed a spell or a curse, one of the dark arts I've never believed in. That I found my mother's portrait in Zedlacher's office as well makes me shudder. Who is this man, and why is he surrounded by my family portraits?

Beneath the portrait, the translator has added additional context: that Zedlacher was, in addition to being a famed mathematician, a respected painter, and that reproductions of his artistic works are included in an appendix.

"His own seminal work in mathematics?" Harriet says. She's peering over my shoulder, reading from the adjacent page:

Foreword

Haskell Gaul is a dangerous man. He is guilty of malicious intervention in our lives and politics and of defying the holiest of constructs, nature itself.

For years, I have studied him. In these pages, I present the full text of every interview I conducted as well as a complete itinerary of his time in Vienna. I interviewed hundreds of men, and not one could speak to his childhood, his education, or his whereabouts before the day his presence was first recorded in the fall of 1933.

I have here not only recorded his habits and routines, but the secret he tried and failed to conceal: the music box, a time travel device based on my own seminal work in mathematics.[1]

I base my claims on solid grounds and put forth my argument in these pages with detailed accounts and supporting evidence. It is urgently important that we find Haskell Gaul, his associate Anton Moritz, and the music box. A tool as powerful as the box should not be possessed by a man who will use it to further his own interests, for Haskell Gaul is a political agitator, made more dangerous by his intellectual abilities. Professor Walfried Engelhardt, himself widely known as a dangerous and tendentious thinker, made the following note about the man in his diary: *Haskell Gaul arrived unannounced at my circle and immediately struck me as one of the oddest and most brilliant men of our time.*[2]

Of our time. Men are defined by their time, and Haskell Gaul's time is *not* ours. Haskell Gaul's time is one I may never know, though perhaps you, reader, are living in it at this moment. Perhaps you can stop Haskell Gaul before he leaves his time for mine.

Reader, I witnessed Anton Moritz use the music box to travel through time. I heard the awful melody and saw him disappear from the present as if it were nothing more than a bedroom in which he no longer wished to sleep.

This is not child's play, and we are not the only players. You must realize how much is at stake—how history can be changed for the better, but only by the right hands.

I extend my open palms to you.

1. I set forth my original work in its entirety in Appendix I.
2. I present the full text of Engelhardt's remarks pertaining to Haskell Gaul, as well as my remarks as to the dangerous nature of Engelhardt's philosophical circle, on pages 567–611.

"He's totally bonkers," Harriet says.

I'm still looking at Anton Moritz's portrait, searching for a detail that would prove the face belongs to someone else—a cousin twice removed, or even a stranger, poorly rendered to resemble my dad.

"If he's Anton Moritz and you're Haskell Gaul, where's the music box?" Harriet asks.

"It's not finished," Manifold says.

"That's what all the Haskell Gauls say," she says. "The Zedlacher Institute has an entire gallery full of 'unfinished' music boxes."

"The difference is that mine can be used—has been used, actually. Otherwise you wouldn't be here." Manifold, too, is looking at the sketch of my father in the Zedlacher book. It's upside down from his perspective, but he seems more concerned that I might damage it.

"You used the box?" I ask.

"It appears that I have."

Harriet laughs. "Are you saying you're in a loop? That you'll forever go back in time and Anton Moritz forever forward, and you're stuck?" She's testing Manifold, poking him like one might a strange beast, to see what it does.

"Not a loop," he says thoughtfully. "Loops imply that nothing can change and we don't have a choice. But we always do—even if we choose to do nothing. Say I decided to wind the music box before you arrived. We wouldn't have met, and I would not be thinking about whatever it is you decide to say, and that will change the story. We needn't repeat ourselves endlessly, and in fact, we do not. But Anton and I are entangled. If I choose to go back now, knowing what I do, it's because I can't be without him.

"I suppose we're entangled, too," he says to me. "Otherwise, you wouldn't be here, either."

"Why wind the box at all?" I say.

"The box has already been wound. I've traveled back, at some point, at least. What I must do is return to where I started—before we're entangled. And for that, I must follow the correct path. Anton and I were working on it. It's not at all straightforward, but I promised I'd disentangle us, undo the damage, erase the mistakes. We're very close—"

"You mean the part that's hopeless?" I ask. Harriet rests her hand on my thigh, comforting or restraining me, I'm not sure. Everything inside me is churning, blending, becoming something else: confusion into anger, anger into defiance, defiance into madness, madness into feeling very, very small.

Manifold's gaze moves to the floor.

"It's not simple," he says, "or easy to explain, but our lives are like notes. They're rendered by any instrument at any time. We belong to infinite melodies. We're nowhere in particular or everywhere at once. The problem is not one of traveling in time, but of placing ourselves firmly into a flow, and, in fact, this is what happens when one winds the music box. By winding the box, a person commits to a particular place and time."

Manifold extends his hands as if to indicate the size or shape of something he struggles to describe with words. "Once you wind the music box, you become part of a new song, and that, it turns out, changes everything."

"An alternate reality?" Harriet asks.

"I think of it more like music," Manifold says. "The notes are different, maybe the key. I suppose the melody you came from is like the past. And the new melody is not the one that was playing when you arrived, because it can't be—because of you—but it can be very similar."

I gather from the rest of his monologue that by winding the music box, one can settle into a time, but from there, one cannot unsettle. Whoever winds the box is constrained at that point and can't move to a different era or return to floating aimlessly. Unsettling is far more complex than settling, and the progress he's made on solving this second, far more difficult problem is due only to the help of a stranger he met online, and with whom he corresponded: Anton Moritz, whose epistolary friendship has been the greatest gift of Manifold's life. Anton Moritz has become more family to Manifold than his own family, who disowned him when he came out as gay. Moritz was the first person in whom Manifold confided the existence of the music box, which he'd built alone while still an outcast and oft-bullied teenager in rural Indiana. Moritz never told Manifold his name, but Manifold deduced it, just as he'd deduced that he himself was Haskell Gaul from reading the Zedlacher book.

"Anyway." His gaze darts between me and Harriet. "There's a certain probability that one note will follow another. But the time and place that note sounds are complex. You might think a melody is familiar, but it's terribly unstable. It's like—take a bridge. We know how much weight it can bear, and where, when building it, to place supports—and yet, it's shaking. There's a mistake, but I can't see it. Anton would, but he hasn't written back, perhaps because you have the letter I intended for him."

"My father's missing."

I say "missing," not "dead," but Manifold seems to hear the latter anyway. He turns his blue-green eyes to me.

"What happened?"

"They found his boat."

"His boat?" He squints at me, as if I'm a puzzle and he's lost a corner piece. Or maybe I just feel lost, as if I am the one missing, not my father, and the whole world is unable to find me.

"They found it adrift, and he wasn't on board, and all his letters are missing."

"Perhaps he destroyed them," Manifold says. "He asked me to burn the ones he sent me. I thought he was being extreme. He always said if it came down to it, he'd disappear."

I follow Manifold's gaze to the bookshelf, where the largest volume, Karl Andelman's *Underground*, is propped up by a star-covered bookend. The others, a mix of philosophy and mathematics, are in German. I can make out the titles, though I don't speak the language as well as I did when I was a child. Mostly, I understand my dad when he talks. I've never failed to understand him.

"That's it?" Harriet says. "That's the music box?"

Manifold nods, and I realize that what I'd taken for a bookend is much more than that.

"It may not look like much, but it's quite intricate." Manifold seems thoughtful but also sad. He's alone, I realize. He's built a fortress filled with whiteboards, but he lives in his head. The writing on his walls means nothing to me. He may once have been close to my father, but my father is missing. "It took months to get the alignment right. If I wind it—"

That any wooden box can carry a person through time is impossible, and yet, the emptiness and stress of the past few days leave me uncertain, almost willing to believe in magical things that might bring my father back to me. In fact, time travel seems no less unlikely than my presence in this room, the curious circumstances that have culminated in this peculiar moment of suspended belief. When Manifold picks up the box, I feel lighter.

"Technology has so many edges," he says. "It's hard to say who's wielding it and who's bleeding." He looks at me the way my father does when I am clearly ignoring him, not with anger but with curiosity, as if whatever distracts me must be terribly interesting. "Anton's not here, but I know where to find him."

He nods toward Josef's book, which remains open in my lap. "And, if I fail, I know what to do—perhaps not exactly, but close enough—to try again."

Then he laughs, but with neither joy nor bitterness. I've laughed in that way when I've burned a dessert or deleted a month's worth of work accidentally.

"Of course," he continues, "Anton still has the music box here somewhere, too. He never mentioned it?"

"The music box?" If what Manifold says is true, and my father is Anton Moritz, and if Zedlacher did in fact witness Anton Moritz wind the music box and disappear in time, then my father must have carried the music box with him. He must have it, unless he destroyed it.

"He wanted me to find something," I admit.

I tell Manifold about the Engelhardt book and the page ID that led to another page, and then another.

"The next page was deleted," I say, "and I didn't know the title, so I couldn't just pull it up in the deletion log. And then the library closed."

"Do you want to use my computer?" Manifold offers.

The melody has ceased playing. I only stream music, so I forget it can end.

"I'll put on another record," Manifold says as I sit down at his desk.

* * *

MY FATHER MADE his edits just a few days ago, so the deleted page must have been removed sometime after that and before I tried to pull it up last night. Thousands of pages have been deleted in that time, but many are just abandoned drafts or obvious garbage. If I scroll through the log, the likely page shouldn't be too hard to spot.

Manifold's keyboard is worn—*A*, *S*, and *E* are ghosts—but I know the keys even without their labels. Harriet watches me work from over my shoulder. Her silence feels like pressure, but it's broken when the music starts again, a melody that begins softly, as if it were water or wind, gentle now, but with the potential of tremendous power.

"How many records do you have?" Harriet asks when Manifold rejoins us.

"Not nearly enough. I collect them—especially unusual ones. This one, for example, only exists on vinyl, and the composer is unknown."

As they natter, I scroll through the deletion log:

deleted page Talk:List of 2007 NASCAR races
deleted page Fart krap
deleted page Category:Food companies of Norway
deleted page Bad sex in literature
deleted page Anastasia Fuller

Most are easy to dismiss. My father would never edit Fart krap. Many seem unlikely, but I look at them anyway: The Greater Battle of Khazjackistan, Black-orange, Orange-black. Some I open with anticipation—Star Arcade or Grady's Theorem—only to be disappointed. Others, I open because I'm interested: Anastasia Fuller, a dancer (No credible indication of importance); Sylvia Snow, philosopher (No evidence of any notability); Jessica Jeong, writer (Article about a real person with no credible indication of her importance or significance); Valerie Keegan, computer scientist (Multiple reasons: speedy deletion criteria); Ines Anouilh, herpetologist (Unambiguous advertising or promotion); Karen Sands, anthropologist (No independent sources, no evidence of notability); Rana Amin, social worker (Re-creation of a page that was deleted per a deletion discussion).

And then I find it. "Got it," I say, because I have.

Katarina Popovic's deleted Wikipedia page is brief—an introduction followed by a section dedicated to her personal life. Nothing about her career, and no links to external sources, but it's illustrated with a portrait that makes me gasp, because it looks so much like the one in my locket. The face is narrower than my mother's, as are Katarina Popovic's lips, but the brows and eyes could belong to either woman.

Katarina Popovic was the wife of composer Gustav Popovic, the father of Viennese modern classical. He fell in love with her when he first heard her play piano [citation needed], and he dedicated many of his compositions to her. Tragically, his life was cut short by an equestrian accident, leaving Katarina a sizable estate.
Upon her death, she bequeathed the property to the University of Vienna.

The page was speedily deleted by a user named RocketMan, because it lacked reliable sources and provided no evidence of notability.

Manifold and Harriet look over my shoulder.

"Katarina Popovic?" Manifold says. "She was a genius."

"She looks like you," Harriet says.

"It's not me," I say. "I didn't travel here with a music box."

Harriet knows I grew up in Berkeley. We shared a nanny and most of our childhoods—though, as I speak, I wonder: What if I did? What if, as Josef Zedlacher wrote, my time is not this time? The whole idea makes me uncomfortable. I can't be Katarina Popovic. And yet, my father sent me to this page. Is this the woman in my locket? I don't think so—I've stared at my mother's portrait so often, I would know. Still, Katarina could have been famous enough in her time—*the wife of the father of Viennese modern classical*—that her portrait would hang in the Zedlacher Institute.

By the page's edit history, only a handful of people know of her today: a user named Stringer, who created the page; SaltedEarth, who requested the citation; RocketMan, who stumbled across the page and deemed it insufficiently notable; and my father, who—just a few hours before the page was deleted—added several lines to the section dedicated to Popovic's life:

> Katarina Popovic split her time between Vienna and her country estate, where she found the peace to compose *Himmelsauge*, an unfinished symphony named for the rose she introduced to her garden. The work was later published under her husband's name.

"One of my favorite pieces," Manifold says. "Every note is exactly right, which is impossible, because right and wrong don't apply to music. And yet, it's true. It's why I used the piece for the music box. A shame it's so often misattributed to her husband."

The music box. Perhaps that's what my father meant to convey with this page, though he could have pointed instead to Haskell Gaul or the Zedlacher Institute, articles that actually talk about it. My father was leaving a message for me, but was he also hoping to set the record straight? To credit Katarina Popovic for her work? *Himmelsauge*, the unfinished symphony and the one part of the strange, sprawling story he shared with me. This edit contains no new page ID, no further path for me to follow. The edit summary—the last thing he wrote—reads only: *Finally adding the rose.*

My father told me nothing of Manifold, or the music box, or the problem he was trying to solve, or Anton Moritz, or Josef Zedlacher and his bizarre book, but I know this music. I have looked at it nearly every day of my life: *Himmelsauge*, the melody named for the rose.

* * *

MY EARLIEST MEMORY is of my father. Other memories—the sting of salt water in my eyes or the taste of lemon yogurt—may predate it, but I can't place those in time. The memory of my father dates back to March 14, 1997, when I was not yet three years old, and my father, who has never been one to arrange parties, decided to celebrate Pi Day.

In my memory, my father woke me from a dream in which I was also with him, and so the waking and dream blended, and I was terrified. My father became two men, one sitting beside me as I played with toy cars and one standing over me with a curious expression that I now understand was anticipation.

At that moment, however, his expression was foreign, and the room quite dark. The sun had not yet risen, and I had the sensation that I'd just awoken not to the day but to a nightmare.

I screamed, and my father placed a hand over my mouth to calm or to quiet me. This only heightened my fear, and I lashed out at him with all my strength. I weighed perhaps thirty pounds. I didn't hurt him, but I upset the plate he'd set on my bed, staining us both with cherry pie filling.

To this day, I have nightmares where I can't speak or cry out, and they may originate from that moment, or not. We are shaped by our times—for me, the hazy hours that don't correspond to either day or night because they're lit by screen glow. The silence of my time is not a pressed hand over lips but the illusion that I'm present.

I don't exist, not in any proper database. My father may, in fact, be another man. I know my mother only through a portrait, done long before I was born, and which may not be her at all.

I sit in Manifold's chair and stare at the image of Katarina Popovic, her eerie familiarity. My father added her rose.

"I know where it is," I say.

"Where *what* is?" Harriet asks.

"Whatever my father hid."

I don't know what my father wants me to find; I just know that he wants me to find it, and I promised to follow his instructions. If he is actually a time-traveling mathematician, perhaps he left me an explanation. If not, he left something else, something important. What matters is that I find it before the Zedlacher Institute does, because whatever my father left is intended for me.

"Can I borrow a shovel?" I ask Manifold, who looks back at me as if I were a dragon or a unicorn, a creature he's seen pictures of but doesn't quite believe in.

"I should never have given the box to Anton," he says. "I should never have been so selfish."

But he leads me to the closet where he stores his gardening tools beside a metal bin that is so full of paper envelopes it won't close.

He's saved every one of my father's letters, knowing my father told him to burn them, and I don't believe the remorse he expressed.

20

Anton

BERKELEY, 1936

Fräulein Popovic watched as I wound the music box, and I knelt beside the chair where the child sat so that she could see, too. The glass caught the light and our reflections obscured the spinning parts, but the child reached forward, fascinated by the gears.

The music began to play as soon as I released the key.

"It's my mother's," Fräulein Popovic said, surprised. "It's her symphony."

I, too, recognized the melody as the one I'd heard Katarina Popovic play at their estate. The notes were made delicate by the small hammers inside the box, but were distinct, and beautiful.

"She never finished it," Fräulein Popovic said.

From the way she spoke, I understood that Katarina Popovic was dead. I stood, intending to express my condolences, but found the room had dimmed. I felt dizzy, light-headed.

I couldn't hear the music, though I saw its motion in the playing mechanism. The office walls pulsed, like a heart. I reached for the desk, hoping to catch myself. Through the strange light, I could see Fräulein Popovic, the pile of student exams on the floor, the office window fastened shut. The burglar could not have left that way, I was thinking, a stray thought in the midst of confusion. I needed to sit, only the child was in my chair. I pressed the music box to my chest. I didn't want to drop it, and I didn't trust myself to set it down. The desk was moving, rising higher, sinking to the floor.

I must not sit, I thought, but already I was falling. I heard the child cry out, or perhaps I did. I was awake but consumed by a nightmare. At the window stood a man I saw only in ugly dreams.

Josef Zedlacher.

I was hallucinating. Josef Zedlacher was in prison, thousands of miles and an ocean away. Yet, he appeared at the window as if conjured by the song.

And then the sky became dark.

* * *

I REMEMBER THE feeling of the box, and that it glowed where the stars had been carved into the wood. I remember closing the lid.

"Please call a doctor," I said.

The ground beneath my feet was moist.

I thought I might stand, but again, I was falling. I was falling so far and so fast, I could no longer feel my own weight. Only the box had substance, and I clutched it to my chest as if it were a sick child and I alone stood between it and death. Or perhaps it was not the box I remember, but the child who clutched me.

I felt dizzy. My vision blurred. I saw a bright light.

Was this death? Was this what death was like?

* * *

THE ONLY THING as disconcerting as traveling through time and space is finding oneself unexpectedly responsible for a young child, and both these events occurred for me simultaneously.

I did not at first understand this, of course.

When Hase and I arrived in Golden Gate Park, I felt ill. My stomach ached and my temples pounded. I felt hot and then cold, and my hands trembled, much as they had the day Josef shot Engelhardt. I wondered if Fräulein Popovic had called for a doctor, and how long I'd have to wait before the ambulance arrived. I imagined a stroke, then a heart attack. Behind closed eyes, I saw muted red, and in my panic mistook it for blindness. The air smelled like compost. I feared I was buried beneath the soil, though by the warmth of the sun on my skin and the familiar press of a breeze, I knew otherwise.

I opened my eyes to the midday sun and was surprised to find a garden. The rows of roses—one just behind me and one two arms' lengths away—reminded me of the Popovic estate, if only because I'd not visited a garden since my time there. From where I sat on the ground looking up, the woody branches formed a thorny enclosure pierced by the bright hues of blooms.

I still wore my leather satchel, and its buckles remained locked. I found this comforting. My right arm bled where it had caught a thorn, but I felt no pain, and I observed the blood as if it belonged to another man. I wondered if I was hallucinating.

A child screamed.

Hase stood at the mouth of the parallel rose beds, clutching the music box—which I must have dropped—as if it were a stuffed toy. Her hair had escaped its ribbon, and her dress was stained with mud, but otherwise she looked much as she had a moment before, when I wound the music box and she bent close to see its workings. The rosebushes towered above her, yet failed to diminish her strength. She appeared less afraid than furious. When she fixed her hazel eyes on me, she did not meet my gaze, but stared instead at the top of my head, where the hair was beginning to thin. She had lost one shoe, a lacy white slipper that looked as absurd in the mud as I, too weak to stand, felt.

I scanned the garden in search of her mother, though even as I looked, I knew she wasn't there. Fräulein Popovic would be beside Hase, or Hase would be running to her.

Hase. Rabbit, an endearment. I didn't even know the child's name. And I knew nothing about children.

"Hase," I called out.

Birds chattered over the hum of distant conversation. The sound of my own voice surprised me.

"Hase," I repeated. I thought the child might run away, but she hesitated, torn between her fear of a near stranger and the unknown.

She was right to regard me with skepticism. I knew no more than she did about our situation, and worse, she had a better handle on it. She was able to move about while I was still too dizzy to walk.

I don't know what I would have done had she run.

As things were, I was scarcely able to crawl to her and wrap her in my arms. I brushed her hair away from her check and recited promises I knew were false: that she was safe, that I'd sort this all out, that she shouldn't worry. Holding her consoled me. I felt her breaths, the soft cloth of her dress, the warmth of her skin. I was not alone. She was here with me, wherever we were.

I stilled the impulse to take the music box from her and turn the key again. I didn't want to upset her, though I felt the hard edge of the wood against my stomach and knew—without understanding why—that the music box was to blame for this. I'd wound it just after noon. Now, by the angle of the sun, it was nearly four o'clock. And we were in a rose garden, far too early in the season for such full blooms.

A car unlike any I had ever seen passed on the paved road at the edge of the garden. Its windows curved with the metal body like fingers in a well-fitting glove, and I knew it was real, because no fabrication of mine could be so original. From the lowered passenger-side window blared unfamiliar music that I later learned was hip-hop.

I was terrified and also shaken. Was this what Haskell wished for me? He'd given me the music box. He knew its powers. The mud on my clothes was real. I could see footsteps: mine, Hase's (one with the shape of her slipper, the other her stocking foot), and others that didn't belong to us.

We were not in my office or at the conference on logic that must be happening now without me. Fräulein Popovic had not come to collect her daughter. My shirt was bloodstained where the rose thorn had cut me.

Hase began to wail. From the road, I heard voices—a group of women approaching, all dressed in stockings (I would later learn to call them leggings) and fitted jackets. Their gazes locked on Hase.

I reached around her and wound the music box, hoping simultaneously to distract her and to return to my office the way we'd arrived, however mysteriously.

The song, scarcely audible over the child's cries, played twice. I heard the clink of loose metal pieces and saw the cracks in the glass. Soil caked the exterior carvings. The ground did not fall away. I saw no bright flash of light.

I knew as it played that the song changed nothing, and yet, I still felt dismay when the music finished and we remained in the grass.

"Are you okay?" the women asked.

"My wife's away," I said, as if this explained everything.

I accepted the animal cookies they offered and extended them to Hase, who refused them. With this failure, I felt even more uncomfortable. I thanked the women and explained that the child missed her mother. There was nothing more to be done.

Ultimately, it was I who had to stand and walk away, though the simple act of leaving required all my strength. Hase thrashed in my arms—I had to lift her, as she refused to walk beside me—and I could barely carry my own weight.

Still, I walked away from the garden, around the bend in the road, past a row of parked automobiles, a half dozen cyclists, and as many pedestrians—all of whom turned a hostile gaze upon me and the tearful Hase—to the edge of the park, where I learned from a placard on a passing bus that we were in San Francisco. The newspaper, visible in the clear window of a dispensing machine, informed me of the date: June 24, 1996.

"Nineteen ninety-six," I said aloud, disbelieving.

"Hell of a year," said a passerby.

I had my notebooks but no money. The music box but no understanding of how it worked; a headache but no medicine; my journal but not my wallet, which remained in the pocket of the jacket I'd left in my office.

I wiped the sweat from my forehead. I was in a strange new world, but there was one place I could go, a place no number of years could make fully foreign.

* * *

THAT FIRST DAY, I walked many blocks, navigated the ferry and bus systems, and accepted the charity of six different parties, all of whom understood that my wallet was lost.

"That happened to me. Some kind soul returned it," I was told, though I heard it as if through a fog. Return meant going home, to my house, my office, my conference in honor of Engelhardt. Return meant Hase would be reunited with her mother and I'd fall asleep in my own bed. To hear the word *lost* spoken in terms of a wallet made it trivial. I hadn't lost my wallet—it was I who was lost. But this truth would not serve me, and so I kept it to myself.

Everything I spoke was false.

"We'll get you home," I promised Hase. "We'll get everything sorted out."

Promising return was as absurd as explaining our situation to the strangers surrounding us, none of whom seemed real, despite the sound of their voices and the shoulders that brushed against me.

If I tried to explain my presence here, who would believe me?

I couldn't even piece the story together myself, though I ran through the day's events—arriving at my office to find my papers strewn across the floor, Fräulein Popovic's unexpected arrival, the gift from Haskell Gaul, Josef's face at my window and the intensity of his stare. The music. *It is my mother's symphony. She never finished it.* Hase, in my chair, the music box's spinning gears.

The child had been as strange and foreign in my office as a mythical beast, yet here she was, more real than anyone around us. Her presence made my own more certain. She, too, saw the tall buildings, the lighted billboards advertising strange products and unfamiliar companies. She saw the brightly colored houses, the tiered parking lots, the shops and restaurants that were both recognizable and totally foreign. Hase and I belonged together, if only because we did not belong here.

* * *

WE ARRIVED AT UC Berkeley just as dusk began to darken to night. The campus had changed, but the library remained at the center, the neoclassical facade a promise that the past remained relevant. Above the entrance, the eerily familiar lettering assured me that, however strange the students in their casual attire, the building still served its original function.

Hase had fallen asleep, and I carried her up the steps to the entrance, her head on my shoulder, her feet dangling just above my belt. She couldn't be much older than two—young enough, with time, to forget all this. I shuddered to think how her mother must feel. I spoke to Fräulein Popovic in my head, where my words were as powerless as I felt: *I will take care of the child, I promise. I promise I won't let anything happen to her.* I worried the child would slide out of my arms even as I pressed her tight against me.

A student held open the library door for us, and I entered the building I'd been inside yesterday, but years ago. The shelves and tables were arranged differently; the nook where I spent hours reading was now a hall leading to the lavatories. The reference desk had moved, as had the portrait of Phoebe Apperson Hearst, the university benefactor. No matter where I stood, she used to stare back at me. Now the wall was adorned with a corkboard festooned with advertisements: music lessons, tutors, lost animals, requests for roommates. I would soon add my own flyer to this collection, offering anyone who came to my table in the North Reading Room an hour of tutoring in either math or German for fifteen dollars. But that night, I simply read through the offerings and considered the possibilities. Even the cheapest housing—a shared room in a communal house "within biking distance" from campus—cost too much.

* * *

I WROTE NOTHING those first few weeks. I had no energy for anything beyond survival—evading the reference librarians who would not be pleased to find us sleeping in the special collections, slipping an extra roll of bread from the dining center, caring for Hase, who stared at me with her mother's wide-set eyes. Even when she smiled, she seemed to be asking a question: What now? What next? Question after question, until she fell asleep, her head resting against me.

I didn't know what next. I didn't know what to tell her. I wanted to bring her back to her mother, but I didn't know how. I'd made no progress on fixing the music box. To work here, now, without tools or an office, and with a young child—impossible! I felt this impossibility so acutely that when I looked for the textbook Fräulein Popovic had mentioned she'd been working on and found she'd published nothing, my first thought was that she'd had another child. She'd be quite old by now—if she was still alive—but not alone.

Only Fräulein Popovic, who'd seen us disappear, would understand the absurdity of our situation: a past that didn't serve us because it was no longer relevant, a present without the comforts of colleagues, friends, family, home. I searched for her at the terminal that had replaced the card catalogues. Hase sat in my lap, marveling at the click of the keyboard and the moving screens. She studied each lighted microfiche as if considering its meaning. I would have thought she was reading, but I knew she could not because I'd only begun to teach her.

She tugged on my pocket, where I kept oyster crackers, though I had only the chocolate bar I planned to share for dessert. She needed dinner, but I was not ready to go.

She slipped the bar from my pocket and smiled, as if she'd tricked me.

Fräulein Popovic must be in the paper somewhere. She would not have left Berkeley, not without Hase, not after the terrible way we'd disappeared. Her name ought to appear in a bulletin or newsletter. She would have given a lecture, or stepped in to teach a class. She would have donated money to the university. She should have left a mark, but I found nothing.

I pulled Hase closer. Her mouth was darkened by the chocolate. Chocolate, the sweetest of desserts. She ate the few remaining squares as I watched her, and suddenly, the bar was gone and she looked surprised.

21

Anton

BERKELEY, 1996

I was at my usual table in the North Reading Room, Hase on the floor beneath it with her coloring book, when a woman approached. She was dressed in a man's suit, cut for a woman, and her hair was tied back with a purple scarf that drew my attention to her forehead, which was high and free of wrinkles despite the gray in her hair. She wore neither makeup nor jewelry, but her nails were polished a pale shade of blue. I thought she might ask me about German lessons—several middle-aged women from the neighborhood had begun to study with me. However, she stopped just far enough away that I feared she'd reconsidered. I was too unkempt; the bags beneath my eyes weighed down her spirits. She carried neither bag nor books, and I worried suddenly that she'd been sent to banish me from the library.

At last she sat, but at the next table, and I realized I'd mistaken her entirely.

I wanted to look occupied, but the paper before me was covered in hash marks, one for each minute I sat at the table and no one arrived to hire me. As such, I could only add a mark once every sixty seconds, or ruin the collection.

I added thirteen hash marks to my paper before the woman spoke. "Are you Herr Professor?"

I nodded. I had given myself the title "Professor of German and Mathematics" on my flyer, but my students simply called me Herr Professor.

"I've been told I could easily find you on campus, in the dining halls, or here at this table. That you and your child are here every day, and that you are very easy to spot. This is true."

"Did you want lessons?" I asked.

She laughed. "No."

I feared I'd disappointed her in some way, but she stood and extended her hand.

"Dr. Monica Ord," she said. "My students speak very highly of you. I'm looking for an assistant—to help with grading, mostly, but some editorial work, if you're interested. Would you be interested?"

Her eyes dropped to Hase, whom—just that morning, before the library opened—I'd bathed in the bathroom sink. Her hair was brushed and she had a full box of crayons, none broken. For breakfast, she'd eaten three hard-boiled eggs as well as every grape from my fruit cup. Her dress was modern, a corduroy jumper I'd purchased at a yard sale. She had no stockings, but none of the children wore them. I was certain she looked every bit an American child, and yet, Dr. Ord seemed troubled.

"If you know of anyone looking for an apartment," she said, "I have a garden house. It's not very large, but comes with full use of the grounds. The last tenant took care of the yard in lieu of paying rent. She was wonderful, but she moved away."

"My wife died suddenly," I said.

I'd wanted to explain myself and Hase—why we were here, why we were in need of an apartment—though even as I spoke this lie, I knew it was the wrong thing to say.

"I'm very sorry," she said.

I cringed at her sympathy. She pulled a business card from her suit jacket pocket, jotted her office hours on the back, and handed it to me: Dr. Monica Ord, Professor of Mathematics. I stuck the card into my pocket.

"Think it over," she said. And then she smiled kindly.

* * *

WAS I WRONG to lie? I did, many times, though by the time Hase and I moved into Dr. Ord's garden cottage, I had real references, if only for recent months. I tried to forget my fabrications, but even as our life became less difficult, I lingered on the dark moments instead of the joy Hase voiced when she claimed the larger of the two beds in our new home, or the first time she called me "Papa," or the conversations Dr. Ord and I had, often late into the night. Life was easier. I stopped counting the days since our arrival. I didn't fear Hase would be taken away. She had a proper nanny now, one she shared with Dr. Ord's daughter, Harriet, who was just a few years older. A friend. The two sat on the back deck of the main house constructing impossible train tracks from interlocking lengths of plastic. Sometimes the track would spiral into itself, a curve ending abruptly. Other times, the girls would abandon a line entirely in favor of a more exciting one, a stretch of track leading into the house or over my foot.

"Papa!" Hase called each time she ran the engine through the track, and I would look up from where I sat grading papers and watch it go.

I was happiest in these moments. Each day brought new adventures, from spray cans of shaving foam to digital photographs, and Hase took to it all. Our life was much better than it had been, and yet the belief that we could return to our real past was the one that sustained me.

We were here only because we weren't able to go, not yet.

* * *

WHEN I WAS at last offered an apprenticeship at Amedeo's Watch Repair Shop, I nearly cried with joy. The work was without salary, and the added expense of the bus trips to the shop and back was enough to cause distress, but we'd manage. The position was temporary. I needed only to learn the craft well enough to repair the music box.

Repair the music box.

I thought of healing, of making the broken whole.

I practiced tightening screws and aligning gears beneath the magnifier until my hands became confident. I learned the tools and laid them out: screwdrivers, brushes, hammers, dust blowers, drills, soldering kit, magnifier, and lamp.

I had no way of knowing if my work was correct, but I fixed the snapped pins on the music box's cylinder and repaired the broken gears. I cleaned the worm shaft and the metal rod that appeared to be part of a fan or cooling device. I repaired a wood crack with glazing putty fashioned from linseed oil and ground limestone. I straightened the key, which was bent, and adjusted the spring, and cut a new pane of glass to replace the broken one. I wiped the top clean with a dry cloth and rubbed it to give it a polish.

* * *

For our return to the past, I took Hase back to the Rose Garden in Golden Gate Park. We would leave from where we arrived, as if we'd never left to begin with.

I said nothing to Dr. Ord or my students. I took nothing more than what we'd arrived with: my leather satchel, the music box, my journal. Hase had outgrown her dress, but I found one that resembled it, at least its white color.

We stood between the rosebushes, and I held Hase close and wound the key. The music box played the sad song that made me think, again, of Haskell and Vienna—the unfinished symphony.

I closed my eyes, pushing doubts from my thoughts, and waited for the ground to fall away beneath us.

Twice the melody played. I heard no missed note, and then the song ended, and I remained where I stood, Hase in my arms.

"No," I said.

I would examine the box again, a thousand times if I must. I would hear the song play as it had the day we arrived here, though it *had* played, just as it had then.

I'd fixed the box. Something else was broken.

I should have listened when Haskell told me he'd traveled through time. I should have insisted he work through his thoughts and calculations. I longed to sit with him again, to hear his voice. If I could return to him, I'd admit how I felt. I'd admit I'd been wrong, a fool.

"A fool!" I said, but I must have looked more like a madman. Even Hase was frightened.

I set her down and then sat down beside her. The air was chilly despite the sun. I ran my finger over my right arm where the long-ago rose thorn had torn my skin. The wound had healed months ago, leaving only my memory of it.

What a fool I was to have hoped for more.

22

Anton

BERKELEY, 1999

I began to volunteer at the Rose Garden. I couldn't leave, but I could leave the grounds in better shape than when I arrived. I turned the soil and cut the dead blooms, and Hase would follow me around the beds, smelling the roses and demanding the name of each. In this way, we memorized them together.

Each day, when I finished gardening, Hase would pick a blossom to carry home, and though I should have reprimanded her, I did not. In truth, I had not moved beyond disappointment. The garden owed us. And so we put the rose in a vase back home so that we could smell its sweetness over dinner.

She looked more and more like her mother. As the months and then years passed, I was increasingly haunted by Sophia Popovic. I could not afford to raise Hase as I'm sure her mother would have, but with some effort and much luck I discovered the jewelers who crafted the locket Fräulein Popovic often wore. The pendants were costly, but our expenses were low, and I began to save so I could purchase one. This much I could do. The rest was harder. I tried and failed to delight Hase with her mother's passions. The child cared nothing for her grandfather's music, despite its fancy packaging, and pouted when our lessons turned to counting and sums. Only her grandmother's symphony delighted her. I hummed the melody as a lullaby, though each time the notes emerged from my lips, I thought of my own sorrow.

I did very little of my own mathematical work. Dr. Ord assured me she'd published nothing for the first four years after Harriet was born, and that I should not be hard on myself. But the truth was, I felt irrelevant. My field had evolved, and my work had not. I was old, already forty. Besides, where would I publish my papers? Under whose name? And who would I work with? Dr. Ord was my companion and friend, but our interests were very different. She offered to introduce me to potential collaborators, but I declined. I didn't wish to draw attention to myself. I didn't want to invite questions.

I had my tutoring and grading work, and Hase. Watching her learn to read and write, subtract and add, and knowing that I had a hand in each of these discoveries was more satisfying than any publication. And though I didn't write new work myself, I continued to follow advancements.

Hase went with me to the Mathematics Statistics Library, where I found an endless supply of books and journals that I read while she used the computer. When I felt sentimental, I descended to the lower floor to look through Dr. Schröder's collection, which he'd bequeathed to the university. Most of these works were in German, and as the demand for such texts was small, I was free to peruse the collection at my leisure: Engelhardt's original texts, and Adler's, much of it never translated into English; my own slim volume and the work of my old students, most of whom were dead.

Surrounded by these books, I could easily imagine Adler walking into the room, or Engelhardt raising his eyebrows as I spoke my thoughts aloud, or Haskell, sitting across from me, waiting for me to finish my work so that we might walk together.

Mostly, I thought of Haskell.

I found his music box as well. Or rather, the star-covered box on the cover of an otherwise unremarkable book: *Zedlacher's Vermutung*.

My heart sank when I recognized the author.

* * *

I READ JOSEF Zedlacher's book in its entirety with both fascination and horror. That there was an entire institute searching for me and Haskell and the music box was alarming. However, the institute's efforts also proved useful, as I could see that their attempts to design a music box were misguided.

Josef Zedlacher believed my mathematical work, with Haskell's additions, was the basis for all time travel. This was clearly false. My work was not at all relevant to the initial problem of traveling from one's present to the past or future. To use the work Josef had stolen as the basis for that was absurd, an embarrassing mistake of imagination, though I could also see how Josef, who'd stumbled on only a subset of my pages, might misunderstand their larger context.

My work, I realized, was relevant only to the second problem, the return.

The music box had never been able to return, and Haskell must have known this when he used it to find me in Vienna. He'd come knowing that he hadn't finished the box and could not go back with it. I wanted nothing to do with Josef Zedlacher or his institute, but it was his book, in the end, that inspired me to return to my mathematical work.

I prayed no other copies of the book had escaped Vienna, and I stole Josef's volume from the library so no one else would see it.

* * *

Zedlacher's Vermutung MIGHT have been consigned to oblivion had it not been for the death of a mathematics student several years later and the media's fascination for the grotesque. I learned about the student's passing in the *New York Times*, where the story appeared on the front page two days in a row before evolving into an investigative series.

The student was described as "a promising mathematician," just two months shy of graduating at the top of his class at the University of Vienna. He was a chess grandmaster and head of the rowing club, where he was well liked and much admired. In the photograph that ran above the first story, he was clean-shaven and dressed in a three-piece suit that seemed too formal for a man of his age. He'd started at the university at sixteen and would have finished his degree in just three years had not tragedy befallen him. He'd died at a mathematical conference, and the cause of death remained under investigation. The piece might not have made the news at all, not to mention the front page, had he not been the son of a German billionaire.

The follow-up story led with a much shabbier image of the young man. Instead of a suit, he wore a white undershirt that betrayed his gauntness, and he gazed at the camera with a hollow stare. The cause of death was determined to be sleep deprivation. Fellow conference attendees testified that the young man had remained awake for the duration of the weeklong conference, and had perhaps been awake even longer. When asked why they had not intervened, the witnesses said that the young man was "in the zone" and that "interfering would have been unethical." The conference organizer, who the reporter noted was not affiliated with the university, claimed that sleep deprivation was common at Zedlacher Institute's events, and that many considered this type of vigilance "the path to truth."

"We were all convinced he was Haskell Gaul," the organizer said. "All the pieces fit."

To see the name Haskell Gaul on the front page of the *New York Times* unnerved me, though even more unsettling was the photo of Josef Zedlacher, taken not long before his death in the mid-1980s. In the photo, he stood in a courtyard surrounded by busts of Austria's greatest thinkers. He glared out from the page, aged but with every bit of his old intensity. The Zedlacher Institute, which he founded not long after the Berkeley conference I organized but failed to attend, was portrayed in the paper as "a cultlike fringe organization" fiercely dedicated to Zedlacher's mission, "to find Haskell Gaul, his associate Anton Moritz, and the mathematical marvel, the time-traveling music box."

The reporter would go on to investigate the history of the "bizarre death math cult" and its "murderous founder," the many men who believed themselves to be Haskell Gaul, and the institute's substantial collection of music boxes that did "not *yet* function." The series would become the basis of a bestselling book, *Genius or Madness: The Story of Josef Zedlacher*, and the attention would inspire the first English translation of Josef Zedlacher's book as well as a new German edition, the original having fallen into the public domain.

I followed these events with horror. Over the course of many months, the story grew from a single unfortunate death into a "mad genius's decades-long quest." Josef's book—containing pages of what many agreed was "indeed beautiful math"—even came to the attention of Dr. Ord.

I don't believe she ever read *Genius or Madness*, but she saw the piece in the *New York Times* because it ran on the Fourth of July, the day of her annual barbecue.

"Zedlacher can't even burn properly," she said when the coals failed to light and the photo of Josef gazed up from the ashes.

She knew nothing about my past. I'd told no one, not even Hase. The silence was a lie, but one I kept vigilantly. I didn't want to be discovered or hounded by the institute. I did not want my work or the music box to fall into the wrong hands. But more important, I wanted to protect Hase. I didn't want her to mourn a life she'd never lived, or the mother she would never know. I didn't want her to feel like an interloper, or to bear the weight of a secret she had done nothing to earn.

She was thirteen, and taller than Harriet, who was headed to college in the fall. I worried Hase would be lonely without her, but she only shrugged when I mentioned it. She looked even more like Fräulein Popovic than she had when she was younger, but, unlike her mother, she didn't command attention when she entered a room. Instead, I'd look up from my work and find her sitting quietly with her laptop, as if she'd been sitting just so all along.

This is exactly how I found her that Fourth of July, bent over her laptop, a gift from Dr. Ord, reading about the Zedlacher Institute and discussing Haskell Gaul with Harriet.

I'd told her nothing, and yet, she'd stumbled upon this history all on her own.

"It's Wikipedia," she told me.

Wikipedia. I knew very little about the internet site, other than Hase enjoyed it and spent hours engaging with its content.

She scrolled through the institute's page to show me, and I saw the photographs of the self-proclaimed Haskell Gauls, the links to their works, the descriptions of their music boxes.

"Here," Hase said, showing me the page history, a log of every change, though so full of acronyms that I understood very little. "Another Haskell Gaul was just added this morning."

"Added?" I asked. And she showed me how I, too, could add content to the page. She showed me that the article was originally only in German, and that the English version had begun as a translation not long after the student's death.

* * *

THANKS TO HASE, Wikipedia became part of my daily routine. By following the Zedlacher Institute page, I could see each new Haskell Gaul. I always failed to find the real one, but, still, I might. As horrible as the institute was, it was also a place that might bring Haskell and me together. The Zedlacher Institute became my obsession.

I studied each Haskell Gaul and every new lead. I learned of the Zedlacher scouts who haunted mathematical conferences, searching for my face (Haskell Gaul's was unrecorded), and of the contests and conferences the institute held to advance the work of re-creating the music box. I learned how the institute's more radical members tapped the phone lines of prominent mathematicians, or lurked outside the homes of the men they believed were secretly working with me.

The question was not if, but when they would find me—though if I could find Gaul first, perhaps we could escape them. We could repair not just the music box but the lives we'd broken.

Perhaps I—we—could find a way to make everything right.

* * *

AS THE ZEDLACHER Institute grew, I stopped seeking out new students and rarely went to campus. I told Dr. Ord I was working on a new and consuming problem, which was both true and false, as I'd started the work long ago. I sent Hase to get groceries. I stopped volunteering at the Rose Garden. I no longer stopped at the café for a croissant and a coffee. How many people had seen Josef's sketch of me? How long did I have before I was found?

When Dr. Ord asked me to move to her sailboat for a few weeks so that she might fix the leaks in the cottage, I packed at once. Anyone—students, librarians, store clerks, neighbors, Harriet, Dr. Ord, even Hase—might betray me. Any one of these people might make a connection between me and Zedlacher, and that would be enough.

On the docks, no one studied mathematics or moved in circles where Josef Zedlacher was discussed.

I grew a beard. I wore a hat. I became invisible.

Hase laughed at me. She told me I was taking the boating life too far. She sat on deck, scanning the sky with Dr. Ord's binoculars or sketching the seagulls and pelicans.

I worried for her. I'd protected her from the truth, but what sort of life had I given her? I'd made every decision for both of us, and she suffered for each of my failures. I'd never burden her with my fears, but I couldn't hide them from her, either.

"What's wrong?" she asked.

"Just work," I told her. "It's a difficult problem."

Hase was never more than a boat's length away from me, and yet, I'd never felt more distant.

"You shouldn't work so hard," she told me.

I agreed, but I worked late into the night regardless.

* * *

After the cottage repairs were complete and Dr. Ord invited us back, I asked if we might stay on the boat instead. We were comfortable enough. The cabin could sleep four and we were just two: I at the front, Hase at the rear in a narrow bunk she called her burrow. Between us was the toilet, though we used it only when we were too tired to walk up the dock to the public restroom, and a kitchen with storage bins locked with bungie cords. I didn't have a captain's license, but Dr. Ord had often taken us sailing, and I knew enough to take the boat out to explore the coast. The world was closing in around us, but we could sail out to sea and back again. Out and back. Out and back.

When I was feeling most melancholy, I added to Wikipedia's mathematics pages. The internet connection at the harbor was spotty and slow, but with patience, I could edit. Wikipedia was the one place I could publish without a name or an institution, and I gladly fixed some of the more glaring errors.

Over time, I met dozens of editors and built what Hase referred to as a social life. Once, after a polite argument about how best to describe deformation theory, I even made a friend, though we didn't start corresponding until we encountered each other on the Zariski tangent space page, as we were both editing it simultaneously.

Manifold's notes to me mostly concerned mathematics, though he would sometimes refer to his isolation: how the library had none of the books I recommended, or how he had no one else with whom he could discuss his work and interests. Once, he apologized for a delay in responding, and mentioned he'd been in the hospital. He'd been riding his bike and a group of boys tossed a chair across his path. Sometimes, he admitted, people were cruel to him. He was nearly twenty years old and still they called him names. Another time, he told me I was the father he never had, that his biological father refused to speak to him. He signed that letter with the word *love*, but from that time on, perhaps embarrassed, he didn't sign his letters at all.

When he moved to San Francisco, he asked to meet me. Of course, I declined. I met no strangers in person. He asked a second time, claiming he had work he wanted to discuss with me and that he didn't want to describe it in writing. He worried I'd think him mad, or worse, that I'd share the message and mock it.

I assured him I would not, and also that I was unable to meet him, and he didn't respond for several days. I thought I might have discouraged him, but he did at last write:

Very well, then.
All my life, I've spent more time online than off. Communicating with people from around the world as if we were all together in a single room made me question my relationship with space and time, and inspired me to construct a tremendously powerful device, but I'm now afraid to use it. I can't provide further details here, but knowing this much: Should I destroy it?

I read this letter several times. Only then did I realize who this young man really was. I'd been looking so intently for Haskell Gaul on the Zedlacher Institute page, I'd failed to see him entirely.

Should he destroy the music box?

How could I tell him to do that when he'd already chosen? We wouldn't be writing now had he not wound the box at some point in his future.

I did not tell him my name—he knew me only by the Wikipedia handle Hase had set up, TheRabbit—but he deduced who I was after he stumbled across the Zedlacher books. *Dear Anton*, he wrote then, and I realized that he'd found the story of the music box and the Zedlacher Institute and understood his role in it, and mine. I had no reason to hide my identity from him—I knew from our time in Vienna that he must discover it, as he knew me when he arrived—and yet, I still felt anxious when he addressed me by my name. However, my unease was small compared to his.

> *What would happen if the music box belonged to everyone? Would there be so many shifting melodies that we'd hear none? Would we lose track of who we are and what's important? Would the world be a better place? Or an empty one? Please, can I see you? I've never felt more uncertain or alone.*

To Haskell, the only danger of the music box was external: that if every person used it, we would lose track of ourselves entirely. He thought of life in terms of song, an abstraction I found troubling. Even one man can disrupt lives, I wrote to him, one man, well intentioned, not to mention one who seeks only to benefit himself.

My thoughts were shaped by loss—Hase's childhood, her mother's sorrow, my own isolation and fear.

I insisted, and he agreed: we must return ourselves, and the lives we'd shifted. We must erase the mess we'd made. History would have no record of our trespass because we'd erase it before it began. Erase. Remove. Forget.

We just needed to solve the problem that imprisoned me, and Hase, in this time.

Hase. None of this was ever meant for her. But we would fix everything as soon as the music box could return us.

I longed for Haskell, but I refused to see him. I was more than twice his age—an old man to him, a father, a mentor, not a lover. I couldn't bear—after all the years and the feelings I'd contained—to meet him in this way. And so we were together only on paper, where our ideas blended, until I could no longer tell what was mine and what his, until we were, in this way, united.

* * *

AFTER HASE MOVED off the boat to live with Jake—not my most promising pupil, but a responsible one, with whom Hase would (I assured myself) be safe—I spent even more time in my head or corresponding with Haskell. He taught me how to restore the music box—which I'd kept all these years, repaired but not correctly—to its original condition, the state it was in when he first wound the box and it carried him to Vienna. Together we continued to work on the remaining problem, the state Haskell hadn't solved yet: how to return.

We'd shared everything we knew about the problem—the work he'd done on the music box before we met, the pages I'd given him in Vienna, and the ones I'd done since then.

"You will solve this before anyone finds us," he assured me. We were working together, my work relied on his, and yet, it was my spiral that promised an answer, a path forward or, rather, a path back.

The Return: I'd wind the completed music box and meet Haskell outside the gathering of Engelhardt's circle. He would have just arrived—as he had—knowing his music box was only half finished, only able to carry him one way. But I would carry the finished box to him, complete after years of repairs and work, and return it before he walked into the Engelhardt circle and my heart fluttered. I would return the box like a library book, a borrowed story, a life lived vicariously.

We'd see each other—I an old man, he a young one—but only for a moment. Then he would wind the box and return to San Francisco. Just like that, we'd complete our circle. Our spiral, as he liked to call it, because a circle, unlike life, has neither beginning nor end, and is—should one repeatedly follow the course of its perimeter—alarmingly dull. He'd leave Vienna before he crossed paths with anyone, before a new melody played. He'd erase everything that once had followed. The song—this song—would never again play.

Our lives were just a shadow that would lift once we changed the light.

* * *

THE ACTOR WHO played me in the feature film *The Music Box* looked remarkably like my younger self. I refused to see the film, but I saw him on advertisements, where he was pictured at a large wooden desk in a lavish office with a leather-bound copy of *Principia Mathematica*. Josef was played by Bernard Kurtz. I didn't know this actor, but his fame—his music topped the Billboard charts—was noted in each of the film's glowing reviews. When the film won an Academy Award for best screenplay, even people who'd never cared for mathematics began to speculate about the music box, and its inventor, and me.

The newspaper ran a full-page story about the mothers' group who'd seen me in Golden Gate Park. A software engineer used a program to age Zedlacher's portrait of me. Her estimate of my age and appearance appeared on Wikipedia within hours. People exchanged information about possible Moritz sightings. The San Francisco chapter of the Zedlacher Institute announced a weeklong event dedicated to "music box recovery," in light of "recent excitement."

I started meeting Hase at different docks. I hoped if I moved frequently, no one would notice me. I felt increasingly tired. I found it more and more difficult to think clearly. When I was stuck in my work, I waited for Haskell's response like a sick child, too weak to pull toys from the shelf without help.

I thought of Hase then, too. She'd grown as tall as me, and far stronger. When she brought groceries to the boat, I had to make two trips to carry what she did in one. I'd worried she wouldn't make it on her own, but she never once asked to move back to the boat. To her, my concern was doubt, but I'd never doubted her. She moved gracefully in the world I shrank from.

The last time I saw her, she didn't have the letter I needed, but I was happy to see her. She stood on the dock, the wind lending her hair a fierce dishevelment, her hand raised in greeting or farewell, the same gesture, the same smile. In her, I still saw the mischievous child who slipped a second cookie from the plate and grinned, either because she believed herself unobserved or because she didn't care if I saw.

I looked back one last time as I pulled away from the dock. She'd crossed the street and was sprinting toward the bus. She could run in sandals. Or perhaps she didn't have running shoes. I'd get her a pair for her birthday, I decided. A pair of good shoes, blue with orange laces, or purple with yellow, bright conflicting colors that suited her so perfectly.

But I did not buy these shoes. I hadn't even settled on which color before I saw the young man at the edge of the pier. He hadn't been there before, I would have seen him, and I'm not sure where he arrived from—the bookstore? The restaurant? A car, just pulled into the lot? Had he seen me through a window? Or known to look for me here? His camera pointed toward me like a gun.

I'd been recognized.

We could fix everything, Haskell and I. We were making progress; we just needed more time.

And my time, it seemed, had at last run out.

* * *

Hase, if you are reading this—not a day passes that I don't think about you. I wish I could repair the damage I've caused. What I haven't told you, I did to protect you, and to protect myself.

But this is your story, too. You look nothing like Engelhardt and entirely like your mother. When I look at you, I often feel as if I'm gazing at the past.

I'm not sure how much longer I can hide. This world is a very different place from the one I was born into. I should destroy this box and this journal, and yet, I cannot bear to.

It is yours, too.

I love you, Hase. I hope you know that. And I am sorry.

23

Josef

BERKELEY, 1936

For his journey to the States, Josef books a first-class cabin. He has money, and he will not spend the transatlantic voyage with paupers. He's never cared for travel, but he enjoys the deference the waiters show him. He passes the hours performing simple calculations and outlining complex problems he does not solve.

The boat docks in Boston, where he knows Sophia lives. He has heard she teaches at a nearby university, but he does not visit her. She is not his reason for coming to America.

As soon as possible, he leaves by train for San Francisco.

* * *

JOSEF FINDS BERKELEY nearly intolerable. The pollen upsets his lungs. The language baffles him. The English he learned in school sounds nothing like the one the people speak around him. He has trouble with the money because it all looks the same. The food is too bland or too spicy. The campus is ugly, clustered buildings overshadowed by hillside.

In the mathematics building, where he arrives before the morning classes start, he learns that Moritz holds office hours on Fridays.

The day is Thursday. The halls of the building are empty. Josef picks the lock on Moritz's door without trouble. Inside, he switches on the light.

The office is small and in need of repainting. The desk is fit for a factory, not a scholar. The single upholstered chair is stained and worn. The desk is covered with piles of papers—student exams and books. Josef brushes them onto the floor. Behind the desk, the shelves are filled with familiar titles: du Châtelet's translation of *Principia Mathematica*, Noether's *Idealtheorie in Ringbereichen*, Descartes's *La Géométrie*.

In his head, he addresses the absent Moritz: *Tell me, where are the rest of the pages?*

He riffles through the desk drawers and finds more student work, department memos, clipped pages torn from a gardening magazine. He tosses these aside.

He searches the shelves, the cabinets. He empties the storage bin and trash.

Disappointment runs through Josef like pain. He has traveled far and received no answer. But he can wait a little longer.

Moritz must keep his papers at home. Josef needs only to learn the address. Moritz can't keep this work to himself when it belongs to Josef.

This truth is simply a matter of who speaks most loudly.

* * *

JOSEF EXPECTS TO wait until Friday to cross paths with Anton Moritz, but the man arrives on campus just as Josef is about to leave the grounds. Stooped beneath the weight of only a small satchel, Moritz doesn't see him. His eyes remain turned to the sidewalk and he appears worn, as if the months in the States have proved trying. His suit fits him poorly, his shirt needs ironing, his hair is in need of a trim.

From across the green, Josef watches him enter the mathematics building. Inside, he will turn right and then left, down the long hallway and into his office. Josef has just followed this path himself, and he can retrace it from outside the building. He will watch through the window until Moritz leaves and Josef can follow him home.

Josef is hungry, but he will not risk missing Moritz for something as trivial as a sandwich. He will not squander this opportunity, though hunger fuels his impatience. He shifts his weight from left to right.

When Moritz reaches his office, he does not turn on the light, but the daylight is enough that Josef sees him clearly. Moritz surveys the mess Josef has left—the scattered papers, the upset furniture. Josef could not work in such disorder. Moritz must feel the same, though his departure is delayed by a woman.

Josef recognizes Sophia immediately, though he's not set eyes on her in several years. Her hair is short and unattractive. If she must bare her earlobes, she should at least wear dangling jewels in them. That she pushes a pram is absurd. The university is no place for children! Josef scowls, thinking of the scholars she has certainly disturbed.

Why is she with Moritz? What are they talking about? Josef steps closer, hoping to hear through the window. He watches Sophia hand Moritz a parcel. He sees Moritz open it, admire the enclosed music box, wind it. He hears the song, a terrible noise that tears through him like a fever. Moritz turns to the window—Josef is too late to duck.

Then the box emits a bright light.

Josef feels a force. It sucks at him, even from where he stands outside, like a tide pulling back toward the sea. The air snaps as if a gun has fired, though there is no smoke and no scent of powder. Josef tenses. He does not look away, and yet, he must have. His eyes dart between the desk and the floor of the office.

Moritz no longer stands by his desk. He has not fallen, he has not stepped forward or back or ducked behind his chair.

Moritz has vanished, and with him, the melody. Gone.

Josef did not hallucinate the disappearance. He is no longer broken by years of dangerous teachings and thought. He has a letter in his pocket that proves he is cured. The tune of the music box beats inside him like an angry child. He is shaking, but he also knows he has witnessed a remarkable thing.

Sophia alone remains across the glass from him, staring into the empty space.

"No!" she says. "No!"

It is then that she sees Josef. The hostility in her gaze is no different from what he feels for her. But they are bound forever now.

Together, they stand witness.

* * *

The police begin an investigation, but they are incompetent. When Josef describes the disappearance to them, they do not even write down the details. Sophia's testimony must corroborate his, and yet, she refuses to speak to him. He does not know what she told the investigators, or if she spoke to them at all. Only one paper covers the story—"Missing Math Genius"—and they don't mention the music box or its mysterious force.

Josef extends his stay in California. He searches Moritz's office a second time and at last finds his home address. The house is poorly tended. The small yard between the sidewalk and front steps is overgrown with weeds. Josef easily breaks in through a back window. If Moritz hid his papers inside, Josef will find them.

* * *

Only after returning to Vienna, where he continues his inquiry, does he begin to piece together the story: that the music box was a gift from Haskell Gaul to Anton Moritz, that Sophia collected it along with Engelhardt's papers from the chair of philosophy's old apartment, where Gaul had resided as caretaker. Between her pregnancy and her grief after Engelhardt's murder, she had delayed this responsibility, but as his assistant, the job fell to her, and she did at last bring Engelhardt's papers to the library, and the music box back with her to the States.

Many who knew Gaul have died or left Vienna, but Josef speaks to those who remain. The administrator is most helpful. He confirms that despite Josef's failure to find coded meaning in Gaul's papers, Gaul may have led the revolt that took his life. The administrator had kept a close eye on the man since he first crossed paths with him at the Engelhardt circle, where, the administrator is quick to add, he'd gone simply to deliver a warning. As a service to the university, the administrator keeps files on all the dangerous and deviant thinkers who gathered in that room, and Gaul joined the list that night.

From the administrator's records, Josef learns that Gaul spent most every evening in the library with Anton Moritz—where they must have worked together on the papers Josef seeks—and that Gaul rarely went out, though he liked to stop at Café Central for coffee.

Josef interviews the waitstaff at Café Central, the newsstand vendors across the street. He identifies the shop where Haskell Gaul purchased groceries, the store where he had his clothes tailored. He finds no employment records, no one who knows Gaul's family or friends, no one who has knowledge of his activities prior to the day he was first seen on campus. He has no known source of income, though a jeweler testifies that a man matching Haskell Gaul's description sold him several grams of gold.

Josef interviews the librarians and learns that Haskell Gaul would often arrive at the library before Moritz and that he always sat at the same table. He learns that Gaul's curious presence intrigued the staff, who would, when work was slow, secretly listen to his conversations. The librarians provide only sketchy descriptions—his work had something to do with inconsistency, or set theory, or Hilbert. Still, Josef records each recollection.

The fragments of the story align. No one from the Engelhardt circle will speak to Josef, but he learns from the meeting notes that Haskell Gaul arrived unannounced and uninvited to the circle meeting, proclaiming he'd been there before *in the past or in the future*.

What's most striking is not what Josef finds, but what's missing: where Haskell Gaul came from, what he did before he arrived, why he came to Vienna. Josef can only deduce this, but his findings confirm his suspicions.

Haskell Gaul came to Vienna from another time.

* * *

JOSEF WRITES TO Sophia to insist that instantaneous travel through time and space is possible. He himself has written the theoretical basis for the device they together witnessed Moritz use. Josef's work is incomplete, but he has done enough to understand that they must continue to press forward. She stood witness to the event. She must work with him to ensure the truth is told.

With his letter, Josef shares a portion of the math he's copied from the pages the administrator gave him—pages he will one day publish. His work is incomplete, he writes to her, but he's certain she has background enough in mathematics to see its great promise. Should she care to provide financial support, she can help him found the institute that will advance the work more quickly.

Sophia is bound to both this work and to Josef. But she does not respond.

He learns of her death a few months later. She was struck by a car in Berkeley. The accident occurred near campus, where neighbors reported they often saw her walking. News of the tragedy was passed from UC Berkeley to the University of Vienna, and from there to the administrator, who then informed Josef.

"She was always opinionated," the administrator says.

Josef remembers how he once loved her and how he imagined his life and hers would forever entwine. He recalls the sparkle of her laughter, the curve of her neck.

"She was—" he begins, but he doesn't know how to finish. The first woman he loved? The only woman he loved? A woman who betrayed him?

He can think of no one with whom he can speak of her death or the unraveling he feels inside, and so he mourns alone.

* * *

He names the institute for himself. Sophia may have witnessed the music box, but she's gone and he has means—not the fortune his father hid, but money he's earned by his own labor. He doesn't require her support. He doesn't require her belief in him, her admiration, or her love.

He hires a secretary to construct a book from his research: the newspaper clippings, and the receipts and itineraries that document Haskell Gaul's steps and prove him an interloper. He includes photographs of himself and his paintings to prove he is a sensitive man, as well as his mathematical work, which—though incomplete—proves he belongs among history's geniuses.

He gathers men to complete the theoretical work and re-create the music box. And he leads the search for the original, now in an unknown time.

He dislikes the thought of another man, enriched by his hard work, stumbling upon the music box before he does. But Josef also knows that the chance of one man solving its mystery is slim.

And so he sets forth his findings knowing that when the box is discovered, it will forever be tied to his name. The box is his, and he will be remembered for it.

24

Hase

SAN FRANCISCO, 2016

The drive from Manifold's place to Golden Gate Park is quiet, but I only notice that Harriet hasn't turned on music when the car stops in front of the Rose Garden and the engine becomes silent. Harriet looks troubled, but more in the way one does when solving a problem than when rent is due and there is no money.

The sky is troubled as well: smoky gray, the light muted. I should have brought along a jacket, though, really, I had no idea when we left my apartment that I'd end up here.

The rose beds haven't changed since my father and I used to come here, or perhaps I just don't remember them well enough, despite the many hours I wandered around while my father gardened and then said that I helped.

"I can park the car and meet you back here," Harriet says, but I shake my head. If she doesn't head back to Berkeley, she'll be late for her class. She might even miss it entirely, and already she's done more for me than I can return.

"I'll be fine," I say.

"Do you think it's true about the music box?"

All I know for certain is that my father's missing. For that, I blame the music box. Whether it works is a separate question, but I believe it does. Zedlacher was clearly mad, and possibly Manifold as well, but that my father would subject me to an elaborate hoax is even more unlikely.

"Yes," I say. "I think it's true."

The car behind us honks.

Harriet honks back. "It's not like he can't go around us," she says.

Then her phone buzzes, and she looks down to see who texted.

"It's Manifold," she says, reading from her screen: "*It's become clear to me that they're getting close and will take the box from me by force if given an opportunity. Fate has compelled me to decide: Do I destroy the box? Or do I use it?*"

"Huh," I say. *Do I destroy the box? Or do I use it?* If Manifold chooses to destroy the box, what will happen to my father? What will happen to me?

And why should this man's choice dictate the course of my life?

And yet, it already has.

The phone buzzes again, and again Harriet reads:

"*It is, in the end, a calculus of the heart.*"

"It's hardly a calculus of the heart," Harriet says. "It's more of a . . ." Her voice trails off as she looks up from her screen. "Hase? Are you okay?"

I'm wondering if I'll disappear—poof!—just like that if Manifold throws away the box without ever having used it, but all I say is, "I'm fine."

She hugs me, like she did before she left for college, when she knew we'd be apart for months, and I become suddenly aware of my own odor, a mix of sweat and the mothballs whoever owned my sweater before me used. The car makes our embrace as awkward as I feel. When I reach around Harriet to return the hug, my chin hits her chest in a way I imagine must hurt.

"Call me tonight, okay?" she says.

I nod.

I miss her as soon as she pulls away.

* * *

I PROBABLY KILL the Himmelsauge rose. I'm alone in the garden, but I feel watched. I dig as quickly as I'm able. The skin between my thumb and palm burns. The afternoon is chilly, but I take off my sweater. Between the soles of my feet and my sandals is a layer of dirt. My jeans are heavy with soil. I feel as if I've just crawled from the ground, though the scratches on my arms and shoulders, where the thorns have torn the skin, make me look more like I've been clawed from beneath the surface.

My father taught me that the Viking sails take longer to make than the ships themselves. Spinning the wool into thread takes a year, he said. Whenever I complained, he would simply point to the sailboat's jib, and I knew he was telling me my complaint was trivial.

I thought I understood my father. I thought I knew him, but even in my head, he now seems blurry, an image of an image of another man, a stranger, a ghost. When I close my eyes, I see not his face as I remember it but the portrait from the Zedlacher book. I'm haunted by the way my father's forehead emerges from the darkness and how his eyes look up from the page but don't see me. He's too far away. He's been gone for too long. I don't know if I can find him.

I dig, my fingernails rimmed with soil. Soil streaks my skin, my face. My hair isn't long enough to tie back, and it falls over my eyes. Each time I push it away, I leave another mark.

Again and again, I plunge Manifold's shovel into the ground, and each time, the roots I hit are solid, whole until I sever them.

But the roots can't be whole if my father dug here first.

Have I made a mistake? I think back to the Wikipedia pages: Rabbit, for me; Karl Andelman—that my father's buried something; Katarina Popovic, for this spot, this rose, the Himmelsauge. This must be the right place, though my path here feels both obvious and flimsy.

Perhaps the clues I followed aren't clues at all, but a pattern I created, a meaning I supplied to strings of meaningless numbers. Perhaps I fabricated this story because I needed it. And now I've reached the end.

But I also think I must be right.

My father loved this rose garden. He would have chosen this spot, though as I imagine him kneeling on the ground with a shovel, I know I'm off. Had he dug where I'm digging now, he would have harmed the rosebush. And he would never have done that.

I've been too hasty.

I take a step back, survey the garden. Under the gray sky, the blossoms glow like stars. The roses are lovingly tended, the soil up and down the beds freshly turned.

The beds.

I study the ground to the left and right of the Himmelsauge rose. Either space is equally possible, but I choose the one that separates the Himmelsauge from the hybrid tea rose named Full Sail.

The soil moves easily.

When my spade hits solid form, I push aside the loose dirt and reveal my father's satchel. He didn't wrap it in plastic or seal it in a box. The leather has already darkened from the damp. I think of the boat, how we stored everything in watertight plastic and still worried about mold and decay. Had I not found the bag, it would have been damaged, its contents spoiled, but perhaps that was his intent.

* * *

I LOOK BEHIND me, down the grassy aisle that separates the rows of rosebushes. How many afternoons had I spent in this garden with my father? Hundreds, probably. Over the years, I'd stolen as many flowers, and not until I told Jake about them and he chastised me for taking the blooms did I ever think it wrong.

A car drives by, then another. No one stops to look at me. I'm sitting in plain sight and am also invisible, a gardener or custodian, a part of the landscape. A woman.

The Zedlacher people aren't looking for me. They only searched my apartment because Jake lives there. I'm not a person of interest, or even a person at all in their story. Still, I fear they're watching, that someone will take the bag from me, and I've not even opened it yet.

But I do open it.

Inside the satchel is a leather-bound book—my father's journal—and the music box, though its wood has discolored and cracked since Manifold showed it to me just hours ago. It has traveled for years since then—first to Vienna with Manifold, and then to California with my father, who has kept it hidden. I open the lid, peer down at the gears under the glass. Where might they take me? For a moment, I think not of my father but of myself. The possibilities.

Then I open the journal:

> *I arrived in Vienna on the twenty-second of April, a Saturday that remains vivid for the stench of burnt wood and the eerie night-dark of smoke. I expected to meet my host at the station, but when I saw the smoldering rooftops and learned from the conductor that a factory fire had been burning for hours, I understood Professor Adler would not be waiting . . .*

I flip through the pages—the blackmail letter from Zedlacher, my father's first visit to the Engelhardt circle, the trip to the Popovic estate, the job in Berkeley, the conference he organized, the visit from Sophia Popovic . . . and then there's me.

Seeing my name, I know my father lied to me. Not in the way I lie—saying "nothing" when he asks what's wrong or insisting, when accused, that I had no part in bringing down the library catalogue system.

My father's lie is silence, as deep and shifting as the ocean. His lie makes plain that all I know is surface. He may have been trying to protect me, but I spent my entire childhood running, and I was not given a choice. Silence is the most haunting lie. I love my father, but what I hear when I think of him now are the words he never spoke.

I turn the pages more slowly now that I'm in them. My father hopes to make everything right, to "fix everything." I can imagine his expression, his lips pressed tight in concentration, his gaze without focus, his attention fully consumed by his thoughts. The Return, he calls it. If he can just solve the second problem—the Return—he can take the box to Vienna and Gaul can return before any of it happens. They will together erase the story. They will strike it from the record before it ever unfolds.

I think of the portrait of my father in Zedlacher's book, the book itself, the institute. All these years, my father's been running. Did he never think to stop?

From the journal slips a letter, for me, I assume, though as I begin to read, I realize it's not.

Dear Haskell,

I don't understand why you left this way. I know you are gone, but I still imagine I'm with you. I'm explaining how foolish I feel for writing this letter. I love you. I have from the moment I first saw you.

I read the letter again. I don't know what I expected, but that my father—a mild-mannered mathematician who spent so little time with people that he appeared to loathe them—had a secret love is as unimaginable as the music box, which I do not fully believe in, even as I reach for it again, the wood solid between my hands.

* * *

I TURN THE key of the music box, of course.

The box is mine. My father left it for me. I don't know that it works, but it might. He claims he—with Manifold's help—restored it to its initial state, a one-way trip to elsewhere, with the hope that he would one day complete the work that would allow him to return to Vienna and "erase the mess we'd made."

The mess.

Mess is a word I use for the broken glass on my bedroom floor, or for the filthy dishes left in the sink, or for those times that I stumble upon a paragraph that's grammatically incorrect or that makes ridiculous claims or is simply incoherent. No one wants a mess. A mess is something one cleans, sweeps up, and throws away.

Mess.

If my father were here, I'd tell him he's chosen the wrong word. I'd argue with him until he acknowledged my point. He can't wind the box and clean up *a mess*, even if he does figure out the Return.

He left me the box because he couldn't bear to destroy it. Did he think I'd destroy it for him? Or that I'd keep it, like an urn or an heirloom, something to remember him by?

I turn the key a second time.

I wonder if he thought I'd wind the box, or if Manifold considered the possibility. I don't think they ever thought of me as part of their plan. But now that I know the details of it, I do have issues I'd like to discuss.

The Return. My father hasn't solved the remaining problem, but then, I'm not exactly returning. I may have grown up in Berkeley, but unlike my father, I never wound the box myself. I didn't, as Manifold put it, "settle into a time" from which I could not now unsettle.

I was merely swept along.

My presence here is an accident, a mistake no one recorded. I'm not mentioned on Wikipedia or in the Zedlacher text. If you search for me, Hase, you will find nothing. No one at the Zedlacher Institute is looking for me. For Anton Moritz, yes, but not me. I was just a little girl, then a young woman, and no one thought I was worthy of note.

Even in my father's journal, I'm just a shadow, the victim of events he intends to prevent—a girl he must return, not one who might travel herself. I'm a person he cares for and loves. But never does he think that I might not wish to wipe away my life.

Never does he admit that his plan will erase me.

He believes the music box is dangerous, that the potential harms are immense. He is right. But harm is only one part of the story.

I see my father in my mind. He sits on the deck of the ship, gazing at the horizon, his eyes seeking the answer to the problem he studies but never seems to solve. In his lap is a letter from Manifold, cradled loosely between palm and thigh where it might blow away.

I have lost many things to the water: hair bands, photographs, magazines. I lost my own baby teeth to the ocean, along with the sack I kept them in. I would never willingly throw away a part of myself, but I have lost some accidentally.

For years, I've been old enough to carry groceries and mail, but not to know my own story. Had the Zedlacher people not found my father, would he have shared the story with me even now?

I don't know, but I don't think so.

Perhaps he thought I would betray him accidentally, or that he was protecting me, or that I would be angry. Perhaps he hoped he could clean up *the mess* before I even knew it was there.

But I am not a mess.

The last message he sent to me was from an anonymous IP address. I don't know where he is or if he is alive.

Is he still running? Still hiding? After all these years. Is he so afraid of Josef Zedlacher that he would deny himself the opportunity to be with both me and the man he loves?

History is easily erased, but it can also be rewritten. Why wipe away change to leave a broken thing intact?

The key is warm between my fingers. I turn it a third time, then a fourth. I feel the resistance strengthen.

The fifth time I turn the key, I hear a click.

The music box plays, but I hear the melody from my father's lips, the song so sad, my tears come, unbidden. When I was a child, this song was my lullaby. When I was feverish, my father sat beside my bed, humming this tune. I know it as if it is part of me, an organ pumping blood or releasing bile.

Why shouldn't I be the one who writes the story? Why shouldn't I decide my own fate? Or that of my father, who would have, had he not failed, removed me from the tale entirely?

I am an expert of subtle revisions. Line by line, each word a choice: "she accepted" or "she chose," "they parted ways" or "their ways were parted," "he wrote a letter" or "the letter was received."

Words are like brushstrokes; details become facts. I can paint a picture like the one in my locket. Complex and beautiful. Surprising.

The sensation I have is not unlike falling.

My muscles shake.

I take a deep breath, feel air fill my lungs. I hear footsteps and the sound of a door snapping shut. I'm not sure if I'm inside or out, but I'm not in the garden. I no longer smell the roses.

I clutch my father's journal and the music box. My shirt clings to my skin.

If I arrive in Vienna, I'll be a stranger. But I will have this story, and I won't let them erase it—not all of it. Not the parts that deserve to unfold.

I feel cold and then feverish. And then a flash of light.

25

Hase

VIENNA, 1934

My favorite place on campus is my mother's office. She's in Boston now with Engelhardt, so I don't worry I'll run into her. I've managed to keep clear of her so far. It's best she never sees me.

I am, after all, only a guest here.

I like to come here at night when the campus is quiet. I sit in her chair, a plain wood, with four legs that don't taper. The seat is cushionless, but beneath the desk, the footrest is padded and embroidered with pink and yellow flowers.

Her office opens only into Engelhardt's, whose door is always locked now that he's away, but Manifold gave me the key. Whenever I come here, I pick up the mail so he can forward it to Engelhardt in the States.

Collecting mail always falls to me.

I don't mind.

My mother's door is never bolted because it has no latch. She could close it, but could never bar visitors entirely. To come and go, she would also pass Engelhardt's desk, and I imagine him looking up at her each time she walks by. In the corner near the door is a pair of her shoes. They are too small for me, and the leather is hard. This may be why she abandoned them. Perhaps one day she walked home barefoot.

Her office is filled with secrets. It is in some ways a secret itself, this space, twice as wide as I am tall and no deeper than my father's sailboat. From the hallway, passersby see her door, but only when approaching from the rear of the building, and only if Engelhardt's door is open as well. Each time I sit at her desk, I think about how many people passed by without knowing she sat here. And yet, her file drawers contain the department's most important records: Engelhardt's letters and the notes my mother took during the circle meetings, each word neatly formed, probably recopied, in her hand. When I look through the transcripts—*How many grains of sand must we gather before they form a pile? What is the relationship between truth and contradiction?*—I wonder if she edited the proceedings when she rewrote them, if all the voices are, at least in some small way, hers.

Her office walls are windowless, but they are covered in paintings and prints, mostly of Vienna, but also of her father: *The Famed Conductor*; her mother: *Vienna's Greatest Pianist*; and her: *Sophia*.

Her portrait is done in violently bright colors. It's not the image in my locket but clearly done by the same hand, the paint so thick it casts shadows. In her portrait, she gazes out, as if concerned by events unfolding behind the artist, who signed his work in the lower right corner.

All my life, I've viewed my mother through Josef Zedlacher's eyes. But only in her office did I learn that. He is not wrong. She is vibrant. She is all the colors he chose.

I know because I've watched her, too.

* * *

WHILE SHE IS in Vienna, my mother goes to the opera on Wednesday nights with Engelhardt and every Friday night alone. I wait in line for standing room so I can follow her past the statue-studded loggias to the balcony. On Fridays, she never sits in the orchestra as she does with Engelhardt, but walks up the stairs to the fourth gallery, where, among the shopkeepers and students, she listens, unaware of the stares she draws.

The music sounds best from there, I am told.

The nights my grandmother performs, my mother goes out with her for dessert, and afterward, they walk arm in arm to their home—our home, though not yet because I haven't been born—which is set back from the street and rises palace-like from the manicured grounds. The fountain in front is always lit and very beautiful, but I prefer the home in the afternoon, when my grandmother practices piano in her third-floor room, and I can listen from the street, anonymous in the gathered crowd.

I watch my mother from outside Café Josephinum as well, at least until the window is broken and then covered with boards, and Engelhardt's table is obscured from my view. She is always conspicuous—her clothing sparkles—and yet, the others at the table seem not to see her. She speaks, of course, and those gathered with her will nod, but even Engelhardt, when he is excited by an idea, turns to Adler or my father.

Does she notice this, too?

Only Josef watches her constantly. Even when he is taking orders at other tables, he manages to fix his gaze on her. I don't think he really sees her, though. He notices only her posture, which is perfect but also artificial, an act she performs.

Once, on the Ringstrasse, I nearly collide with her, but she is with Engelhardt. They are clearly lovers—everyone must know—but, as they walk, they never hold hands or lean close. They don't have to. When I watch them together, I can see no one else exists.

They are arguing that day. He's forgotten to do something important. I can't hear what.

"I'll take care of it," he keeps repeating.

I doubt he's referring to me. Still, I think of myself and our relationship. My mother loves him, I can see, but this man in his gray suit and gray overcoat and gray hair seems a poor substitute for the man who raised me.

* * *

I SEE ANTON Moritz as often as possible. "Promise you'll always be a part of my life," I say, and he looks at me kindly and a bit bemused, as if I'm a window that distorts the light, a glass he wants to peer into but can't see through.

I want for us to be entangled.

We were never a mess.

To his landlady, Inge—who arranged for my room two floors above her apartment and helped me find needlework, as a favor to my father—I am a cousin visiting from America, though I see her eyes dart between us. She believes I am something more.

"How long will you be here?" she asks, and I tell her I don't know, which is easier than explaining that my mother is just now pregnant with me.

I am like the spiral my father is describing. Pieces of my life will be unrecorded, erased, unwritten, missing. Or rather, as my father likes to say: not missing, but unseen, invisible.

* * *

MY ROOM LOOKS out over a wall, much like the one outside the library where my father and Manifold sit most nights, though here in Vienna, they did at last finish the music box. It can return one or take one elsewhere.

I don't think either my father or Manifold likes that I use it, but they owe me that much. I don't belong in the Vienna of this present, or the San Francisco of my past, and they are to blame for that.

I'm in between, I tell them. My only time is other.

Eventually, they agree.

I like to wind the box and travel to my former haunts to make a tweak or two to old narratives, though often I simply observe. Today, for example, I peer through a window and see my mother as she holds me, newborn.

She kisses the top of my head and speaks my name.

Vera, she says, *from the Latin*, and my grandmother, who's the one with my mother when I'm born, agrees it's the perfect name for me.

Our lives are just a shadow that will lift once we change the light.

If Manifold had wound the music box and returned to San Francisco before he crossed paths with anyone, before the new melody played, he could have disentangled our lives—or at least attempted to. The Return, my father called it, but why?

Why shouldn't we be together in this moment, this song?

* * *

IF I REMEMBER only one thing from my time here, I hope it's the moment when I find the door to the library of the philosophy building ajar. I'm still very new to Vienna, and I've been wandering the campus since I recovered enough from my journey that I can walk without shaking too much. The building is quiet, the campus closed, but this one door is propped open at the hinge with a torus like the ones my father loves.

Inside the library, two people are talking: Manifold, who's seated with his notebook, and my father.

"Dad?" I say. He's not much older than I am, and far more handsome than I would have guessed he could be. His eyes are not yet ringed with dark circles; his forehead is not heavy with lines. He seems light, buoyed with hopes and expectations, but also troubled.

He looks back at me with concern—of course, he does not know me; he has not yet wound the music box or written much of the story I read in his journal—and I know, even as I feel joy and an irrational sense of well-being, that I must appear a lunatic.

"It's me." I step toward him. "It's me, Hase."

I turn to Manifold. "Tell him."

My father's eyes move from me to Manifold, and Manifold looks at me quizzically. He didn't expect to see me here. Had he wound the music box before we met in San Francisco, I would not already be in his thoughts—he told me this himself—but I don't think he ever considered that our meeting could affect me, too.

"Me. It's me," I say. "Don't you see, Dad? It's me, I have your journal."

My father's gaze turns to the leather-bound book I carried with me from the Rose Garden.

I open to the first page and read: "*I arrived in Vienna on the twenty-second of April, a Saturday that remains vivid for the stench of burnt wood and the eerie night-dark of smoke. I expected to meet my host at the station, but when I saw the smoldering rooftops and learned from the conductor that a factory fire had been burning for hours, I understood Professor Adler would not be waiting.*"

I close the book and hold it out.

"Take it," I say, and he does.

He flips through the pages. I see his doubt. I see that he doesn't believe me, and also that he can't explain my presence or his handwriting on these pages—the ones he's written, the ones he hasn't yet.

He searches my face as if for a sign of himself. He will not find one.

We look nothing alike. I might as well be a ghost or spirit. I might as well be made of ice, or ectoplasm.

The tall shelves dim the light. The floor is shadowed, the air filled with dust.

"Would you believe me if I told you I traveled back through time to see you?" Gaul says, but he sounds far away.

I am watching a woman. Her complexion is fairer than mine, but her features—the narrow nose, high cheekbones, deep-set eyes—belong to me. She carries a stack of books, and she's looking down, reading as she walks, which I do sometimes when I'm searching for a line or a fact I know but have forgotten.

I imagine she cups my cheek in her hand, that she kisses the top of my head, that I'm cold and she's wrapped me in a blanket. Or perhaps this is a memory.

Beside me, my father is reading the letter he's pulled from his journal.

"What is it?" Manifold asks him.

My father doesn't pause before answering, and yet, his words emerge as if he's considered them carefully, as if he's thought about Manifold his entire life.

"It's for you," he says, extending the letter, deeply creased but now unfolded.

It's for you. The words sound inside me, too.

This is for me—not as I am now, a strange woman in a foreign city. This is for me as I will be, a young child who grows up here, the life I haven't lived, not yet.

I will leave the library before my mother sees me. Only those of us who've wound the music box will ever need to know its details. That is, in my experience, for the best. But I linger one moment longer, watching her.

"Apparently," my father continues, his confusion clear but—as he looks at Manifold—also his delight, as if he's just struck his head with a rock and found, against all reason, that he enjoys the feel of it, "it's for you."

Acknowledgments

I became fascinated by 1930s Vienna after reading my grandfather's memoir, *Reminiscences of the Vienna Circle and the Mathematical Colloquium*. The tension between the intellectual pursuits he describes and the rising Austrofascism struck me and, ultimately, inspired this novel.

The Vienna Circle was led by Dr. Moritz Schlick, who—like Walfried Engelhardt in my novel—was the chair of philosophy at the University of Vienna. Also like Engelhardt, Dr. Schlick was murdered by a former student. The arguments Josef Zedlacher's counsel makes are inspired by the clemency petitions filed by people who felt Dr. Schlick was not a suitable educator.

Dr. Moritz Schlick was murdered on June 22, 1936. A few weeks later, my grandfather was offered a position at the University of Notre Dame in Indiana, which he accepted. Over the course of the 1930s, many other participants of the Vienna Circle also left Austria.

In his memoir, my grandfather writes:

> It was a tragic spectacle to observe the atrophy of the previously vigorous intellectual life in Vienna. . . . The extreme nationalists ruled in the faculty as well as in the student body in the university. The Schlick Circle, which already had a world reputation, was disparaged and maligned. . . . For liberal-minded people who had loved Austria, life in Vienna became harder with every passing month.

After the war, my grandfather returned to visit Austria, but he never moved back.

On a lighter note, among my grandfather's recollections, I also discovered the "send more money" puzzle. I hope that it would have pleased him to know that this puzzle appears in my novel, too.

Other books about the time that I'd like to acknowledge include Friedrich Stadler's *The Vienna Circle Studies in the Origins, Development, and Influence of Logical Empiricism*; David Edmonds's *The Murder of Professor Schlick: The Rise and Fall of the Vienna Circle*; Ilona Duczynska's *Workers in Arms: The Austrian Schulzbund and the Civil War of 1934*; G.E.R. Gedye's *Fallen Bastions*; Karl Sigmund's *Exact Thinking in Demented Times: The Vienna Circle and the Epic Quest for the Foundations of Science*; and *Interwar Vienna Culture Between Tradition and Modernity*, edited by Deborah Holmes and Lisa Silverman.

This novel would not exist without its editor, Amy Einhorn, whose insights improved the story tremendously. I would also like to express my deepest appreciation to the team at Crown: Lori Kusatzky, JoAnna Kremer, Chris Tanigawa, Heather Williamson, Natalie Blachere, Christopher Brand, Dyana Messina, Julie Cepler, Annsley Rosner, and David Drake; as well as the team at Holt: Hannah Campbell, Micaela Carr, Kathleen Cook, Jason Reigal, Janel Brown, Christopher Sergio, and Kelly Too.

Many thanks to my agent, Heather Jackson, for believing in this story. I will forever be grateful for her wisdom, kindness, and support. Thanks also to Emma Kaster for her feedback and enthusiasm.

To the talented people who read and responded to the novel's pages over the course of many years and revisions—Eve Menger-Hammond, David Thau, Daphne Kalotay, Lenore Mohammadian, Alison Bing, Julie Wells, Ethel Rohan, Janis Cooke Newman, Susanne Pari, Cameron Tuttle, Kathryn Ma, Jason Dewees, Laurel Leigh, Jilanne Hoffmann, David Marx, Michele Mortimer, Liz Darhansoff, Helen O'Hare, Laila Lalami, Michelle Arkin, and Meredith Davis—thank you!

Thanks to my parents, teachers, family, and friends. And finally, thanks and love, always, to Dave, Ada, and Asher.

About the Author

Kirsten Menger-Anderson is the author of *Doctor Olaf van Schuler's Brain*, a finalist for the Northern California Book Award in fiction and one of *Time Out* Chicago's top ten books of the year. Her short stories and essays have appeared in publications including *Ploughshares*, the *Southwest Review*, *Lit Hub*, and *Undark*. She currently lives in San Francisco with her family.